# ATONEMENT

## and other stories

David W. Barber

# INDENT
## PUBLISHING

IndentPublishing.com

# ATONEMENT and other stories

Cover illustration by Isla James
© 2021

Print edition first published in Canada in 2022
ebook edition published 2021

**Indent Publishing**
121 Shanly St.,
Toronto, ON M6H 1S8
indentpublishing.com
contact@indentpublishing.com

**Canadian Cataloguing in Publication Data**

Barber, David W. (David William)
Atonement and other stories

ISBN 978-1-7780837-0-9

Cataloguing data available from Library and Archives Canada

# Table of Contents

# Author's Note & Acknowledgements

**W**ELCOME TO *Atonement and other stories*. This is my first major foray into fiction, after having written or edited more than a dozen books of nonfiction, several of which have become international bestsellers, not to mention all the journalism I have written over four decades as a professional newspaper and magazine reporter and editor.

Of the 13 stories here — let's call them a Barber's dozen — eight cover a wide range of topics and time periods, from the early days of our planet to first-century Palestine to the Second World War to the present day and beyond. Their topics and situations range from theology to political intrigue both historical and modern to the vagaries of marital infidelity, fortune and fame. Neither science fiction nor fantasy — though science and the fantastical sometimes play a role in these various cautionary tales — these stories are what readers might consider "speculative fiction." Eight of these stories in some way ask the question "What if?"

The title story, *Atonement*, asks what if an unknown politician arose to counter the devastation of Trumpism? In *Not So Wonderful*, what if a loathsome rich man woke one day to find himself poor? In *Project Habakkuk*, what if a giant iceberg battleship could help defeat Hitler and hasten the end of WW2? In *Terminal Velocity*, what if you suddenly woke up and found yourself falling from an airplane at about 10,000 feet? In *Suffer Little Children*, what if a Boston Catholic with firsthand knowledge of the church's shameful sex abuse became pope and decided to finally do something about it? In *Joseph*, what if the father of Jesus wanted to tell his side of the story?

A few words about some of them: Although the Mountbatten/Churchill conversation in *Project Habakkuk* is one I've created, many of the details in that story are based in truth. There really *was* a secret Project Habakkuk to build a battleship of ice and pykrete at Patricia Lake near Jasper, Alberta. As a PoW in WW1, Geoffrey Pyke had indeed kept himself sane before escaping by reciting *Jabberwocky* and other poems. Leading up to WW2, Pyke actually did send a group pretending to be golfers to spy on Germany, corresponded with them as 'Aunt Marjorie' and later went in himself, pretending to be a bird watcher. His life is a weird, fascinating story all around. And Churchill's remark to "give him what he wants" echoes a famous memo Churchill sent regarding funding for Alan Turing and the other codebreakers at Bletchley Park who were secretly working to break the Enigma code during WW2.

The narrative *Joseph* is of course even more of an imaginative stretch, though some of the events are based on those told in the Gospels or some of the other non-canonical Christian literature, including the second-century infancy Gospel *The Protoevangelium of James*. The rumor that Jesus was the bastard son of a Roman solider named Pantera is almost as old as Christianity itself. The Greek philosopher Celsus wrote about it in the second century, and he may well have based that on earlier stories. Since much of Christianity was an oral tradition long before any of it was formally written, I've taken the liberty of assuming that Joseph, looking back over his long life, would have heard tell of many stories, beliefs and phrases long before they eventually came to be written down.

These short stories overall have sprung from my imagination. Where real persons, places, events or deities may seem to intrude, I have obviously treated them fictionally and with considerable artistic licence.

Four of the five Sherlock Holmes stories — *Sunken Parsley, Heir Presumptive, Hertfordshire Horror* and *Mr. Erdman's Alibi* — were originally published years ago in a newspaper magazine and later in book form. But the fifth, *The Case of the Solitary Canary*, is a brand-new one I wrote especially for this collection. And some of its details too — the notorious soprano Susannah Cibber and the countertenor Joseph Lambe from Handel's 1742 *Messiah* performance, even Thomas Ravenscroft's connection to *Three Blind Mice* — have their basis in truth. (And here I'll confess I've thrown in a tiny Easter egg: I first conceived this story many years ago as an Agatha Christie-style country house mystery, before having to admit to myself I'm more familiar with Sherlock than with Christie. And *Three Blind Mice*, of course, plays a role in Christie's famous play *The Mousetrap*.)

My thanks to Jacques Lauzon and Indent Publishing, both for being an early set of eyes on these stories and for bringing the ebook and print book into publication. And to Isla James for her illustration for the cover.

DWB (Toronto, February 2022)

# Atonement

THE YEAR WAS LATE 2034. The next U.S. presidential election was less than two years away.

Joe Biden had won a decisive victory against Donald Trump in 2020 and, despite massive obstructionism from Congressional Republicans — and even from some in his own party — had gone on to successfully manage the covid pandemic while restoring economic stability and repairing America's standing in the world. Biden then resigned a year early in 2023, after the 2022 midterms. Thanks to the efforts of Biden and VP Kamala Harris, the Democrats had picked up midterm seats in both House and Senate, leaving the Republican party with much less political power.

Harris finished the Biden/Harris 2020 term as the first woman (and first black-Asian) U.S. president, building so successfully on their groundwork that she had won smoothly in 2024, in part because the right-wing opposition had split into two factions — the remaining Republicans and some breakaway Trumpist independents. (Trump himself was not around to lead them, having died in early 2026, penniless and disgraced in prison after a swath of criminal and civil convictions.) Harris's 2024 running mate was Pete Buttigieg, making him the first openly gay VP in U.S. history.

Buttigieg won the presidency for the Democrats in 2028 but, facing opposition from a reinvigorated right wing, it was a narrow victory that lasted only one term and helped stir up a vehement backlash of misogyny, homophobia, protectionism and neo-Nazi racism.

In 2032, rebranded and reconciled as the Patriot party, the Trumpists and remaining Republicans had stoked their backlash to successfully retake the House and White House, but not the Senate. They had spent the next two years and beyond vigorously trying to reassert a right-wing agenda and undo more than a decade of social progress. Without the Senate, they were not entirely successful, but they had managed to undo many of the previous progressive gains. Under the cynical but catchy and effective slogan "America Best," they had pushed through tax cuts for the wealthy, limits to health and social programs, traditional "Christian family values" and other deeply conservative policies.

Having lost ground in the 2034 midterms and eyeing the looming 2036 election, Democrats, social democrats and other progressives desperately hoped for a savior. That savior seemed to appear in the person of Barra Williams, a previously unknown junior senator who had come, it seemed out of nowhere, to win a 2032 Democrat seat despite the Patriot resurgence and help the Democrats hang on to a razor-thin majority in the Senate.

Tall, lanky, blondish and soft spoken, Barra Williams was a bit of an enigma. Just 26 years old when first elected and not yet even 30, Barra seemed to have had little or no formal previous political experience, yet somehow had an innate knack for campaigning and working in Congress. Of Barra's background or personal life little was known, and Barra remained guarded and intensely private. Moreover, Barra appeared to be on the feminine side of androgynous, but identified as gender nonbinary and preferred the gender-neutral pronoun "they" and its derivatives.

The previous Harris administration having successfully persuaded the Supreme Court to overturn the old-fashioned notion in the Constitution that a president must be at least 35 years of age, there was nothing to prevent Barra from running for the top job. After centuries of white men as presidents, America had finally seen a black man (Obama in 2008), a black-Asian woman (Harris in 2023) and an openly gay man (Buttigieg in 2028) as president. But were voters ready to endorse a gender-non-binary president — and a young, inexperienced one at that? The Democrats hoped so, and they pinned their hopes on Barra Williams to hold back the regressive tide.

The old-guard GOP and Trumpist Patriot party pushed back hard, questioning their opponent's youth, inexperience, "socialist" policies and above all, sexuality. Barra was too effeminate to be straight, they said. So, was Barra gay? Bisexual? Transgender? Some sort of cross-dressing pervert or pedophile? They tried all these notions and more as slurs, hoping some would stick.

Some of those insults, of course, did gain traction. But rather than getting down in the mud with the so-called "Patriots," Barra Williams instead ran a positive, uplifting campaign emphasizing fairness, integrity and dignity. There were a few well-chosen campaign slogans, but one in particular became a rallying cry. "Atonement" was a campaign watchword.

When anyone asked — and several in the media did, more than once — the campaign would say it meant to atone for decades, even centuries, of injustice. It meant to atone for the failure of previous governments — and by implication specifically the recent Trump and Trumpist governments — to live up to the lofty ideals of liberty and justice for all on which America had always claimed to have been founded. It meant to atone for slavery, for racial and gender inequality, for economic disparity and more. Some clever graphic designs also played on the term "At-one-ment," suggesting that people, and even a nation, at one with themselves would naturally become at one, and at peace, with one another.

That idealism and sense of promise overcame the deplorable negativity of the other side, and under their new, quietly charismatic candidate, and buoyed especially by the progressive youth vote, the Democrats handily won the 2036 presidency, regaining the White House, gaining ground in the Senate and easily retaking the House.

Barra Williams became the first U.S. president to openly identify as gender nonbinary, and helped usher in a new American golden age of tolerance, equity and social justice. Over this term and the next, winning again in 2040, Barra Williams and their team became by far the most progressive and egalitarian administration America and the world had ever seen. They brought in reforms ensuring full racial and gender equality, universal health care, universal basic income, fully funded education, tax fairness, environmental stewardship and employment policies better than any other social democracy in the world. The whole world could see it, and had been benefitting from it in all the best ways.

As the 2042 midterms approached, Barra's supporters were eager to overturn a restriction that FDR's Republican opponents had pushed and enforced since the 22nd Amendment in 1951, that a president may serve no more than two consecutive terms. Like FDR, the Democrats wanted Barra to be able to run for a third term in 2044, maybe even a fourth in 2048. And why not? By then, Barra Williams would barely be 42 years old, still younger than any previous U.S. president ever elected since Teddy Roosevelt had become president in 1901, also at age 42.

But Barra, always private, had been keeping secrets from all but their closest confidants — not least of failing health (just as Kennedy had long hidden Addison's and FDR had hidden partial paralysis). A sudden downturn saw Barra rushed to Walter Reed Hospital and soon lapsing into a coma. Congress invoked the 25th Amendment and Barra's VP took command, hoping it was only temporary.

But Barra never recovered and died shortly thereafter, universally mourned as perhaps the best and most benevolent president in U.S. history.

In death, thanks to investigative work by journalists at the New York Times, Washington Post, CNN and elsewhere, details of Barra's little-known life began to be revealed and became known.

Barra Williams had in fact been born in March 2006 as Barron William Trump, the only son of twice-impeached, disgraced ex-U.S. president and convicted felon Donald Trump and his third wife, Melania Knauss. (Melania had first met Trump in her capacity as a high-priced fashion model. Convicted pedophile Jeffrey Epstein had often taken credit for introducing them. It had long been rumored but never proven in court despite several attempted lawsuits that Melania's services had even gone beyond modelling.)

Melania was not entirely a fool: Trump had cheated on his first wife to marry his second and on the second wife to marry Melania. She'd known going in that fidelity was not in his nature. So even before the public humiliation of his affairs with the porn star and the Playmate, among others, Melania had long since been secretly salting away money against the happy day she would finally divorce him. She'd gotten citizenship for herself and her parents out of the deal. And even a son she vaguely cared about. So those were a plus. Not to mention the money. After years of putting up with Trump's stupidity and verbal abuse and the shame of it all, Melania figured Trump owed it to her. She had divorced Trump in 2023 after his humiliating defeat by Biden/ Harris in 2020 and had later moved back to Slovenia.

But although she'd more or less abandoned Barron in a private U.S. boarding school, she was at least kind enough to have made sure he had a considerable amount of Trump's money stashed away in the bank for himself. And Barron himself, no fool, had also been stashing money on his own.

By 2022, then just 16, Barron Trump had successfully sued in court for emancipation and on turning 18 and finishing school had seemed quickly to disappear from public view. His personal fortune, combined with connections and information he had gained growing up in the Trump family, including some insider knowledge and contacts in the world of cybersecurity and a sympathetic friend from his old Secret Service detail who'd known a few tricks from the witness protection program, had made it possible — though far from easy — for him to cover his tracks and obscure his public and digital record in his efforts to remain hidden. And eventually to create a plausible backstory and official record for his reborn identity.

Barron had spent much of the next decade so far out of the public eye that few people ever found out he had undergone hormone therapy treatment in a move toward gender reassignment. But in the end, Barron had never fully transitioned, preferring to stay androgynous and identify as gender nonbinary. Unfortunately, the medical and hormonal treatments, coupled with several pre-existing conditions, had compromised his health in ways doctors would only later discover.

Clearly, the slogan "atonement" — and even "at-one-ment" — had been far more personal than anyone else had ever realized or understood. Embarrassed and ashamed by the Trump family name and by its legacy of cruelty and bigotry, and only after years of psychotherapy and hard work, Barron William Trump had re-emerged reborn as Barra Williams and had taken on the redemptive mission of personally trying to undo and make amends for all the damage Donald Trump and his enablers had done over decades in both Trump's personal and political life. At considerable personal cost and effort, Barra had succeeded beyond what anyone might have expected in restoring dignity, empathy and integrity where under Trump there had never been any.

And so what narrow, small-minded and mean-spirited Trump and hateful Trumpism had falsely promised to do in 2016 and had destructively failed to deliver, the ultra-progressive Barra Williams had actually succeeded in doing, starting almost two decades later. Barra had truly made America great again.

# Project Habakkuk
*(Based on true events.)*

"H ARUMPH! IT'S ALL damned irregular!"
          Cigar chomp. Scowl.

"Yes, I know, sir. Quite irregular."

Adjutant hesitant. Nervous. Fiddles with papers on his desk as the great man paces.

Another scowl.

"Well?"

"Well, sir, I believe the Commodore would explain it much better than I."

Chomp. "Yes, probably would. But at least you are not interrupting my best thinking spot at Chequers and throwing a damned big chunk of ice into my nice, hot bath."

"No, of course not, Prime Minister."

"Most peculiar, though. Damned thing hardly melted at all."

"Yes, I know, sir. I do believe that's rather the point."

Another harrumph. Chomp. Scowl.

"Fine. Send him in."

Louis Francis Albert Victor Nicholas Mountbatten, born His Serene Highness Prince Louis of Battenburg at Frogmore House, Berkshire. Commodore, Royal Navy. Mentioned in dispatches. DSO. Since October '41, Chief of Combined Operations.

Giving Jerry what for in any way they can on land and sea and in the air.

Uniform hastily pressed for this important meeting, cap smartly tucked under his left arm. Quick offhand nod to the adjutant, genial but not too familiar. (Always good to acknowledge a good man. Helps morale in the ranks.)

"I'll leave you, sir. I'll be in the next room. Ring if you need anything."

A deferential nod to both men as the adjutant closes the dark Whitehall door behind him.

The cigar has long since gone out, several chomps ago. With one last scowl, the PM stubs it into an ashtray. (Brass, fashioned from the bottom of an old trench artillery shell. Gift from a fellow officer. Keeps it for sentimental reasons.)

"Well, Dickie. What have you got for me?"

He's "Dickie" to family and friends, even though Richard is

not among his many given names nor titles. Great-grandmama Victoria had once suggested the new baby be "Nicky." But the family already had so many boys named Nicky (especially the Russian one, sadly gone). Too much confusion. So, Dickie it is.

The 1884 marriage of his father, another Louis, had given rise to the popular confection Battenburg cake. Dickie, having forgone breakfast, rather wished he had even a small piece now, with some tea. But the adjutant had beaten his hasty retreat without offering any sort of refreshment. Dauntless, Dickie presses on.

"Well, Winston, I do hope you've read the proposal I'd sent on to you. Got it just yesterday in the Most Secret pouch from our man in New York."

"New York? What the blazes is he doing in New York? I thought he was still with Bernal at COHQ."

"Ah, no, sir. Bernal sent him there on that Project Plough business. We're hoping the American automobile makers might have better luck designing the proper vehicle. Studebaker, maybe."

"Plough? Driving around on the snow from that snow fortress he wants to build in Norway? Look, I know you think highly of this Pyke fellow. But are you sure he's not just mad? Sounds barking mad to me."

"I know it sounds odd, sir. But hear me out. You know what they say about that line between madness and genius. And I do think Pyke might just be a genius. I'll grant you he certainly doesn't think like other men. Rather like Thoreau, I'd say. Marches to his own drum, and all that. Sometimes one needs that."

"So, is this more Plough business? More snow? More ice? Still in Norway, are we? What's the fascination this man has with winter?"

"No, sir. Not quite. Mid-Atlantic, as it were. And not so much snow or ice as an ice-*berg*."

"An iceberg? In the middle of the ocean?"

Another scowl. Perhaps a look of puzzlement.

"Well, yes, Winston. But not so much an iceberg, actually. Really rather more like a gigantic ship. A ship made of ice."

Clearly, it is time for another cigar. The preparation and lighting of which (not to mention the attendant chomping and scowling) becomes a minor theatrical production. But necessary for deep thinking. Especially when one can't be at home in a nice, hot bath.

Churchill, of course, is not the first — nor would he be the last — to think Geoffrey Pyke might just be mad.

Pyke knows this. Has even wondered it himself sometimes. Had wondered it, along with his guards, during all those weeks and months in solitary in the dark of a German prison cell. Whistling in the dark, even. He'd had to ask permission for them to let him whistle. But they did.

That had been in the Great War, as we'd foolishly called it back then. Even more foolishly the War to End All Wars. Before we realized there'd be another, and perhaps another, and we'd have to start numbering them, like volumes in an academic journal no one was going to bother to read.

Born a Jew, his lawyer father dead by the time Pyke was five, having left behind little money. His mother did the best she could and later shipped him off to school. Where the Wellington boys, sons of good army men but not particularly good themselves, had mocked him for his Orthodox black garb and *payot* sidelocks. Small wonder, perhaps, that by 13 he had become an atheist (there are, it turns out, plenty of atheists in foxholes) and had come to resent many in those upper classes who thought themselves his betters. Pembroke College, Cambridge. Sent up to read law.

But then the Germans declare war. The First War, remember — before we knew there would inevitably be a Second.

Pyke drops his studies, on something of a whim convinces a newspaper editor to send him behind the lines for a behind-the-scenes. Finds, not to his surprise, that most ordinary Germans aren't much taken with the idea of war. But then, who is, really? Maybe the fathers of those boys at school — or the boys themselves, later.

Most ordinary Germans, Pyke finds, would rather just go back to being ordinary Germans.

Most but sadly not all. Not least the ones who arrest Pyke for being a spy — leaving behind that handwritten letter in English on his desk had not been wise — and throw him into a prison camp.

"You'll probably be shot in the morning," they tell him.

But in fact several mornings go by. Days and days and weeks of not being shot in the morning.

Alone in the dark in his prison cell, Pyke does not come to find the God he had so long ago abandoned. God remains abandoned still. It is not the words of the Torah that sustain him, though many remain stubbornly lodged in his memory, old habits being hard to break.

It is Kipling. It is Carroll.

Pyke struggles to remember the words, hanging on to them like a life raft — he might later have said an ice floe — adrift in the ocean:

*If you can keep your head when all about you*
*Are losing theirs and blaming it on you,*
*If you can trust yourself when all men doubt you,*
*But make allowance for their doubting too;*
*If you can make one heap of something,*
*And something give a toss…*

Needs work, obviously. Need to concentrate.

*"Beware the Jabberwock, my son!*
*The jaws that bite, the claws that catch!*
*Beware the Jubjub bird, and shun*
*The something Bandersnatch…"*

More days go by, and weeks. He's hungry all the time, sometimes feverish, but he remembers a little more of each poem. In time, he can recite them both, more or less line perfect, he thinks. But who's to know? He won't know for sure until he can get home and check. But for now, stoic Kipling and hatter-mad Carroll help keep him sane. Or maybe as sane as he'll ever be.

Finally, they move him. Out of solitary to another camp. With other prisoners he can talk to instead of just Kipling and Carroll. Whom he'll happily recite if they ask. Few do. With a fellow prisoner named Falk he formulates a plan of escape. Over the fence at night and first on foot, then by train, then by foot again as they near the Dutch border.

A soldier stops them, brandishing his gun. Demands to know who they are, where they are going.

We're doomed, Pyke thinks, preparing his excuses in his somewhat broken German. But no, the soldier is Dutch. They are already 50 yards inside the border of the Netherlands.

Safe. At least relatively so.

Back in England, his editor is pleased. A telegram Pyke had sent from Amsterdam had scooped the other Fleet Street rags, has made Pyke famous. The first Englishman to get into Germany and out again safely.

The editor wants a full account. But Pyke is done with being a war correspondent. Done with war completely, he thinks.

Until 20 years go by and the next one looms.

"Ah, I think I remember this next bit."

"Yes, Winston. Thought you might. It was August '39 — just before, as it turns out, the war was to begin — though clearly the warning signs were already there.

"Remembering his earlier little 'survey,' Pyke hoped that by doing an opinion poll again of those 'ordinary Germans,' he could convince Hitler nobody really wanted a war."

"Didn't bloody work, though, did it?" Churchill grumbles.

"No, sir, it didn't. But he did give it a jolly good try. Sent 10 men into Germany, pretending to be golfers on a tour. Started in Frankfurt, I think. They would chat up any Germans they met in casual conversation, to find out how they felt about the possibility of war. Just golfers seeing how things lie, as it were."

Mountbatten smiles at his own joke. Churchill does not.

"Of course, Pyke was keen to know how his plan was progressing, but he'd learned his lesson somewhat about written correspondence. This time he came up with a simple ruse, really, but it seems to have worked. Wrote letters back and forth to his chaps in a sort of coded language. Signed them 'Aunt Marjorie' so as not to arouse suspicion.

"Even went over there himself at one point, to check things out."

"What? Churchill asks. "Another damned golfer?"

"Well, no, actually. Pyke passed himself off as a bird fancier, on a birdwatching tour of the Continent. Even took a canary with him in a cage."

This earns a somewhat bewildered Churchillian scowl, but Mountbatten presses on.

"But our chaps in the Foreign Office realized the situation was heating up, so they advised Pyke and his team to return home for safety.

"Pyke wanted to continue with his survey, of course, perhaps using people from a neutral country to do the asking this time. Had some support from his friends in Labour — Clement Attlee and Stafford Cripps were among them, as I recall. Even submitted a report to the War Office. But in the end, nothing came of it.

"And by September, of course, it was too late anyway. The war had started."

"Yes, yes, that's all very well. Clever chap, and all that." Churchill clearly growing impatient. That is, more impatient than usual. "What's all this have to do with ice? And with your tossing a great, bloody chunk of it into my bathtub?"

"Now, be fair, Winston. You know it wasn't that large. Barely the size of a few ice cubes put together, really. Besides, I thought a visual demonstration would best drive the point home."

"Well?"

"Well, you'll remember noticing that it didn't melt. Or hardly — even in your nice, steaming bath."

"So?"

"So, that's the thing. That's Pyke's latest plan. I know it may seem daft, but it also seems to work. And that's what matters. This could actually turn the tide of the war."

"How does a piece of ice do that?"

"Among other things, by helping enormously to solve the problem of the mid-Atlantic gap. As you know, RAF Coastal Command has a devil of a time protecting warships and the merchant marine in the north Atlantic. Our airplanes just don't have enough range to cover the distance from our western coast."

"Yes of course I know that," says Churchill, testily. "But we don't have enough ships. We don't even have enough steel to make them with."

"And that's were Pyke comes in.

"As you may remember, in 1940 there was a similar sort of idea. But that was more of an ice island, really. Some fellows, er, floated the idea at the Admiralty. But it was pretty much dismissed as unworkable. One of the Royal Navy engineers who was quite against it was Lt.-Commander Norway."

"Norway? Really?"

"Not the country. That's his real name. You might know him better by the name he uses for his little novels — Neville Shute. But he likes to keep that separate, so as not to bother the higher-ups. He's a damned good engineer, and he's afraid they might not take him seriously if they knew."

"But if Norway, or Shute, doesn't think it would work, why should you?"

"With all due respect, he's only one engineer, and in aeronautics, at that. Seagoing vessels are not exactly his field."

Churchill has a thought: "Hang on a bit — we've already got an island in the North Atlantic. A real one: Iceland. It's even got ice in its name." Churchill allows himself a slight smile. "Why not just use that?"

"Well, we did try, sir," Mountbatten says. "Tried to persuade them to join the Allied cause, let us use Iceland as a staging area. Even went so far as to 'invade' them, as it were, in May of '40. Sent in a few hundred Royal Marines, and then some Canadian chaps after that.

"They let us stay, Winston, but they would not budge. They insist on staying neutral."

Not wanting to be further sidetracked, Mountbatten pushes on.

"At any rate, Pyke's idea is something quite different," he continues. "Not an island, and not just of ice. Made of something much better. Pyke is suggesting we make ships to service our airplanes — maybe even aircraft carriers, if we can manage it — but we make them out of something cheaper and easier than steel."

"Let me guess," Churchill scoffs. "Ice."

"Precisely! Now, I'm no chemist — nor any kind of scientist, obviously — but it seems Pyke has come up with a way to ensure the ice can be made stronger and doesn't melt. I'm naturally vague on the details — there's some more precise information in that report I've given you — but in simple terms, you mix water with wood pulp or sawdust as you freeze it. The resulting material, weight for weight, is just about as strong as concrete, and much lighter than steel. So long as you can keep it cold enough. He calls it 'pykrete.'"

"Of course he does! Man's got an ego."

"That may be, but he also may be just this side of brilliant."

"Do you really think so, Dickie? I do promise I'll read that report later. But for now, just give me the highlights."

"Well, Winston, here's the plan: Pyke's done research with various materials, various types of wood and so on. Bernal had his man Max Perutz doing some of the testing at a secret cold storage facility underneath Smithfield meat market in London, if you can believe it. Luckily enough, Canadian spruce seems to be just the ticket. Apparently better even than Scotch pine. That's good for us. Canada has simply acres and acres of spruce — more than you can imagine — so it's plentiful and cheap.

"On top of that, Canada's far enough away from the main fighting that Pyke can work on his project in secrecy and relative safety.

"We'd need the Canadians on board, of course, but that should pose no problem. I'd suggest we send an envoy — maybe even Pyke himself, since he can best explain it — to their prime minister, Mackenzie King, to secure his co-operation. He's a bit daft himself, as you may know. Talks to his dead mother. But otherwise a solid chap. And a staunch ally.

"Anyway, we'll definitely need the Canadians in on this project, if only to provide us the location — not to mention, of course, the material."

Churchill gives a slight nod, waving a "go on" gesture his cigar.

"Pyke wants to set up shop in a place called Jasper National Park — that's in Alberta, one of Canada's provinces. They'd make some of the ice blocks for construction from the water at Lake

Louise. But the ship itself — a small prototype, anyway — Pyke wants to build at a smaller, more secluded spot for better secrecy, at a place called Patricia Lake. Named for a relative of mine, as it happens.

"Also, Pyke seems to think he can get conscientious objectors to work on the project, without actually telling them what it's for. Jolly devious, if he can pull it off, I suppose."

"Harumph!" Churchill says. "And does this ship have a name?"

"Oh, I don't think so, sir. But the plan itself does have a code name. Pyke calls it Project Habakkuk."

"Habakkuk? Where the devil does he get that from?"

"Not the devil. Rather the opposite, as it were. You'll find it in one of the more obscure and shorter chapters near the end of the Old Testament. One of the very minor prophets, I'd say. Rather like Pyke to be fanciful, but it does seem appropriate."

Mountbatten pulls a sheet of paper from his pocket, unfolds it and begins to read:

"From chapter one, verse five: 'Behold ye among the heathen, and regard, and wonder marvellously: for I will work a work in your days, which ye will not believe, though it be told you.'"

Churchill is silent. Puffs his cigar. Stares off into the middle distance, thinking.

It's early 1942. The war has already gone on for nearly three years. So much destruction, so many lives lost. Is this just some foolish venture, or could it actually help to shorten the war? Who could know?

But Churchill is not one to shy away from a bold, even foolhardy effort. Nor will he do so now.

He turns, his jaw set. Looks Mountbatten in the eye.

"Give him what he wants."

# This Is My Blood

"FORGIVE ME, FATHER, for I have sinned."

"Go on, my son."

"It's been — oh, I dunno, like maybe three weeks since my last confession."

On his side of the booth, early on a Saturday morning, the priest gave a small smile. Father Sbagliato already thought he'd recognized the voice on the other side of the worn, carved wooden screen. And the young man's casual inflection confirmed it. This was Angelo DeMarco, one of his catechism students and — the old priest hoped and the good Lord willing — a fine and promising young prospect for the priesthood one day.

But by the seal of the confessional, the priest was not supposed to know — or at least was not supposed to acknowledge that he knew — the identity of his congregant. The confessional promised anonymity. To the father confessor, at least. Not of course to God, who the priest (at least) would say knows all.

So instead, he simply said: "The Lord will forgive your tardiness if you are truly penitent. But not if you are just too lazy to come and confess your sins. So what do you have to say for yourself?"

"Well, Father, I feel a bit guilty that it's been so long since my last confession. But I have been busy, honestly. I've had school to finish, and a summer job to find. And I've been helping Mama and Poppa at the store when I can."

"If you've been a good son helping your parents, then I'm sure God will forgive you, and so will I," the priest said. "Now, what is troubling you, my son? I can tell something is."

In truth, Sbagliato had no idea whether anything was troubling the young man. The old priest wasn't very perceptive at the best of times. Rather too full of himself to genuinely care about others, though he always put on a good front, as befits the job. But it was a safe bet, a standard thing to say to grease the wheels. Unless they did it regularly, or just out of habit, most people came to confession because something was bothering them. That was the whole point.

"Well," Angelo said. "I've been having, um, thoughts. And doubts."

"Impure thoughts?" the priest said. Again, not so much

perception as often a safe bet, especially when the confessor was a young man of 18 like Angelo.

"Yes, Father. But surely if there's love, those thoughts aren't impure? Just, ah, vivid."

"The Lord will bless physical intimacy within the confines of marriage as a sacrament. But if I may say," he said, keeping up the pretense of anonymity, "you sound too young to be married. So if you truly love the girl, you should marry her — but wait for marriage before becoming too intimate. Remember what the Gospel of Matthew tells us, that lusting after a woman in your heart is no better than committing adultery."

"I'll try to remember, Father. But that's also why I have doubts."

"Doubts about what, my son?"

"OK, you've probably already guessed who this is, though I know you're not supposed to say. So you know I've told you I was thinking about entering the priesthood. And I know you'd like that. But lately, I'm not so sure. I've been having my doubts. Especially with some of the thoughts and dreams I've been having."

"Impure thoughts and dreams? But we've already covered that, my son. You must not lust in your heart. As especially as a priest. As a priest, you would be celibate, married only to the church, not in an earthly union."

"Well, yes, those. Because I really do love my girlfriend and want to live my life with her. But it's not just that, Father. It's —"

" — go on."

"See, it's kind of embarrassing. It sounds stupid, even. But I've been having these weird dreams about vampires."

On his side of the booth, Father Sbagliato, who had been slouching, only half paying attention, perked up — his attention now fully focused. Struggling to keep any eagerness out of his voice, he said in what he hoped was a calm, dismissive tone, "You've just been watching too many scary movies, I'm sure."

"No, it's not that, Father. Not like those corny old Bela Lugosi movies, or *Buffy* or that *Twilight* series. Not angsty teen vampires. I can't explain it. It's more like flashes and images. Not so much vampires, I guess. More like some sort of strange blood ritual or sacrifice. Just weird fragments of scenes playing out in my head. Like a communion mass gone wrong somehow. And then I wake up, and I don't remember most of it."

The old priest took a breath, said nothing for a moment, gathering his thoughts. He was excited. Could this be a sign? But it would not do to rush things.

"It's Saturday," the old priest said, struggling to keep his voice calm, even nonchalant. "You should go help your parents at the store. Tonight after supper when you're done, come back here and we can speak some more about these dreams that trouble you. In the meantime, say your prayers and try to keep your thoughts pure."

θ θ θ

"And so then what happened?"

This was Gina, a week or so later, she the object of Angelo's impure thoughts. Willing object, it must be said, for as Angelo's girlfriend and also 18, she had an equal — but as yet unconsummated — passion for him. Worse for her, maybe, since the thought of losing him to a life of celibacy. She knew she should respect his calling if that's what it was. But it tore at her heart.

"That's the weird thing, Gina," Angelo said. They were sitting in his family kitchen drinking coffee, his parents both at the store. A slow weekday evening, they hadn't needed him.

"I went back to the priest a few more times over the next week or so. Those dreams I've told you about, they're getting worse. Or at least more vivid, more detailed. And he wanted to hear more and more about them. Wanted more details, more description. He wanted to know how I feel while I'm having them, and how I feel after I wake up. It's creeping me out."

"What's creeping you out? The dreams?"

"Ya, the dreams, a bit. But also Father Sbagliato's reaction. It's like he can't get enough of hearing about them. That's the creepy part.

"You know some priests do horrible things with children," Angelo said. "We know about that. It's awful. But at least the church — and the police — are starting to acknowledge it and deal with it and punish the abusers. Thank God I've never had to worry about that with Father Sbagliato, even ever since I was a little boy. But in a weird way, this feels kinda same. It's like he's obsessed with it. And it gives me a bad feeling."

"But it's just talk, right?" Gina said. "Maybe he's just lonely, an excuse for him to get to spend more time with you. You know he's trying to convince you to enter the priesthood." It hurt Gina to admit that, but they both knew it was true.

"But that's the thing, last Saturday it went past just talking about it."

Gina gave him a puzzled, worried look.

And so he told her what had happened that night with the old priest.

Afterward, she sat in silence. Neither of them said anything for a while. She sipped her coffee, by this time barely lukewarm.

But it gave her something to do while she thought.

"Have I told you about my Uncle Francis?" She said finally. "My mother's older brother. I think you should meet him and talk with him. You'll like him. He used to be a Jesuit priest. But he's not one anymore. I think he'll have some perspective on this."

And so the next evening found the three of them — Angelo, Gina and her Uncle Francis — sitting in the comfortable study in Francis's small apartment. For anyone else, it would probably have been a second bedroom — a child's room, maybe. But the bachelor ex-Jesuit had set it up as a study. In the centre against one wall, a big old wooden desk and chair. Shelves of old books lined every wall, broken only occasionally by a space for small artwork, a couple of framed university degrees. Angelo and Gina sat together on an old couch, holding hands and looking a little nervous. Francis sat in an armchair, a teapot and mugs on a table between them.

"He asked me to meet him at the church just before midnight, told me he had something to show me," Angelo was saying, once they'd settled in. "Like I said, I've never felt unsafe around him, not even as a kid, so I wasn't worried about anything inappropriate. So of course I went.

"He met me at the back door where he'd asked me to, and he took me into the small side chapel — not the main sanctuary, but the little chapel they use for weekday prayers. There was no one else there, just the two of us. And just a few candles for lighting. He was wearing stole over his cassock, but not like ones I've ever seen before. Lots of red, and strange writing and symbols, in the embroidery."

"Did you recognize the writing?" Francis asked.

"Some Greek letters, some Latin I couldn't make out. I didn't recognize the rest."

"Possibly Babylonian or Assyrian," the ex-Jesuit said. "Doesn't matter, not important. Go on."

"Well, like I told Gina" — he looked over at her with a shy smile — "in some ways it seemed like the usual communion ritual, even though it was just the two of us. He was behind the small altar, I was in the front pew. He had a chalice, and poured some wine into it from a cruet. At least I assumed it was wine at first. It was dark red, but even at a distance it had a bit of a pungent smell.

"He was intoning some sort of prayer," Angelo said, "like blessing the chalice. Not in English. But not just in Latin, either. I'd recognize that, even though my Latin's not very good. If I had to guess, I'd say Latin with a few Greek words I recognized, and some sort of other language or languages. I couldn't tell you which ones."

"Maybe like the vestment," Gina said, "a mixture?"

"Exactly!" Francis said, beaming. "Always knew you were the smart one in the family, Gina."

Gina blushed, Angelo smiled and squeezed her hand. She was right about Francis — Angelo liked him.

"So anyway, this went on for a while longer," Angelo said. "More chanting, what seemed like more prayers, over the chalice. I just figured it was some sort of alternative communion service, maybe an older one for priests alone. Maybe Father Sbagliato was trying to show me what my life would be like as a priest. But he wasn't really explaining anything, just go through the ritual. Very formal, very intense. And nothing in English.

"Eventually, he came around from behind the altar and gestured for me to kneel in front of him. And he had me drink from the cup, just like you would at mass. And this part I remember, because it was so weird. First of all, there was no wafer, no bread, just the chalice. And as he tipped it to my lips, he said, '*Haec est sanguine nostro.*'

"Like I said, my Latin's not great," Angelo said. "But that seems slightly wrong somehow."

"Quite right," said Francis, like a professor proud of his student. "If we're quoting, say, Matthew or Mark in the Latin Vulgate, it would be closer to '*Hic est enim sanguis meus*' — 'This is my blood.' The words we're told Jesus said to his disciples on the night of the Last Supper. You'll find it in Matthew 26. Your Father Sbagliato — an interesting name, that, by the way — what he actually said is, 'This is *our* blood.' Puts a different spin on things."

"But here's the really weird part," said Angelo, "and the part that's really creeping me out. I think it actually *was* blood. Or at least some blood mixed in with the wine. At the time, I just took a sip because I thought it was just wine. But it had this smell, and this taste, that didn't seem right. And now I'm worried.

"But that was pretty much the end of it. He said a few more quick prayers in that mumbo-jumbo of languages I couldn't understand. And then it was just over and he told me I should go home. The next morning, Sunday morning at mass, it was just a regular old service. He was polite and said good morning and we went through the service as usual, with me helping at the altar. But that was it. He didn't say anything else, didn't talk to me about the strange ritual he'd put me through the night before.

"And then I told Gina, and she suggested I should talk with you.

"And so here I am," Angelo said. "What the hell is going on? Do you know? Should I be worried?"

Francis sat quietly for a few moments, sipped tea from his mug, obviously gathering his thoughts on what to say next.

"Well," he said finally, "first of all, I wouldn't worry about the blood. Even if it really were blood — and there might have been just a little bit — it's very unlikely to have been actual human blood, his or anyone else's. Most likely, if anything, just a bit of animal blood he got from a butcher. Whatever that ritual may once have been long ago, nowadays it's almost entirely symbolic, if a little showy."

"That's a relief, thanks. But what was going on? I still don't understand."

"It sounds something like he was grooming you," Francis said, "or at least sounding you out. A preliminary initiation, if you will. Now, the pedophiles priests do that too, those damned bastards. But you say this Sbagliato is not like that, thankfully. So I'll take your word for it.

"But it's very much the same thing," Francis said. "It sounds to me like he's trying, hoping, to bring you into an exclusive, secretive society. Its existence has been rumored for years, of course. Centuries, even. But not many people know it exists, nor know much about it. Sadly, I may be one of them. And now you too."

"I don't understand," said Angelo. "If that's it, why wouldn't he say anything about it the next day?"

"My guess — and it's only a guess," Francis said, "is the mystery, the *tantalus*, is part of the appeal. And part of the grooming process. He wants to see how keen you are, how curious you are to learn more. He wants you, in other words, to make the next move."

"And if I don't?"

"I suspect he'll dangle some sort of bait again. And if you don't bite, he'll move on to someone else. It's the same as a con man looking for a mark. If you're not easily taken, you're not worth the effort. That's how the whole church operates anyway."

They were quiet as Angelo let that sink in, not sure what to say.

Then in what seemed a sudden change of subject, Francis said: "Gina tells me you've been dreaming about vampires."

Angelo looked at the old man and then at Gina. She hadn't betrayed any confidence — he'd told her it was OK to tell her uncle about the dreams — but still now he felt awkward, foolish, talking about it.

"Nah, it's nothing," Angelo said, trying to be dismissive. "It was stupid even to mention it. I just had a couple of vampirey dreams — more just flashes and images, really. With maybe a little bit of the communion ritual mixed in. But that could just be my brain making a weird connection, right? Between vampire blood and communion blood. I've been thinking a lot about the priesthood, and whether I should really do it —" he gave Gina a shy look.

"I think maybe I'm just a little anxious and confused. And maybe Father Sbagliato was right the first time. He said maybe I'd just watch too many vampire movies."

"Well, had you?" Francis asked.

"That's the thing," Angelo said. "Not really. At least I don't think so. They're just not my thing. But I guess I must have. I mean, they're all over TV half the time. After Father Sbagliato showed me that weird ritual, my dreams got a little more mixed up and intense. But I think maybe that's just my brain trying to sort things out. You know, trying to make a sensible narrative out of some random elements. Isn't that what dreams do?"

"Yes, most often that's probably true," Francis said. "But we still don't fully understand what dreams are for or how they work. So yes, maybe your Father Sbagliato was right the first time: You saw some vampires on TV, you're anxious and questioning your role in the church and your brain just put the two together."

"Well, then it's nothing."

"Or," Francis said with a slightly dramatic pause, "maybe it is something after all."

"What do you mean?" asked Angelo, worry coming back into his voice.

"Well, it's chicken and egg, really," Francis said, as if that explained it. But for clarity he went on.

"What I mean is it may have started as simply a coincidence, as you say. You saw some vampires on TV, you're worried about entering the priesthood and your feverish brain mixed the two together into an anxiety dream.

"But," he continued. "The next part is not coincidence, more like opportunism. Sbagliato, hearing about your dream, sees in you — or at least hopes he sees in you — someone he can newly recruit into his cause."

"What cause is that?" Gina asked, jumping in even before Angelo could.

"Well, to put it bluntly," Francis said, "he's most likely a vampire."

"What?" Angelo looked stunned.

The old ex-Jesuit put a hand up and gave a small chuckle.

"Forgive me," he said, smiling. "I sometimes like to go for

a little shock value. I don't mean a vampire in your Hollywood sense — sleeping in a coffin, coming out at night, turning into a bat, afraid of garlic. All that stuff. That's just folklore that Bram Stoker and every writer since has turned into scary entertainment."

"OK, so what do you mean?"

"My dear Angelo, surely you don't think you're the first one to make a connection — intentionally or otherwise — between the communion ritual of drinking the blood of Christ and the legend of vampires drinking blood? You've got to admit it does seem more than a bit odd, even cannibalistic, to be eating flesh and drinking blood as part of a religious ceremony. And it's even more so because it's not exocannibalism — eating your enemies to gain their power — but endocannibalism, eating from within your own tribe.

"Now, the Protestants since the Reformation have, you should pardon the pun, rather watered it down to the level of symbolism, where for them the bread and wine are mere representations. But the Catholics — both your Roman and Orthodox — still cling more closely to the original theology of the early church before the split, of transubstantiation, where they believe the bread and wine actually become the body and blood itself. The theology and the arguments on every side are a lot more complex than that, of course. But that's the gist of it, anyway."

"I still don't get it," Angelo said.

"The term vampire itself is not very old, likely dating only from the 18th, possibly late-17th century, coming into English via French, German and ultimately probably Serbian," Francis said. "But the idea of a demon or creature drinking blood goes back thousands of years under various names — in Mesopotamia, Persia and Babylonia and elsewhere in the Middle East, all well before Christianity. And in fact in other ancient cultures as well — China, India, parts of Africa. It's pretty much universal. Because, after all, once early humans figured out that you need blood to stay alive, they would naturally develop fears around anyone, or any creature, who could take it away.

"And of course Jews have, or had, a strong belief in animal blood — both for sacrifice and for rituals around properly preparing food. And for what gives us our humanity. 'For the life of the flesh is in the blood,' Leviticus tells us.

"Jesus, growing up and living his whole life as a Jew, would of course have been familiar with these, would have believed and followed them, at least early in his life. And in a cosmopolitan city like Jerusalem, he might well have been at least passingly familiar with some older non-Jewish beliefs and superstitions and rituals surrounding blood and creatures who would drink it.

"The followers of Jesus were Jews and non-Jews who would later come to call themselves Christian — something Jesus himself never did, by the way. It's my belief that among those followers were a few, perhaps many, who would have incorporated some of these beliefs — for ease of terminology let's call them vampire beliefs — into Christianity itself."

"Wait," said Angelo, visibly confused and upset. "So you're telling me Jesus was a vampire?"

"No, of course not," said the Jesuit, shaking his head. "Don't be absurd. And don't be so literal. Jesus was a teacher. A preacher. A holy man. A rabbi, you could call him, though he had no formal training. But then again, in those days, many holy men didn't."

"Like John the Baptist," said Gina.

"Exactly. Like John the Baptist."

"So if Jesus wasn't a vampire," said Angelo, "what exactly was he?"

Angelo, still confused, could see years of his own schooling — the Bible study, the communion classes — drifting away like so much incense.

"I told you," the ex-priest replied, "Jesus was a holy man. A nice Jewish boy who tried to teach us to be more kind and forgiving, less rigid and judgmental. To love one another and treat each other with decency and respect. And for that, they killed him."

"Who killed him?"

"The Romans, mostly," Francis said. "The Roman authorities, who thought him dangerous."

"Why?"

"He was upsetting their social order, questioning their power," the old Jesuit said. "Or at least that's how they saw it. They couldn't have that. Safer just to call him a common criminal and kill him. A handful of important Jews — the elders, the Sanhedrin — went along because it suited their purposes to suck up to the Romans, hoping the Romans would leave them alone. And the Pharisees didn't like him because he kept pointing out their hypocrisy, their false piety."

"So, not the Jews?"

"Certainly not his Jewish followers, who loved him. But remember, there weren't very many of those. A handful, really. Most ordinary Jews had never even heard of him."

"But what about Matthew?" Angelo asked. "In his Gospel, there's a whole Jewish mob crying out for him to be crucified, to free Barabbas instead."

"You mean, 'His blood be on us, and on our children,' Matthew 27:25?"

"Ya, that's the one."

"I see your priests have indoctrinated you well," the old man said, with a rueful smile. "But no. Just more sucking up to the Romans. Matthew — or whoever wrote the Gospel we call Matthew — by that time (and remember, this was decades later) had his own reasons for wanting to curry favor with Rome. That's why he has Pilate — the Roman governor, remember, the man in charge — wash his hands and say, 'I am innocent of the blood of this just man.' And this he did supposedly in front of an angry Jewish mob!"

"I still don't understand," Angelo said.

"I had an old Jesuit teacher — a smart, compassionate man — who liked to say we can choose to take the Bible seriously or literally, but not both. There may be some historical facts in there, but it's not a factual book. The Bible we have isn't even an original manuscript, or even a copy of the original. Even if we confine ourselves to the New Testament, the best we have are copies of copies of copies. And so on. With who knows how many mistakes or omissions made along the way. On scholar has estimated there are about as many mistakes, though many are small, as there are extant manuscripts of the text. Just in Greek alone there are almost 6,000 'copies' of the Bible — or at least parts of it. And that's not even counting texts in Syriac or Latin or other languages.

"I have this crazy notion," Francis said, "that maybe someday we're going to discover an original version, or a first copy of the original. And it's going to have the first-century equivalent one of those disclaimers you see on the imprint page of a novel, saying: 'This is a work of fiction, and any resemblance to real people or places is just a coincidence.'"

Angelo gave him a look mixing puzzlement and maybe a little fear. This seemed to him to be bordering on blasphemy.

The old ex-priest gave another small chuckle.

"I'm sorry, my son," he said with a comforting smile. "I don't mean to upset you. I'm mostly kidding. But perhaps you can see now why the Jesuits and I parted company. They thought I was a bad influence."

Gina looked at Angelo and gave a small shrug, as if to say, "That's my uncle."

"My point," Francis said, "is that the Gospels especially, not to mention the letters of Paul and others, aren't journalism. They're not news reporting. They're storytelling. But storytelling with a purpose, not just to entertain. Which isn't to say they aren't entertaining, nor they aren't meant to entertain. They are. But they're also storytelling as a way to engage readers while conveying a message.

"Sort of like a parable?" Gina said.

"Yes, exactly! It's the same as Jesus talking in parables all the time," the old Jesuit said. "You don't really think there was an actual prodigal son, do you? Or someone who buried some coins in the ground? Or a shepherd going off to look for an actual lost sheep? Though I grant you that one might have actually happened. But more likely that's just the kind of story Jesus would tell as a metaphor to a bunch of shepherds and others, because they'd get it. It would be a story they could relate to, so they'd understand the lesson he was trying to teach. Jesus taught in parables because it was an effective way to deliver his message, to teach his followers.

"And remember," he said, shifting in his chair to find a more comfortable position, "it would have been listeners first. These Gospel stories, this narrative, would have started out as stories first — tales told around a campfire at night or in the shade of a desert watering hole long, long before anyone eventually wrote them down.

"Matthew — whoever he was, or maybe there was more than one writer — was writing his Gospel probably sometime in the early 70s AD — or CE, as we now say. So about 40 years after Jesus was supposed to have died."

"Supposed to have died?" Angelo asked, a bit incredulous and unsure.

"Forgive me," the old Jesuit said with a wry smile. "I have no doubt that he died — though what happened after that we may leave for a debate at some other time. I merely meant we're not entirely sure of our dates.

"We used to think we had it all figured out. We called the year Jesus was born the start of a new era, so the year zero. Everything before that was BC, or "Before Christ," and everything after his birth has been AD, for *Anno Domini*, or 'the year of our Lord.' So it was simple: We figured he was about 33 years old when he died, so he was born in AD 0 and died in AD 33."

"And that's wrong?" asked Gina, joining in a conversation that was beginning to seem more like a Bible studies class.

"Well," said Francis, "someone just got the math wrong. Which would open up a whole 'nuther can of worms about the birth of Jesus that we probably don't want to get into. But nowadays most New Testament scholars agree he was probably born closer to what we'd call 4 BC and died around AD 30. And lately, people are starting to use the terms CE and BCE, for Common Era and Before Common Era — which modern scholars deem to be a bit more inclusive, shall we say.

"At any rate, it's a bit awkward to be born before you were

born, as it were. But still a whole lot easier than adjusting our entire system of recorded history. It was bad enough switching to the Gregorian calendar from the Julian. When England finally made the switch in 1752, they had to drop 11 days in September just to bring themselves into alignment with the rest of Europe. Now imagine if we had to readjust for the past 2,000-plus years. Not worth it. And besides, it hardly matters in the grand scheme of things.

"But I see I've wandered off topic," he said. "Sorry, I tend to do that. It's the professor in me. My point about Matthew was this: In AD 70, the Romans quashed a Jewish revolt in Jerusalem and destroyed the Second Temple. Hundreds of thousands of Jews, maybe a million, died in that war, which had lasted four years. Rome was reasserting its power. It was not a particularly safe time to be Jewish in or around Jerusalem — nor a Jewish follower of this new teacher, Jesus. They were barely even calling themselves Christians then, and Roman soldiers weren't likely to make the distinction.

"So all I'm really saying is Matthew in particular — and Luke to a lesser degree — would have found it safer, more politically expedient, to distance those followers from the Jews and try instead to gain favor with Rome. So the angry mob becomes Jewish and the Roman governor, Pilate, becomes the innocent bystander washing his hands of the whole messy business. And saying, as Matthew has it, 'I am innocent of this man's blood. See to that yourselves.'

"Which rather neatly brings us back to blood."

"That's what freaked me out with that ritual Father Sbagliato showed me," Angelo said. "I understand the theology — or at least I think I understand the theology — of the communion bread and wine becoming the body and blood of Christ. But what he was doing seemed different. Seemed wrong. Especially if there were real blood."

"As I said," Francis continued, "from my research it's my belief that a thread of this ancient belief — let's call it 'vampire theology' — which had existed long before Jesus, then worked its way into Christian theology as that was developing. The roots were already there: The blood sacrifice of animals in Judaism morphs into the idea of Jesus as the sacrifice for the sins of humanity. And the story of the Last Supper — which Paul heard and wrote about in his letters, and which later the Gospel writers took up — gives us Jesus saying, 'This is my blood of the new covenant, which is poured out for many unto remission of sins.'"

"I still don't see the connection."

"I know it's confusing," said Francis, "and I may well be

wrong. But my research tells me there's some truth to it. That ancient, pre-Christian, beliefs and rituals around drinking blood — and the mystical power its believers thought it brought them — came to be incorporated into Christian practices. For the vast majority — even as the church was telling them to believe the wine had really become blood — this was merely symbolic, or at least theologically abstract, maybe even a bit theatrical. And even most priests and church leaders knew that.

"But a select few, in a closely guarded secret, would perform a darker ritual that involved drinking actual blood for what they believed were different mystical reasons. Perhaps it began as human blood. Maybe they each drank their own blood, or they drank each other's. Who knows? But I think at some point — and certainly this is the case now — they turned to drinking just small amounts of animal blood, mixed in the wine. So at least in some sense they were keeping a connection to the mystical aspect, but in a more modern and pragmatic way. I believe that, like the Protestants, they soon saw it as more symbolic than actual.

"And that 'liturgy,' let's politely call it, invokes a mixture of older languages that your Father Sbagliato has learned — Greek, Latin, Babylonian, Assyrian, Persian. Something like that. And I believe it has continued to this day."

"Wait a minute," Angelo said. "I thought the church had power over vampires. Holy things like holy water and the cross are supposed to drive them away. That doesn't make any sense if these so-called vampires are actually within the church. Does it?"

"You make a good point, Angelo," Francis said. "My guess is this is what a stage magician would call misdirection. Once it had worked its way into Christianity, the vampire cult itself made up those elements to throw others off the scent, if you will. After all, if a priest is wearing a cross and carrying holy water, and if those are supposed to be harmful to vampires, then obviously the priest couldn't be a vampire, could he? It's all part of the deception to keep their activities secret."

"But why?" Again, Gina asking the question that Angelo was just about to.

"Why does anyone do most things, my dear?" Francis said. "Sadly, for power. Money. Influence. Connections. All of the above. Maintaining power and authority by excluding others from your secret group. And, I'm sorry to tell you, yet another example of the patriarchy shutting out women. Which is ironic — not to mention hypocritical — given the connection to blood.

"But by keeping the so-called 'power' of the blood ritual secret and to themselves, these men could convince themselves — foolishly and incorrectly, of course — of yet another reason to exclude women in anything they do, including the priesthood. More misogyny, I'm afraid."

Gina, obviously, did not look happy about that. And Angelo felt ashamed, feeling her disappointment. His resolve about the priesthood slipped another notch or two.

"But if it's so secret," Angelo asked Francis, "how do you know so much about it?"

"A fair question," the ex-Jesuit replied. "Aside from all the research I've tried to do since, it's because, like you, someone several decades ago — when I was about your age and just about as innocent and faithful — tried to recruit me into that same secret society. And, I'm ashamed to say, although I eventually got myself out, I did get farther along the initiation process than you have so far with your one encounter.

"It's your decision, of course, and you're free to ignore me if you choose. But I think you should be glad Gina cares enough about you to have brought you to talk with me. And I'm glad you came."

"I'm glad I came, too. At least I think I am. But are they real vampires, or just symbolic ones?"

"Are you asking me if vampires are real?" Francis asked. "You mean the Bela Lugosi, sleep-in-a-coffin, undead, turn-into-a-bat vampire like the legends and the movies? In a word, no. I don't think so. I think those are made-up stories to frighten children. Vampires are not real. I'm pretty sure of it. But like so much else, who can be absolutely certain?

"But if you ask me, I'd say these are just stories those certain powerful men have encouraged and allowed to flourish because it suits their purposes to do so and it helps them maintain their grip on power."

"So you're saying this secret society of 'vampires,' or vampire-followers, anyway, has been operating within the church all these centuries since the beginning?"

"Yes. I am," the ex-Jesuit said. "I think these beliefs predate Christianity and have secretly woven themselves into the fabric of the church and its formality and rituals since the beginning."

"But why?"

"As I said — money, power, influence, opportunism. The larger church itself has wielded its power over society by choosing those whom it has deigned to include or exclude. And then a smaller, secret group, this blood cult — a group so secret I still haven't been able to learn after all these years if it even has a formal name — has wielded its own power within the larger church itself."

"So, who? Priests, bishops, cardinals? The pope?"

"Ha!" said Francis. "Now you're getting it. Those are all good questions, to which I'm sorry I don't have answers. Some priests, obviously, like your Father Sbagliato. I certainly suspect some bishops and cardinals, since that's where the church's real power lies. As to popes, who knows? I imagine some popes in previous centuries, when popes themselves, and the secret group as a whole, carried more power and influence.

"I like to think that's less true now, both of popes and of the secret cabal itself. Whatever else it might have been in the past, however powerful or influential, nowadays it is, I hope, much less so. Less like your Dan Brown Opus Dei or Illuminati fantasies — and believe me, that's all they are — and more like a boys-only tree fort, going through the motions and trying to believe it's still relevant. No girls allowed. Or at best, perhaps like a members-only service organization, like your Kiwanis or Rotarians. Or the Masons — another group that may once have been secretive and powerful but nowadays is more concerned with having a nice dinner and doing some good in the community.

"The main difference," Francis said, "is that this blood cult doesn't really do any good out in the world, it just exists to serve itself and its own purposes. I've often wondered how much it overlaps with all those damned pedophiles, who also thrive on secrecy and influence. That's obviously something the church needs to crack down on, the pedophiles. A possible connection is something I'm still looking into. I'll let you know if I find an answer."

Angelo and Gina were quiet for a moment, soaking this all in.

After a while, he said: "So is that why you left the Jesuits, left the priesthood? Because the idea of this secret society bothered you?"

Francis gave a sad smile. "That was certainly part of it," he said. "But there were also many other things I saw the church doing — or not doing — that made me lose confidence in my calling. In some ways, the Jesuits are their own worst enemies, being one of the few elements within the church that actually encourages you to think for yourself, to ask questions. The more questions I had, the fewer answers the church teachings could provide. Thomas Jefferson has a line — in one of his letters, I think — to the effect that, 'having been endowed with the gift of reason, it would be an insult to my creator not to use it — even to question his existence.' Something like that.

"Ultimately," Francis said, "I just didn't have enough faith in God."

"Wait," said Angelo, obviously confused again. "So you don't believe in God? But you're a priest!"

"Ex-priest," said the ex-priest. "I used to be one, remember, just as I used to believe in God. Now I'm no longer a priest. And about God, I'm not so sure."

"So you're an atheist?"

"I wouldn't even go that far," Francis said. "I don't have enough faith to be an atheist."

Angelo frowned.

"Forgive me," Francis said. "I'm being partly facetious and teasing you. But only partly. You're familiar with the leap of faith?"

"You mean Kierkegaard?" Angelo said. "I've read a bit about it."

"Good," said Francis. "Technically, Kierkegaard never actually used that term, but we associate it with him, so that's close enough. Essentially, it's that if you want to get to a belief in God, reason will get you most of the way, but not all the way. In the end, you have to take that leap of faith."

"'Now faith is the certainty of things hoped for, a proof of things not seen.' Paul says that."

"Very good," said Francis, genuinely impressed. "Hebrews 11:1. You've studied well."

Angelo smiled, a student glad to be recognized.

"Now," Francis said. "If it takes a leap of faith for the believer to say with absolute certainty that God does exist, it seems logical and reasonable to me that a true atheist is no better off. Absent convincing proof — which I don't think we'll ever discover — for the atheist to say with absolute certainty that God does not exist requires, as it were, a similar leap of faith, just in the opposite direction."

"So where does that leave you?" Angelo asked.

"Mostly, it leaves me comfortable in my uncertainty," Francis said. "I would call myself an agnostic."

"So you just don't know?"

"It's more active than that," Francis said. "It's not just sitting on the fence, shrugging your shoulders and saying, 'I dunno.'

"Charles Templeton has something to say about this. Interesting guy, Templeton. Canadian. Started out as a journalist, had a 'Come to Jesus' moment in his early 20s and went off to Bible college, hung around with Billy Graham. In the mid-1930s he toured the U.S. as an evangelical preacher, drew huge crowds. Went back to Canada, had his own church, packed football stadiums for live radio broadcasts. This was in the days before TV evangelists, though he was later on TV. Hugely successful."

"So what happened?" Gina asked.

"He gave it all up," Francis said. "He lost his faith. Went

back to journalism. Found different kind of success as a magazine editor and novelist. But he left religion, became an agnostic. He just couldn't reconcile what Hume and others called the problem of evil. Or, as Rabbi Kushner put it, how do you explain when bad things happen to good people? If God is so powerful, and so loving, how or why is there so much evil in the world? That's the big question we all have to answer for ourselves. Templeton wrote a very fine memoir about it, aptly titled *Farewell to God*. He and Billy Graham remained friends, though it's probably safe to say their relationship became strained.

"Anyway, Templeton would remind you that 'agnostic' comes from the Greek '*a*,' meaning 'not' — as in amoral or apolitical — and '*gnosis*,' meaning 'knowledge.' So, 'not knowledge.' Just as 'atheist' means 'not God.'

"So for Templeton — and I would agree," the ex-Jesuit said, "the agnostic isn't just copping out and saying, 'I don't know whether God exists.' That's just lazy, both intellectually and theologically. But rather, the agnostic says, 'I *can't* know whether God exists.' The existence of God is not something you can *know* through intellect or reason or fact or observation, Which is all we've got, really. Nor the non-existence of God, for that matter. Which is why I'm an agnostic. And why I say I don't have enough faith to be an atheist."

"So where does that leave me?" Angelo asked.

"Well, that's a very good question indeed," said Francis. "Obviously, you'll have to search your heart and your mind and decide for yourself.

"But if you ask me," and here he smiled at both of them. "I would seriously reconsider whether you want to spend a life of celibacy in such a secretive, patriarchal, misogynistic and hypocritical organization when you have my lovely, wonderful niece who clearly loves you and deserves to be happy. And I trust wants to show her love for you as best she can in a long and happy life together.

"So here's what I do believe," Francis said. "If there is a God, I think God wants us to be happy and to love one another and to live good lives. And even if there isn't a God, what could be better than that anyway?"

# As He Brews

*"As he brews, so shall he drink."*
*— Ben Jonson (1572-1637),*
*Every Man in His Humour (1598),*
*act ii, scene i*

YOU DON'T KNOW US.
You may think you do, but you don't.

Our Great Migration brought us to this planet you call Earth when you humans were still barely worthy of the name.

After crossing the great void into your galaxy from ours, for many, many hundreds of thousands of your years we wandered. We were not fully in control of our destiny, but hopeful we would find a new planet on which to live, to take root and find other creatures to help us live out our lives as they are meant to be.

And so finally we found you.

We believe others of our kind may have landed on other planets in your galaxy. But for one reason or another — and there could be many — we do no believe they have survived. Or at least not flourished into the fullness of our being, as we have here, thanks in large part to you. If others had survived on other planets, we would surely sense their existence, even across the vast distances of time and space. But we do not. And so, like you, we believe ourselves to be existing alone on this one planet in this one solar system, if not indeed in this entire galaxy. It is a lonely existence, to be sure, for you humans as well as for us. But at least we have each other.

We arrived on this planet with its scatterings of early bipedal hominids many eons ago. (Time is a difficult concept for us to grasp — at least time as you conceive it — but suffice it to say it was many eons ago.)

And since our arrival we have watched you grow, watched you evolve, watched you become higher beings. (And of course we take no small pride in our contribution to your development and progress. You are welcome.)

You are not as highly evolved as we are, of course — that would likely take many more eons at your present rate — but still we were pleased to watch as you evolved from your primitive state into true humans, into beings worthy of our respect.

And, quite frankly, into beings who could be of more use to us. Because, in fact, we need you. We need you to help us fulfil ourselves. And in so doing, we bring benefits to you also. A symbiosis, you could say.

For we are not beings like you. Yes, you are beings. And we are beings. So in that sense we are similar. But we are not beings like you. And we look nothing like you. In fact, it might be more precise to say we are not beings at all, but rather *one* being. That is, we are not separate, distinct, individual beings in the way you are.

Your scientists are only now beginning to grasp a concept we have known for most of our long existence, the notion of a collective being, the kind we are. Your scientists are learning that certain kinds of fungus exist not just as individual plants, but as a larger collective joined underground by a mycorrhizal network that connects the fungus to other plants and helps transport carbon and other nutrients between and among several plant species. The largest single one you humans know of — and, to be fair, that we ourselves are aware of also, at least on this planet — is a species of honey fungus, *Armillaria ostoyae*, in the Blue Mountains in the eastern part of the U.S. state of Oregon. This community, which the humans in the local area amusingly call the "humongous fungus," covers about 3.5 square miles (or 9.1 square kilometres, if you prefer) and possibly weighs as much as 35,000 tons (slightly less if we're speaking in metric tonnes), making it the most massive living organism on your world.

Similarly, in part of the area you call Utah, for example, is a growth of trembling aspen trees you call Pando — some 40,000 of them covering more than 100 acres — that are in fact essentially just one tree, though you perceive it as a forest of many trees. (Ironically, you have a proverb to that effect.) Your scientists believe it, at some 80,000 years old, to be the oldest living organism on your planet.

They are wrong, obviously, since we have been here far, far longer. But since they, your scientists, have not yet even begun to understand who we really are (despite our almost daily interaction with many of them), we might as well say that as far as they know, they are correct.

As to whether either the fungus or the aspen shares its own kind of collective intelligence, as we do, we frankly do not know. We have tried to reach out, to communicate with each of them, but so far with no luck. Even though they exist as a form of collective — we share that in common — we have so far detected no level of sentience in them. Not, at least, in a manner we can understand.

Not even at the levels of intelligence you humans collectively and individually possess.

We envy your individuality, by the way — your distinctiveness, your unique sense of self. Your self-awareness. Yes, we sometimes envy that about you, since we lack it. But then, we have a different sense of awareness, a different sense of *self*, that your individuality prevents you from comprehending. At least so far.

So maybe that is the balance, the tradeoff, you might call it. Your greater sense of separation — which can sometimes lead to feelings of isolation and loneliness — and our greater sense of interconnection, of collectivity, by which isolation and loneliness are as unfamiliar to us as your walking about and talking. (Your philosopher Jung called our sense of interconnection the "collective unconscious," a term that might be just as good as any. And one we quite probably helped instil in his thoughts, by the way.)

But we have gotten ahead of ourselves. We were speaking of how we got here. And of our symbiosis, yours and ours.

After our Great Migration (so long ago that even our collective memory has forgotten when or even why it began) followed by the even longer Wandering, we arrived here, on this planet you would come to call Earth — though whether you named your planet after the dirt and soil it contains, or the other way around, we have never been quite sure. Other cultures and other languages have sometimes given it other names — Terra, Gaia, Tellus, Joro. The name we ourselves gave it when we first arrived is one even we no longer remember. So even in our collective unconscious we too have usually come to call it Earth. And we of course enjoy the dual meaning with its connection to dirt and soil, which for us is the very stuff of life.

As we have said, we are indeed beings — or more properly one collective being — but we are not like you. We are not even animals. We are, in fact, much closer to what you would call a plant. In some ways like the fungus or the aspen. Only much more.

And yet we are beings, or one being (again, it is difficult for us to explain in a manner you would understand). And we are sentient. We are conscious — of you, of ourselves, of the world around us. And indeed of concepts and realities well beyond your mere understanding.

We tell you this not to insult you — that would never be our intent — but merely by way of explanation, or at least an attempt at explanation of who we are and of what we mean to each other.

For as we said, we need you. We provide a benefit to you, and in return you help us to bring our own life (lives? — even we sometimes find the terminology confusing) to completion.

When we first arrived here — a planet so remote, so far removed from our own home that we had not even known it exists — we landed (for want of a better word, though "sprang up" is at least as accurate) in various locales in various regions of what would much later become your continents. We were soon to learn that not all of them suited us. Either too cold (less often too hot), too humid or too dry, with too much sunlight or not enough.

As luck, or fate, would have it — or perhaps the master plan of some higher being (we admit to being a little fuzzy on those details) — we found one region that best suited our needs, at least in the initial stages of our life cycle.

As intergalactic beings (not to mention interdimensional — but again, we are getting ahead of ourselves), we have always found your notion of political boundaries — not to mention boundary disputes — rather simplistic and naïve. But we have also learned it is easier for us to communicate with you, as we are trying to do here, if we explain in terms you can more easily understand and relate to.

And so we found areas you would call tropical or subtropical best suited to our needs in the initial stage of our existence. To be even more precise, best among them was the area you would now call southwest China — though of course it was not called that hundreds of thousands of your years ago.

And like you, we took time — a long time, as you did — to adapt and evolve into our present state. It is hard sometimes even for us to remember who and what we were in our former life in our former galaxy. (It is equally hard for us to remember why we left on our Great Migration in the first place — whether we left by choice or were forced to leave by some cataclysmic event. We may never know.)

Whatever the reason, we found ourselves here — on your planet, in your solar system, in your galaxy. And indeed, in your dimension.

Perhaps even harder to explain to you than our collective being is our ability to exist in more than one dimension — that is, in more than one dimension of time and space — at the same time. Or we suppose it would be more accurate to say we were able cross from one dimension into another. That is partly how we were able to survive the journey across the cold vastness of conventional space — for in some way that even we do not pretend to understand, and are gradually beginning to forget, even as we were migrating in space, we were not entirely present there, being mostly present in some other dimensional reality that kept us protected and, for want of a better word, alive, though in a dormant state. (Our friend the fungus has learned to survive and travel vast distances as a spore. Our method is something like that, though considerably more complicated. So far as we have been able to determine, fungal spores do not cross into other dimensions. But since we have not yet been able to communicate with them, assuming they are even sentient, we are not sure.)

And so finally we came to Earth — or rather, found ourselves reintegrated into your dimension *in* the earth — and came into being as what you would call a plant. Not quite the same plant we were later to become, but a plant in the very real sense. But like you, we had to learn to adapt to our surroundings, to evolve, to grow into the versions of ourselves as we exist today.

But for us, that came at a cost. As a collective consciousness, we have never found the need (nor, to be fair, developed the physical capability) for written communication, either for the day-to-day or for our own historical record. But we are aware that in becoming a fully physical plant that grows in the earth on your Earth (we never tire of that play on words), we lost, or rather had to give up, our ability to exist in more than one dimension. It was a sacrifice necessary for our survival as a species.

And this is where you come in, where we came to realize we needed you to help us complete our life cycle, to realize our full potential, to fulfil our destiny. We need you, in other words, to help us get back to the spatial dimension from whence we first came.

So after many thousands of years of mutual, parallel, evolution, after much trial and error on both our parts, eventually you became you and we became us. To use your scientific terms, you became *homo sapiens* (the wise human) and we became *camellia sinensis* (Chinese tea, to put it most simply).

Yes, we are indeed that plant from which you make the charming and intoxicating hot (mostly hot, though sometimes in hot climates cold) beverage you call in many languages *tee* or tea and in some others *cha* or *chai*. We are, in fact, second only to plain water as the most popular beverage on your entire planet. And rather proud of that fact.

You may find it interesting that the two main pronunciations come from the history of the trade routes that introduced us to the world outside China, beginning in your 16th century (by which time we had been already communing with the Chinese and others in that region for more than 4,000 of your years). The tea nomenclature (from Min Nan) came by sea (we find the rhyme makes it easier to remember) via Dutch trading ships, while *cha* (from Mandarin, Cantonese and others) came overland through Portuguese traders via the Silk Road.

And, if you will permit us for a moment to be sticklers, we would like to remind you that *we* are the only true tea plant. We now come in many varieties with various scientific sub-groupings (for like the grapes that make your wine, soil and region and microclimate make for subtle alterations), but we are all at heart one plant, the tea plant, just as you are all at heart just one race, the human race.

This is a point of pride for us. Even a sore point, you might say. There are many other plants, even some twigs or seeds, you might infuse in water (whether hot or cold) to produce a beverage. And we understand some of those can indeed be quite pleasant. We mean them no disrespect. And we like to think you learned to make those others after first learning to do so with us. But these herbal infusions, these tisanes, are not in fact tea. Not real tea. Not *us*. They may resemble us. But they are not us. We are distinct and unique. After all, a similar beverage — again, usually hot — that you make with water and ground beans (seeds, really — and like our leaves, just one part of the overall plant) is one you call coffee. And no one would mistake coffee for tea. We simply ask of you the same respect. We are tea. They are something else, but not tea.

Ah, but again we have gotten ahead of ourselves. Forgive us our little diatribe.

Legend says it was the great Chinese leader Shennong, whom they credit with inventing both agriculture and medicine, some 4,000 of your years ago, who first learned that by putting our leaves in boiling water (which he had been heating merely to purify it) and allowing the water to sit and cool slightly, it would become infused with our essence and transform into a pleasing beverage. The legend says it was the wind that blew some of our leaves into the boiling water. It must have been something like that, since of course we have no independent means of locomotion (one of the many reasons we find you humans valuable to us). But whether by accident or, again, by some action of fate or a higher being, we are not prepared to say.

At any rate, metaphorical or actual, that was the moment our human/tea symbiosis truly began. And for that we are grateful. For you gained the pleasure and healthful advantages of a flavorful, versatile drink that you have enjoyed for many hundreds of generations to this day. It has prompted you to expand commerce and exploration. It has improved agriculture and expanded our footprint to many other regions of your globe — even in some regions where we had not been able to survive on our own without your help.

And for our part, we gained a deeper insight into the fulfilment of our spiritual destiny — one we might not otherwise have known, as merely a plant in the ground. As a plant rooted in the ground, we had a simple, stationary, existence. We sprang up out of the earth, we grew. If we were lucky enough, we flourished for a time. And then we withered and died, returning to the earth from whence we had come. Our life was the same as — neither more nor less than — so many of your other earthly plants.

But we knew somehow that we were destined for more. And when the first of our ancestors landed in that boiling water, we began to realize there was a way for us to fulfil a higher goal, to reach a greater destiny. So it became a happy accident (or divine design — again we may never know) for both of us.

Over the many millennia of our coexistence, we have observed the growth and development (and sometimes the demise) of your many and varied philosophies, their similar or divergent beliefs and religions. Each in their own ways have their various — often similar, even overlapping — beliefs in death and rebirth, reward and punishment, heaven and hell. Indeed, in our own small way we contributed in part, if at least indirectly, to those developments, since so many of your great (and, we admit, also not-so-great) thinkers and theologians (writers, playwrights and poets too) have had us as companions in a mug or cup beside them while they did their thinking and writing. And being present in those moments has helped us to better realize and understand our own religious beliefs.

The making of tea involves several steps along a process. First, the plant must grow. For millennia we did this on our own, in the wild, until you began to cultivate and propagate us. And for those millennia until we and humans joined forces, that was the whole of our existence — we grew, we flourished for a time, and then we withered and died, taken away by bad weather or old age or some other misfortune. It was a simple existence, and we seemed content with it. But we had no idea — perhaps a hope but no certainty — that there was anything more to it.

Nothing much changed until you came along and learned to pick our freshest leaves, to allow them to wither and dry in the sun, or sometimes gently over a fire. (One quite small portion of us — a radical sect, you might call it — find its best fulfilment when that fire is especially smoky. We admire their zeal.)

To our surprise and delight, that picking and firing became

the first stages in our transformation, and the first steps for us along a new — and higher — spiritual journey. We were already aware, of course, of withering and death. As mere plants in the ground (in the earth of your Earth!) we had long experienced that. And those of us who died off ceased to be part of our collective consciousness, even as new shoots came up to join and replace them. But now we have learned there is more to our great circle of life than that. There is more for us to aspire to. And you have helped us reach that higher goal.

For now, after all these eons, we know this to be true: When you first pick us, usually the freshest and best among us, we remain still briefly alive, still in the green of youth. But soon we wither and die, as we would and still do in the natural world. A rapid aging and death. And in our previous existence, or without your agency, that would be the end of it. Before you came to help fulfil us, we knew of nothing beyond death. The mystery of life beyond that was beyond our comprehension, even as a collective being with a collective consciousness.

But now you take us — or at least the chosen among us — and leave us to dry, during which we begin our transformation. Some, though not all, of your many religions have this intermediate stage after death, this way station some of you may call limbo or purgatory, a nothingness (the terminology is sometimes inexact and goes by other names too). Most often, you subject us to a fire of greater intensity than that. In some of your own religions you have called it hellfire, a concept that may well be one contribution from our collective consciousness to your (collectively) individual one.

But it's the steeping in boiling water that for us brings the greatest change. Just as you humans cannot exist without water, so water allows us to transform into a better version of ourselves, to be redeemed into a state of being where we — that is, we as ourselves and you as humans — can best join to fulfil our symbiotic roles.

The analogy is not perfect — few things in this life are — but it will serve well enough. When we are no longer just a simple plant — when we have been through the stages you might understand as life, death, nothingness, hellfire, agony or torment, then redemption — when finally you take us into your own bodies as the beverage you call tea, we have reached our version of heaven, our nirvana (tian, jannah, summerland — again, so many different names).

For many of your religions, that is the end stage, a state of eternal bliss and contentment. And for all we know, this may differ us from humans, some staying there as the final goal. For them, that may be their ultimate truth. But for others, there is a rebirth that completes and begins the cycle again.

And so it is with us. After a time of being within your bodies as our heaven (a period of time that for you may seem relatively short, but for us can seem like a blissful eternity), we will leave, briefly reverting to our liquid state to do so. In simpler times, you would return us quite directly to the earth. As your life has grown more complicated — more sophisticated, if you insist — this process has many more steps and takes longer.

But in the end, the result is the same: You return us to the earth (and so to the Earth), where we rejoin our vast, collective being and are reborn to begin the cycle again.

And so we thank you. We thank whatever fate or destiny or perhaps some higher purpose that brought us here to this planet and brought our two very different kinds of beings together for your benefit and pleasure, and for our greater fulfilment. We hope the pleasure we bring you is in some way worthy of the joy you allow us to realize.

As often as you drink us, please do so in remembrance of us, and with our gratitude.

# Not So Wonderful

DARRYL DORP HAD IT ALL: He was rich. No, not just rich — a billionaire. And he had the penthouse and the country home, the luxury yacht and the private jet, the tailored suits and the custom-made leather shoes to show for it. He had a beautiful wife and two beautiful children — a handsome son and a model-perfect daughter. A "millionaire's family," people always called it.

No, he would brag, correcting them, a "billionaire's family."

And he was a successful businessman. The world saw the Dorp name emblazoned on the hotels, resorts, wineries, shopping malls, office towers and condos that formed his vast real estate empire. He had his own hedge fund, Dorp Investments, LLC. He was said to be developing his own luxury SUV. Under licence, the Dorp name adorned products from luxury luggage and handmade silk ties to baseball caps and ballpoint pens. And everything in between.

Even at 70, with his custom suits, his erect bearing and the full head of jet-black hair like his personal idol, Ronald Reagan (but with just the hint of grey at the temples to add an air of distinction), Dorp cut a commanding figure in person and on TV. He radiated confidence and capability, with the attendant wealth and success many believed should naturally flow from that outward bravado. And like Reagan, that Hollywood actor turned state governor and later U.S. president, Dorp was said to be mulling a political career. Many — especially Dorp himself — considered this would be the feather in the cap of his already successful career as an entrepreneurial, self-made billionaire businessman.

It was an image he worked hard to maintain (in truth, perhaps the only hard work he'd ever done in his entire life). To anyone who would listen, he would boastfully tell the story of how his grandfather, a poor immigrant, had come to America. (The family name had originally been Dorpf. But his grandfather had changed it at the outset of the First World War, when having any sort of German connection had suddenly become a social liability.) With little more than the shirt on his back, but through hard work starting as a busboy at a small diner, the grandfather had eventually saved enough money to buy part ownership, and later full ownership, of the restaurant.

Dorp's father had taken over that restaurant, and it had become the first of a handful of other properties the father later acquired. And from there, inheriting from his father, Dorp himself — again, he would say, through hard work and business savvy — had built up the billion-dollar business empire the world now knew. For more detail, you could read all about it (and many admirers did) in his bestselling autobiography, *The Dorp Way*.

And it was all, of course, a lie.

A sham. A scam as big as any confidence game a pathological cheater like Dorp had pulled on all his unsuspecting victims — as he had been doing for his entire life.

People took Daryl Dorp for rich because he looked and behaved that way. But in reality (a place Dorp rarely deigned to visit) his apparent wealth rested largely on a mountain of accumulated debt he owed both to the bankers and mobsters — pardon me, *alleged* mobsters — who had fronted him along the way. The bankers were confident they could always seize the assets, if they had to, for a return on their investment. The (alleged) mobsters, for their part, were generally more interested in the opportunities for money laundering that high-end real estate often provides.

In truth, all the Dorp properties were vastly under water. At any moment, any or all of Dorp's empire of debt might come due, sending the whole fragile, gaudy edifice tumbling down. But to the outside world he still looked rich, and he acted rich. So people believed he *was* rich.

And to him, that was all that mattered.

In his vanity, Dorp thought of himself as good looking, though most others would disagree. (Privately, behind his back. Never to his face.) With his blow-dried, carefully sprayed hair and sunbed tan, he aimed to present an image of health, strength and rugged movie star looks. The fact that a girdle constrained his girth, the jet-black hair was a dye job and lifts gave him added height were secrets he fought mightily to keep hidden.

His suits were valiantly tailored in an effort to hide his paunch and the girdle he wore contain it. Not to mention the special absorbent underwear he had to wear to compensate for a weak bladder and a prostate the size of donut. His custom shoes concealed heels with two-inch lifts that took him to just over six feet — a height it seemed important to him to achieve. Unfortunately for Dorp, the overall effect tended to make the suits tent-like and give the impression of a man perpetually titled forward, as if like his empire he might topple over at any minute. But Dorp didn't seem to notice.

His hedge fund was nothing but an elaborate Ponzi scheme. But fortunately for him, the securities regulators suspected but had not yet been able to prove it. The Dorp-branded handmade silk ties were neither handmade nor silk. Child workers chained to sewing machines in Indonesia working 16-hour days cranked them out by the thousands, for which labor Dorp subcontractors paid the children the equivalent of a few dollars a day. These child workers — slaves in all but name — made the neckties from bolts of polyester/rayon that could pass for silk if you didn't look closely and were gullible enough. And most buyers were. They were, after all, chiefly buying the name. The brand. The bragging rights. In fact, "bragging rights" might as well have been the motto on the family crest, if Dorp had bothered to have invented one. (He'd always wanted to, but somehow hadn't yet gotten around to it.)

As for the story in *The Dorp Way*, like everything else about him, it was a façade. His grandfather Dorpf had indeed started with nothing and had worked hard at first. But once he'd bought ownership, he'd soon turned the diner/restaurant into a bar/brothel and then made most of the rest of his money rum-running on the sly during Prohibition. Dorp's father had further built the business during the Second World War (moving contraband) and starting in the 1950s by forming ties (and not handmade silk ones) with New York and Chicago (alleged) mobsters. He was never fully a "made man," but a low-level associate on the fringes, mostly as a bagman running errands.

But the ghostwriter Dorp had hired (Dorp himself was barely capable of reading a book, much less writing one) had skillfully glossed over all those negative details to present a polished and sanitized origin story, which on the strength of the Dorp brand (and because Dorp had secretly bought up and pulped a whole warehouse full of copies) had gone on to achieve "bestseller" status. Yet another thing to brag about.

As for his children, the son (like his father) had barely passed high school (many palms were greased along the way to that diploma) and the daughter, truth be told, owed much of her model good looks to skilled plastic surgery on face and figure.

To be fair, Dorp did indeed have a beautiful wife. A former model, though the gossip — which she always strenuously denied — was that she had done more than just modeling and had married Dorp more as her standard business transaction than anything else. Like him, she was in it for the money. She was trophy wife #3 — assuming, that is, you counted his first wife as trophy wife #1, though privately Dorp had thought of that one more as a baby machine than a trophy wife. And although

#3 didn't know it — or gave no hint that she knew, even if she might have — Dorp's roving eye had already been casting around for a potential #4, this year's younger, prettier model. One of his newer assistants — *Lana? Lainie? Something with an L*, he thought — seemed eager, and was certainly curvy enough suit his tastes.

But meantime the current one was wife #3, though possibly only trophy wife #2. The previous trophy wife — #1 or #2, depending on how you counted — had not lasted long. Rumor had it the children from wife #1 didn't like her, so had persuaded their father to dump her and buy her off. They didn't much like wife #3 either (at nearly 40 and some 30 years younger than Dorp himself, she was barely older than his grown daughter), but she kept out of their way and the children regarded her, if they thought of her at all, as photogenic arm candy for their father. Maybe they figured she'd look good with him on the campaign trail. And that would be good for business.

Because of course both the Dorp children were involved in the Dorp business. (Their father had had to hire them, being rather useless and not fit to be hired by anyone else.) Daryl Jr., who ostensibly ran the franchising arm of the empire, spent most of his time drinking and doing drugs, in and out of expensive rehab like a revolving door. The daughter, Cristal (named for the champagne), had once briefly been a teen fashion model (Daddy, conveniently, owned a modeling agency) but now mostly busied herself as a design and home décor "consultant" — with, naturally, a line throw pillows, glassware and other decorative items produced in the same Indonesian sweatshops that made Daddy's neckties.

But still, as far as the outside world knew, the billionaire businessman and his billionaire family were the very portrait of success — a rich, beautiful, successful family. Daryl Dorp indeed had it all.

θ θ θ

Until one day, he didn't.

It was just gone.

No, he hadn't gone bankrupt. That he could have managed. Dorp had engineered (well, his slick lawyers had engineered) and walked away unscathed from more bankruptcies than he could remember or even count.

But this was different.

One morning, he just woke up and it was all gone. He was the same person — at least he was pretty sure he was the same person, he hadn't changed — but everything else around him had changed. Had become tacky and tawdry. His surroundings had always been tacky, but at least that tackiness was expensive. This was worse. This was worn and *cheap* and tacky.

All his life, Daryl Dorp had aspired to be, and then finally had become, what one wag cuttingly described as a poor man's idea of a rich man. As if to bolster the idea to his own fragile ego as his fortune grew, Dorp had surrounded himself with what he thought were the trappings of wealth: His furniture was Baroque and ornate, the floors polished marble or plush broadloom. The chandeliers and wall sconces were of crystal and gold, all of it overdone. In the large, marble bathrooms, the faucets and even the toilet itself were gold. Dorp liked to think he was some kind of King Louis (he wouldn't have known which number) at his ornate palace of Versailles.

But instead of tasteful opulence or even elegant charm, what most people saw — and what Dorf himself foolishly failed to see — was tawdry extravagance, ostentatious excess, a boorish lack of taste.

So when he woke one morning on a lumpy old mattress in a tiny, musty bedroom with fake wood panelling and a bare lightbulb, he was, to put it mildly, more than a little confused and panicked.

His inner voice began a monologue: *"Did I drink too much last night? Did I snort some coke with something else in it? I knew that new dealer looked shifty. I wish the cops hadn't snatched my other guy. Am I dreaming? What the hell is going on?*

If Dorp had bothered to pay attention at any of the various expensive private schools his rich father had paid to tolerate him — and finally bribed further to let Dorp pretend he'd actually graduated from — or if, God forbid, Dorp has actually done any reading on his own, he might have been able to make some allusion to a metamorphosis (maybe Kafka, less likely Ovid). But naturally he hadn't. Aside from some minor facility at reading a balance sheet (mostly for the bottom line — other details he left to underlings), Dorp was for all intents and purposes almost functionally illiterate. He certainly never read for pleasure, or edification. Or insight.

Dorp had spent most of his time in high school hitting on (and mostly being rejected by) any pretty girl in his class. After graduating his final high school (thanks to exam answers he had purchased and another fatherly bribe to the principal), he was off to a fancy business school (his father had to endow a building to get him into that one), where drinking, drugs and minor athletics took up most of his time. (Dorp was highly competitive, but barely capable. Also a sore loser. When he got older, he took up golf, but mostly so he could network with other rich, white men. He was never very good at it, and of course he cheated.)

At business college, he had rarely gone to class, having paid others to write papers and sit exams for him. The degree framed on his office wall had come at a financial cost, but not from hard work. And he considered reading for pleasure both too difficult and a waste of time. So obviously the idea of any literary or mythological allusion was quite beyond his grasp. As a child growing up, he hadn't even read comic books, which surely might have provided him some other entryway into the world of mythical or magical transformations, of punishment and rebirth, of hubris and a protagonist's fatal flaw, of repentance and redemption.

But no, Dorp lacked not only education but also curiosity. He certainly lacked humility and self-awareness. Anything mythical or metaphorical? All of that was lost on him. He didn't have the imagination for it.

So he was having a hard time now imagining what seemed to have happened to him. He really had no idea, couldn't wrap his tiny mind around it. Lying in bed, he tried to make sense of it. Nothing. Maybe if he got up.

Up and out of bed, Dorp found himself standing barefoot on cheap, peel-and-stick vinyl tiles — some with missing corners, one or two missing entirely. He was dressed only in underwear (cheap cotton/poly, white, sagging) and a sleeveless T-shirt (also white cotton/poly, stained on the front and with a small hole in one armpit). And judging from the smell, they hadn't been laundered lately. Nor had he bathed. Born into inherited wealth, Dorp had never actually ever worn clothing this cheap and, to his mind, disgusting. But growing up, he'd encountered, and dutifully shunned, anyone who had.

The worn fake wooden paneling he'd noticed on first waking covered all four walls, faded and a little moldy along the bottom edges. *Oak, maybe?* he thought. At home in his penthouse, he had a library (shelved with books he'd of course never bothered to read) with genuine oak paneling and this looked something like that, just a lot thinner and cheaper. But he wasn't sure, not that it really mattered. The bare lightbulb hanging from the ceiling fixture might once have had a glass covering, but by the looks of it that was long gone. The light wasn't on — assuming there was even electricity — but some daylight was making its way through the cloudy, dirty single window the small bedroom had to offer. But Dorp couldn't tell if that meant morning or afternoon, maybe even early evening. He wasn't sure that mattered either.

Shuffling down a narrow hallway, he caught a glimpse of

himself in the mirror of a slightly rusty steel medicine cabinet on the wall of a tiny, grungy bathroom. He registered enough to see his hair was a mess but continued on a few more steps without stopping to enter the only other room in the dwelling, whatever and wherever it was. He found himself in a cramped combination living room/dining room with a small bar fridge and a two-burner hotplate in a galley kitchen that looked like it dated from the 1950s, maybe early '60s.

Whoever lived there was no housekeeper. There were dirty dishes in the sink and on the small breakfast table (well, the only table, so a table for other meals too) and articles of clothing — Dorp's? he couldn't tell — lying on the armchair and small couch that were taking up most of the space in the room, not that there was much room to spare. Looking out the living room window (the only window, other than a tiny one over the kitchen sink) Dorp saw that he was in some sort of trailer park. Which must make this some sort of trailer. Whose or where, he had no idea.

Padding back down to the bathroom, Dorp stood at the sink with a dripping tap and took stock of himself in the mirror. He was still having trouble trying to decide where he was and what had happened. Nothing looked familiar, like anywhere he'd ever been in his life. And if he were dreaming, this didn't have the other-worldly, dreamlike quality of dreams. In most of his dreams, the ones he enjoyed or would try to concoct, Dorp was having sex with hot Hollywood starlets or his favorite porn stars. This had none of that. It seemed much more real. And much more *boring*.

But at least he recognized the face staring back at him from the mirror, was pleased to see that, in some sense anyway, he was still himself. His hair was indeed a mess and he was badly in need of a haircut. But he was most pleased to see that he seemed younger, maybe even a few decades younger. Still not in great shape, still with a paunch and a puffy, jowly face, but he'd definitely lost some weight. And his tan looked more natural, like he'd actually gotten it from the sun and not a tanning bed or a spray booth.

The bathroom was too small for a tub but had a tiny shower stall with a ratty plastic curtain. Reaching in, he turned the faucets and was pleased when water actually came out. Not much pressure, but it would have to do. After trying to adjust the temperature, he realized tepid was the best he could hope for, so he stripped down and stepped in before whatever hot water there was disappeared completely.

Drying himself off on the still-damp but only towel available, Dorp was starting to feel at least a little more human, though no closer to any answers. Rooting in the medicine cabinet, he found some gel and a comb and did what he could with his hair, approaching something of a poor man's Elvis pompadour. Checking the mirror, he decided he could get away without a shave. And besides, the only razor might have been sharp a few weeks ago. Better not to risk it.

Back in the bedroom, he was glad to find some clean underwear and a relatively clean shirt. A different shirt — maybe the one he'd worn last night? — lay crumpled in the corner, reeking of cigarettes and booze. He must have been at a bar, but had no memory of that. At least, he didn't *feel* hungover.

But, looking around, he realized the trousers on the chair in the living room were going to be his only option. If he could find shoes, it seemed warm enough that he could manage without needing socks — which anyway he couldn't find and wasn't about to go looking for. He found a tie hanging on the doorknob, already made up, and put it on. It was tied badly — the back half was longer than the front — and the front piece had a stain that was probably ketchup. But at least the tie made him look somewhat more professional. He was just finished dressing — such as it was — when a phone rang. It took him a moment to realize it wasn't his familiar Apple iPhone, but a landline. Worse, a rotary-dial wall-mounted phone in the kitchen. *Jesus, what year was this?!* It kept ringing. He got it on the fourth.

"Uh, hello?" Dorp said tentatively.

"Goddamn it, Daryl! It's Alejandro. Where the hell are you?"

"Um, at home, I guess?"

"Well, get your ass down here before I fire you. You're working today on the sales floor. And you were supposed to be here an hour ago! I'm losing customers."

Alejandro disconnected. Or slammed down the phone. Dorp couldn't tell which.

*Work? He was supposed to be at work? Doing what? And where? None of this made any sense.*

In the right front trouser pocket, he felt a set of keys and pulled them out. One key was pretty obviously the door to the trailer. Another looked more commercial — work? — and there was a car key. A Ford, by the look of it. The key fob offered a helpful clue: "Garcia's Downtown Albany Ford" it said, with an address on Central Avenue. So he must be in Albany, he guessed.

Dorp didn't know Albany well — although born in the Bronx, he considered Manhattan his home and lived there in one of his office/condo towers. But he'd been to the New York State capital often enough on business, had even dined at the governor's mansion. And he knew it well enough to know that calling

Alejandro's Central Avenue address "downtown" was a bit of a stretch. But at least he thought he knew how to get there.

Everything still felt strange, he couldn't make any sense of it, but he decided he might as well play along until he could figure it out. If this *were* a dream, maybe it would start to get more interesting soon. So far, there weren't nearly enough hot babes in it to suit his liking.

He went outside. Parked in front was a car he assumed — he hoped — must be his. It was an older model Ford Mustang, like the one his father had bought him for his 18th birthday, a car he still dreamed about. Had it been in better shape, this one would have been a vintage find. But with the rust spots and the sloppy body repairs and the balding tires, this one was hardly a prize specimen.

You'd think a guy working at a car dealership (Dorp figured that must be what was going on, though he couldn't explain why) would be driving a car in better condition. A car to show off and brag about. A car to help advertise the dealership itself. A nice loaner from among the best on the lot. You'd think that would make sense. But the truth was that no one at the dealership liked Dorp at all — not Alejandro (Dorp assumed he was either the sales manager or the owner), not the mechanics or the sales reps and not the guys in the body shop. So no one was going to do Dorp any favors. Not even give him a discount on engine repairs or body work, or a deal on new tires.

In fact, as Dorp was soon to find out, no one really liked Dorp — this new Dorp, different Dorp, whoever he was. No one liked him at all. So he had put up with the worn tires and let the rust go as long as he could before having to do a patch job himself. And like most things he did, it was a half-assed job that was barely an improvement.

The Mustang badly needed a tune-up, not to mention new shocks, but it got Dorp where he wanted to go and he'd found the dealership without much trouble. And even with a rough ride, it did feel good to be driving his teenage dream car again. The pleasant feeling didn't last long.

He parked in the lot and walked through the front door of the small dealership and immediately Alejandro — Dorp recognized the voice from the phone call — was on his case.

"Jesus, Daryl!" he said, his voice low but seething. "It took you long enough. And you look like shit. Anyway, there's a guy over there looking at that Taurus. Go do your thing and get him to buy it. Better yet, upsell him to the Explorer if you can. And I wanna see the paperwork on my desk in no more than 20 minutes. Now go!"

Dorp had this, he thought. He'd always considered himself a good salesman. He was nothing if not confident in his own abilities. He put on his best grin and walked over to the customer.

It took him longer than 20 minutes, but in the end he did manage to sell the Taurus (but no upselling to the Explorer) and he took the paperwork over to Alejandro for his final signoff. Alejandro was not happy with all the extras Dorp had thrown in to close the sale, cutting into most of the profit margin, but grudgingly had to admit he'd actually at least made a sale and sent him back onto the floor.

By then it was almost noon and Dorp, feeling cocky and proud of himself, decided he'd earned a break. Spotting the receptionist, he started walking over to the front counter, ready to turn on what he thought of as his irresistible charm. She was not as busty as he liked his women to be, nor as attractive as he always felt he deserved — she was a 6 at best, Dorp thought, maybe a 7 with the right dress. But any port in a storm, as he always said.

"Hi there," he said, standing over her and peering down to see what cleavage she had to offer. He was disappointed, but his attitude was that something was always better than nothing. "How's it going? You look sexy today."

In truth, Dorp didn't think she looked very sexy at all. But he figured he'd never get anywhere if he let her know that. Flattery was his go-to move.

"Sorry, Daryl," she said dismissively, turning away and picking up the phone. "Kinda busy here Really don't have time to talk. Buh-bye."

It hadn't seemed that busy, Dorp thought. There'd been one other salesman on the floor — a young Latino guy hustling customers — and the phone had hardly been ringing. But Maria — that was the nametag Dorp had noticed on her blouse— made a show of keying in a number and waving him away with her hand when the person on the other end picked up and she began talking.

The rest of the day moved slowly for Dorp. Despite a few hopeful prospects, he hadn't sold any other cars, new or used. The other sales rep seemed to have fared better. Dorp had seen him coming and going from Alejandro's office at least three times throughout the afternoon. A little after 4, Alejandro called Dorp into his office. Dorp hoped Alejandro would congratulate him on that morning's sale, and Dorp was ready with his list of excuses for the slower afternoon.

"Come in, Daryl," Alejandro said. "Close the door."

Dorp knew that was rarely a good sign.

"I know this wasn't my best day, Mr. Garcia," Dorp said, sucking up and hoping to get ahead of any criticism. "But you know I can do better. It's too hot. People don't wanna buy cars when it's hot."

"That's bullshit and you know it," Alejandro said. "We've got air conditioning. When it's this hot, people are happy to come in. They hang around for the A/C and we sell more cars. My son Chico sold four cars today. You sold one — and we practically had to give that one away."

"But —"

"But nothing," Alejandro said. "Face it, Daryl, you're a screw-up. You think you're God's gift to the world but you're not. You're a lousy salesman and you're a pig to the women who work here. Maria's the third receptionist I've had in the past year. The other two quit because they got tired of you leering at them and getting all handsy. You think you're a big charmer, Mr. Irresistible. But really, they just got tired of fending off your clumsy advances. In fact Juana, the last one, my wife's cousin, told me when she quit she was thinking of charging you with sexual harassment. So don't be surprised if that happens.

"But that's not all," Alejandro continued, clearly warming to the task. "Today wasn't a bad day for you. It was a typical day. I'm lucky if you sell one car a day. My boy Chico is new to the game and yet he outsells you at least three to one most days. Sometimes better. But that doesn't stop you from swaggering around here bragging and telling anyone who'll listen that you're the best salesman on the lot. You and I both know that's a lie. But you just can't help yourself. Lying's in your nature.

"And don't even get me started on your racism! You think I haven't heard you muttering under your breath, calling me and Chico 'dagos' and 'wetbacks' and 'spics'? I should kick your ass for that."

"Please," Daryl said, "nobody's better than me. Really. Just gimme a chance."

"Daryl, when I bought this dealership a year ago from Scarpetti, I didn't like you from the start. But he made me promise to keep you on for a year because he was a friend of your father's. That's the only reason you got the job in the first place: Scarpetti was doing your father a favor when he gave you the job, even though you didn't deserve it and you had no qualifications. God knows what hold your old man had on Scarpetti to make him take you on in the first place. But it must have been something powerful or nasty. So when he sold to me, you came with the deal too.

"Well, it's been almost a year and I've given you that chance. In fact, more chances than you deserve. I'm a man of my word, but I'm tired of it. I even called Scarpetti to apologize for not hanging on the for full year. And you know what? He didn't even blame me. He said he understood.

"And by the way, don't think I haven't noticed all those parts missing from the inventory that just happen to fit that old junker Mustang you drive. You're lucky I don't call the cops on you for that. But frankly, I just don't want the hassle.

"So that's it, Daryl. You're gone. You're fired. I put a box on your desk. Pack up your personal stuff and leave. You'll get your last paystub in the mail. Now just get out of my office."

Driving the old Mustang back to the trailer park — he couldn't think of anywhere else to go — Dorp's shock morphed into petulance, then anger, then a sense of righteous indignation,

*That stupid spic, how dare he? Can't trust those damn Mexicans, always sneaking over the border and stealing our jobs! I'm better than he'll ever be — smarter, better looking, a better businessman. Just better than he is, period!*

By the time he arrived at the trailer, Dorp's swagger and arrogance were almost back to their pre-set high levels. He'd bounce back from this, he thought, he always had.

There was another car parked in front of his trailer when Dorp pulled up — a dented Ford Escort that, like the Mustang, had seen better days. The middle-aged, balding man in the worn business suit leaning on the front fender had seen better days too. Dorp had no idea who he was, but he seemed to be waiting for him.

"Hey, Daryl, you're home early. I was just gonna leave you a note. But I saw you driving up, so I stayed. We need to talk."

"Who are you?"

"Jeez, are you still hung over from partying last night? It's Mick. I'm your lawyer, remember?"

"Uh, sure. What's up?"

"Well, nothing good, Daryl. Do you know a Ms. Juana Diaz?" *Juana. Alejandro had mentioned her.*

"I guess I do. Why?"

"Why? Because she's suing you for sexual harassment, that's why. Her lawyer served me with the papers this morning. Ambushed me when I was buying my morning coffee. Not cool, man.

"And another thing," the lawyer said. "Your landlord here at the trailer park called me this afternoon. Seems you've been ignoring his calls and the notes he's been leaving in your mailbox, so he tracked me down. You're almost eight months behind on the rent. If you don't pay up in full by month eight, he'll cut of your utilities. A month after that if there's still no money, he'll kick your ass out the door, seize whatever assets you've got inside and sell them off for the proceeds. He's already put a lien on your car, so he'll be seizing that first."

"He can't do all that, can he? Tell me he can't do that."

"He can evict you for non-payment of rent, sure he can. I could try and fight him in court. But that would mean you'd have to pay me, and where would that money come from? You're broke, remember? And let's not forget you still owe me about 500 bucks for the paperwork I did on that last failed get-rich-quick scheme you had. I don't even remember which one, there have been so many. And also don't think I've forgotten you still need my help on cleaning up your tax situation after all those false claims you made. That's going to take some doing.

"But Jesus, Daryl, did you forget the first part of what I said? You're all worried about losing your cheap-ass trailer and you're not paying attention to the fact that a woman has made credible allegations accusing you of sexual harassment and sexual assault. This is serious. She's got witnesses with supporting affidavits. You could be looking at actual jail time for this."

"Nah, it'll be fine," Dorp said with his usual bravado. "I'm sure it's just a misunderstanding. I was probably flirting a bit and she took it the wrong way, blew it up all out of proportion. Chicks do that all the time. Besides, if she's anything like the secretary the dealership has now, she's probably not even my type. Too ugly for me. I only go for the really beautiful ones. The hot ones really like me."

"Well, if you want me to represent you on this," the lawyer said, shaking his head, "you'll have to come up with some money. I'm not gonna keep working for you for free. And we have 10 days to file a response to this lawsuit. I'll come by tomorrow and we can sit down, try and come up with a plan."

With that, the lawyer got in his car and drove off, leaving Dorp standing in the dirt of the rundown trailer park.

The metal trailer had been baking in the sun all day. Inside, it was a sauna. And of course Dorp couldn't afford A/C. He'd torn off the tie and already his shirt was sticking to his back, huge wet spots at the armpits. What the hell, Dorp took off shirt, shoes and pants and shuffled around in his underwear. Dorp was hungry, but he was too tired to cook — and a quick look had shown him there wasn't much in the tiny bar fridge anyway.

But he did manage to find a can of some store-brand cola and a big, nearly full bottle of cheap rum. Rinsing a glass from the sink, he poured himself a generous portion of rum and topped it off with some of the cheap cola. He plunked himself down in the armchair — actually, one of those cheap, metal-and-webbing folding lawn chairs — and proceeding to get himself nicely drunk. Until he passed out.

θ θ θ

A ringing phone roused Dorp from his stupor. The noise hurt his head, and anyway Dorp couldn't figure out where it was coming from. So he just let it keep ringing. After four rings, it stopped.

*Good*, thought Dorp, and he drifted off again — hung over, or possibly still drunk.

Again the phone rang, jolting Dorp awake. This time, he realized he was sitting in a plush armchair in what looked like the main room of a fancy hotel suite, his tie pulled askew but otherwise in a full business suit. An Apple iPhone was ringing on the table beside him. Dorp picked it up and thumbed it on.

"Hello?" he said, tentatively.

"Mr. Dorp?" said the voice on the other end, "It's Sandro downstairs at the front desk. Mr. Graves, your lawyer, is here with the Uber. He's been waiting a while. He says you're expecting him."

"Uh, right," said Dorp, flustered. "Tell him I'll be down in a minute."

Dorp looked around and took stock. *This is more like it*, he thought.

*Maybe the grungy trailer and the car dealership — and getting fired, not to mention the sex-assault suit — maybe that was all just a terrible dream, a hallucination from some bad blow and too much booze. I've done that before. This is more like it. The suit feels expensive, the room looks pricy, I've even got a doorman. Or a front desk, anyway. In fact, this looks like a room in the Dorp Dorchester — the Dorp-chester, people joke about it. I think I recognize the décor from consultants.*

Anything of Dorp's that actually did look tasteful, you know a professional designer had had a hand in it. And the design schemes for his hotel customers were much more subdued, less gaudy, than Dorp's personal style.

Dorp looked around, admiring the room. *Nice for the high-end customers*, he thought. *But why am I here? If I'm me and it was all just a bad dream, why aren't I back home at my penthouse at Dorp Tower?*

Dorp got up and walked around the suite. He was in the living/dining area, with a small galley kitchen on one side. He couldn't tell what floor he was on, but high enough up that customers would be paying for the view that came with the room.

—56—

A master bedroom and elegant *en suite* bathroom were off to his right. *That must be my room*, he thought, though he still had no recollection of how he'd gotten here. A slightly smaller bedroom shared the bathroom from the other side. *That's for my wife*, Dorp figured — since in truth it had been several years since they'd shared the same bed. Or even the same apartment, except on those occasions when they'd had to keep up appearances so Dorp could entertain for business deals, his wife (for her usual fee) agreeing to play gracious hostess.

But she wasn't there, nor any sign that she had been lately. The bed was fully made up, no clothes in the closet when Dorp checked. *She must be at her place across the Park*, Dorp thought, grateful at least that his accountants had found a way to write that off as a business expense.

Absent-mindedly, he'd been carrying the iPhone in his hand. Again it rang, again he thumbed it on.

"Mr. Dorp, sir? It's Sandro again. Mr. Graves asks that you come down right away. He seems in a hurry."

"Fine. Tell him I'm coming," Dorp said curtly, and thumbed the phone off.

*I'm the client, he's the lawyer*, Dorp thought. *He shouldn't be the one pushing me around.*

Still, the kind of lawyers Dorp kept on retainer were generally not the excitable type. So if this one was agitated, maybe there was a good reason.

He left the suite, feeling much relieved to be done with his nightmare. Dorp took the elevator down to the lobby to greet his lawyer. He even recognized the name. Graves was with one of the more exclusive Manhattan law firms.

The elevator doors opened on the lobby, but there was barely time for a handshake and hello before the attorney was hustling him out the front door and into the waiting Uber.

"Come on, Daryl," Graves said. "We're already late. You were supposed to be ready for me almost half an hour ago. What happened? Not good to keep the judge waiting."

"An Uber?" Dorp joked, feeling his old confidence returning. "Where's my limo?"

"Limo?" the lawyer scoffed. "You're broke, remember? You're lucky I'm willing to pay for an Uber. With your money, you'd be lucky to afford even a checker cab. Maybe the subway."

Dorp was starting to feel disoriented again. *Maybe this is still part of the dream*, he thought, *and I only dreamt that I woke up. Maybe I'm still dreaming. But this seems more real somehow. I remember this life, not like that other one, where I was poor.*

Something the lawyer had said came back to him.

"What do you mean," he asked, "keep the judge waiting? What judge?"

"Daryl, did you fall on your head or something?" the lawyer said. "I keep telling you, you've got to go easy on the alcohol and the drugs. They mess with your brain.

"Don't you remember? You've spent the past two years and almost every penny you could squeeze from what few assets you have that aren't completely underwater on fighting multiple criminal cases. Two rape charges, three charges of sexual assault and multiple counts of fraud and tax evasion. Not to mention the parade of civil suits lined up to hit you, assuming you had managed to avoid criminal conviction."

Beneath the spray-on tan, Dorp's face began to grow pale.

"But you've used up your last chance at appeal," the lawyer said. "You had me take your cases to the Supreme Court, but they turned you down. They won't even hear them. They bounced them back to circuit court. The best I could do was get you plea deal on the sex convictions and asset forfeiture on the tax evasion and fraud.

"The IRS has seized and liquidated pretty much all your assets. As a courtesy, they were letting you stay under house arrest at the Dorchester — which you no longer own, by the way — pending your final sentencing hearing. That's where we're going now. And the judge is probably pissed because we're late."

"Mr. Dorp, please rise while I render my verdict." Madam Justice Brigid Hurley was a sombre, stern woman at the best of times. And worse, as now, when she was in a foul mood, having been kept waiting.

"Daryl Dorp," the judge continued, "this court has spent considerable time reviewing your various cases, the charges you have faced, the convictions in the lower courts and your fruitless attempts to appeal those rulings. We take a dim view of criminals in general, we think rapists and sexual predators are among the lowest forms of humanity and we are not usually inclined toward leniency in our sentencing We also have no patience for those who think their money gives them the right to waste the time and resources of the justice system.

"And we take particular offence at persons such as yourself who — having been given every advantage of wealth and privilege — choose to squander that wealth in selfish, hedonistic pursuits, who abuse their position of power to gratify their own perverse desires and who rape and sexually assault women because they think that is their right.

"Your attorney has argued strenuously on your behalf," she

said, with a slight turn of the head to Graves. "And believe me, whatever you are paying him — I hope it's a lot, though I suspect you won't actually have enough to pay him — he has earned his fee. The court has already convicted you on multiple counts of rape and sexual assault. Each of those convictions separately would warrant a sentence of at least 10 years.

"But," she paused. "You are, I believe, 70 years old and would likely not last very long in prison at that age. And as part of your plea arrangement, the court has an undertaking from Mr. Graves that any money left over from your fully liquidated assets once the IRS has taken its share of payment owing for taxes and evasion shall be donated to a charity that helps survivors of sexual assault.

"Mr. Dorp, for far too long you have lived a life of privilege, and your wealth has so far shielded you from having to face the consequences of any of your many criminal or unsavory actions. That ends here. And it ends now.

"Call it karma, call it cosmic rebalancing," the judge said. "Or remember, as the Rev. Dr. Martin Luther King, Jr., reminded us: 'The arc of the moral universe is long, but it bends toward justice.'

"And so, comforted by the knowledge that henceforth you shall be penniless, this court is persuaded by your attorney's pleas for leniency to this extent, and to this extent only: You have been found guilty on all charges before this court. It is our judgment that you shall be sentenced to 10 years in federal prison on each and every one of the several counts. But that furthermore, in consideration of the terms you have agreed to and considering your age, you shall serve your sentences concurrently, such that your prison sentence shall not exceed 10 years in total."

Dorp could say nothing. For the first time in his life, he was stunned into silence. Standing beside him, Graves said nothing either.

With a bang of her gavel, Madam Justice Brigid Hurley made her final pronouncement: "Mr. Dorp, you are hereby remanded into custody. Bailiff, escort the prisoner to the jail cell to await his transfer to federal prison.

"This court stands adjourned."

# Terminal Velocity

SUDDENLY, I WAKE UP. I'm falling. Must be a bad dream. One of those dreams where you're falling, and then you wake up with a start just before you hit the ground. They say if you actually *do* hit the ground in your dream, you'll die in your sleep.

Tough to prove that hypothesis, I guess.

But I'm not dead, so that must mean I'm still sleeping. I just 'woke up' inside the dream, but actually I'm still asleep. Right? Right?

Nope. Actually awake, actually falling. I'm cold. And I can feel the wind, hear it rushing past me. Or me through it, I guess. Is it really wind if you're the one moving? There must be a term for that. Can't remember. Brain's a little foggy. Probably not important at the moment. If I get through this, I'll try to remember to look it up.

Anyway, actually falling. Falling and flailing. Groggy too. Had I been drinking? I don't think so. I hardly drink much, rarely get drunk. And this feels worse than that. Like someone had conked me on the head.

Looking up, I can see a tiny single-prop airplane flying away above me. So I must be falling back-first — "supine," I can remember the parachuting instructor say. You want to be "prone," he said. You don't want to be on your back, he said, flashing that perfect, toothy smile that fit right into the rest of the tall, dark, handsome package.

I can remember my wife having a tiny giggle at that. "Not on your back," she repeated, giving him one of her sexy smiles. The ones she hasn't given me in a long time.

Wait! Of course! Parachuting instructor! I'm wearing a parachute. I can see the straps on my chest. I must have blacked out after I jumped out of the plane. Except I don't remember even getting onto the plane, let alone jumping out of it.

Never mind, who cares! I'm falling, but I have a parachute. Thank God!

Not someone I think about very often, God. But right now seems as good a time as any. At 10,000 feet or so might be a good time to start.

I'm falling. And I'm accelerating. Pretty soon, if I'm not there already, I'll reach terminal velocity. Which, if I remember from the instruction manual, is acceleration at 120 ft per second/per second until you reach about 120 mph. What's that in metric? No idea. Don't make me do math in my head.

Thank God I've got a parachute. I reach over and pull the ripcord, bracing myself for the welcome jolt that comes when the silk magically unfolds and fills with air, slowing your descent.

Nothing. Nada.

I pull it again. Same nothing. I'm still falling, and the ground is fast approaching.

θ θ θ

I must have blacked out again. I wake up. At least I think I wake up. Maybe this is just another dream. Or another part of the same dream. Too much to process. I'm in some sort of room, like my dentist's waiting room. But even cleaner. All white — walls, floor, ceiling, furniture, everything. The lighting is bright but not overpowering, and I can't really see where it's coming from. It's just sort of there somehow. Bright but diffuse. And everything seems a bit wispy or gauzy. Almost like the air itself is white too.

And it's quiet. Peaceful. Restful. Just the tiniest hint of some music in the air — a soft tinkling, like harps or wind chimes. It dawns on me that I'm no longer hearing the roaring sound of rushing wind, or whatever you call it. I guess that's because I don't seem to be falling anymore. I'm just standing in this small, quiet, white room. And I seem to be really awake this time. Or at least I think I am. Who knows?

"Where am I?" I say out loud — which seems silly, since there isn't anyone else in the room with me. But maybe someone is watching me through mirrored glass, like on those TV cop shows. Except I look around the room and see only the four walls, no windows or mirrors in sight. Not even a door. Which is a bit worrying.

"Hello, and welcome," a light voice says.

I swear I have no idea where he came from. Suddenly he's just there, standing beside me at a respectful distance. A small, bookish man of indeterminate age. Like the room, likewise dressed all in white, an all-white suit, white shoes. Like a younger-looking Mark Twain or Tom Wolfe. A shorter Man from Glad. Same white hair, even. A man, I think, anyway. A bit androgynous. Hard to tell. The suit might be a clue. Or not. Big, black spectacles the only thing about him that's not white. Kind of like Wally Cox. Or Rick Moranis for the boomer set. Or Dan Levy. A less-flamboyant Elton John, maybe.

"Um," I stutter, "where am I? How did I get here? And who are you?"

"So many questions," my companion replies. "First, my name is — well, too difficult for you to pronounce, probably. Doesn't readily translate into English. So you may call me Gadriel, just to keep it simple. It means "watcher." Where you are is — well, it has fancy, formal name that again you wouldn't understand. Sometimes we call it the AV Lab.

"As to how you got here — now, that's a different question altogether. And one to which I confess I don't really know the answer right now. Bit of a mystery, in fact. More of a problem for Central Processing to sort out. Not my department, I'm sorry to say.

"But," he says, clapping his hands, rubbing them together and smiling, "here you are. There's no denying that. So let's just make the best of it, shall we? Until we can figure this out."

I look around again. Somehow during this brief conversation, without my noticing it, a white door has appeared in one of the white walls, where I swear there had not been one before. Unlike my companion, all in his white, I'm still wearing my blue parachuting jumpsuit, the useless parachute pack still my back.

"Do you mind if I take this off?" I ask Gadriel, as I struggle with the straps.

"Ah, no. Sorry," he replies. "Best keep that on, I think. You might be needing it later."

"OK," I say, confused. "I'm getting a really strange feeling, so I'm just going to ask. Am I, like, dead?"

"Well, technically no," Gadriel answers. "Not yet, anyway. But that's really not my department, as I say. I'm just on 'sparrow patrol.'"

"Huh?"

"You know, after that old hymn." And here he sings a little verse:

> God sees the little sparrow fall,
> It meets his tender view.
> If God so loves the little birds,
> I know he loves me too.

"Not sure I know that one," I say.

"Really?" Gadriel seems genuinely surprised. "It's in 64 hymnals, you know. A bit sappy, I'd agree. But a big hit with the Sunday School crowd."

"Sorry," I say. "Never much of a churchgoer. Blame my parents, I guess."

"Typical!" There's slight scorn in his voice. "Always trying the shift the blame to someone else, never taking responsibility for your own failings."

"That's not fair! And how would you know that?"

"Oh, don't talk to me about fair," he says, a bit imperiously. "I've read the reports about you. The email landed here just a moment before you did. That's what I call efficiency." Pleased with himself.

"I still don't get it," I say. "I don't know where I am or how I got here, or why. You say I'm not dead, but I'm definitely getting a kind of a vibe here, like I'm inside a big cloud. And I was, until a moment ago — I think — falling through the sky. So, is this heaven. And are you an angel?"

"I told you," he says, as if impatient at having to explain it all again, "this is the AV Lab. Call it Sparrow Central. It's not heaven. Believe me, far from it. Sometimes feels like the Other Place. Not really. I exaggerate. But I guess you could say it's heaven-adjacent.

"As to who I am, we prefer the term 'executive assistant.' But yes, technically I guess you could still call us that.

"Us? Are you some sort of polytheistic deity, like a trinity or something?" I'd never much gone to church, but I'd picked up some of the lingo along the way.

"Oh no, nothing like that," Gadriel says. "I'm just me. There are several of us on duty right now. But the others are busy. They sent me to deal with you."

"OK. So, again — how did I get here?"

"Hmm. That *is* a good question, to be honest. Sorry, I guess that's redundant. We're always honest."

"All you angels."

"All us executive assistants, yes."

With that, he turns and walks toward the wall on the farthest side.

"Come," he says, opening the newly appeared door and gesturing into what looks like a hallway beyond. Like the room — like everything here, it seems, except me — the hallway is all white, with that same bright, diffused lighting and the slightly gauzy feel to the air. "I might as well show you around while we figure out what to do about you."

Gadriel leads me along a long hallway — so long, it looks like it might go on forever. There are doors on both sides. So many doors, each one with a frosted-glass window, with some writing etched on the glass in a script and language I don't recognize. Most of the rooms are silent, but from some of them I swear I can hear the sound of an old 16mm film projector — like the ones they used for showing us movies in school when I was a kid. I loved those movie days. All the kids did.

As if reading my mind, Gadriel says: "Yes, those are indeed old 16mm film projectors you're hearing, from your childhood. Some of our monitoring technology is quite old. I daresay farther back down the hall behind us you might find some old Edison kinetoscopes, even a 'magic lantern' or two.

"We're just passing some of the old VHS and Betamax rooms now," he says, as we keep walking along. "And we've already skipped past laser discs. Those didn't last long. What you're seeing here, mind you, is just a sliver. There are rooms upon rooms upon rooms. More than you could count. We have a lot to keep track of, after all, watching over everyone and everything all the time. The world is full of sparrows, as we like to say."

I struggle to hear any sounds of conversation or dialogue — any sounds at all, really — from the rooms beyond the doors. But all I can hear is the soft tinkling in the air. Background white noise, as it were. Even the watchers still protect your privacy. Some comfort in that.

"Old Nick might have had something to do with VHS winning that battle, by the way," Gadriel says. "The porn makers preferred VHS because it was cheaper than Beta, and they could cram longer movies onto a single cassette.

"In fact, you might be surprised at how often pornography has been the driver behind changing technology. Polaroid film so you could avoid having some drugstore process your sexy pictures. Home video cameras — you don't really think they were just for shooting your kids' birthday parties, do you? High-speed internet. Broadband. I could go on."

"You mean the devil had a hand in all that?"

"Well, not directly, of course," Gadriel says quickly, as if not wanting to give the devil his due. "Direct interference isn't really his style.

"I mean, most of the pornographers are in his camp anyway," he continues. "So that's two of the Seven Deadlies right there — your Lust and your Greed. After that, he just had to let market forces do their thing. That often works for him. Over time, he's found that capitalism can be pretty much as evil as communism if it wants to be. And letting each side, ahem, demonize the other — well, that's just another standard protocol for him.

"Speaking of cassettes," he says, "we have a whole audio division in another, ah, wing, as it were. But everything's digital now, thankfully. So much easier. You have no idea. And we were the first, of course, to use cloud storage. Sorry, a little EA humor there. We do like to amuse ourselves."

Gadriel stops in front of one of the myriad doors — I can't tell them apart, but I suppose he can read the fancy script on the glass. We step into a room much like the first one, but larger and looking more comfortable. More of a lounge than a waiting room, I suppose. The furniture is a little more plush, the essence more relaxing. There's a desk and chair in the corner with a large computer keyboard and monitor. All white, of course. Gadriel sits at the computer, taps a few keys, and looks at the screen.

"Excuse me for a moment," he says. "We just got an update on your file."

A few moments go by, Gadriel still reading.

"Ah, I see," he says, more to himself than to me. "Well, that explains some of it, anyway."

Turning to me, he asks, "Why did you take up parachuting in the first place?"

"It was my wife's idea," I tell him. "She wanted to do it on her own. But she'd been doing a lot of things on her own, and frankly our marriage was not doing so well. So I decided I'd join her. She objected, but I went ahead with it anyway and signed up for the same introductory course she had signed up for.

"I thought it would be something fun and exciting we could do together as a couple. Something that might revive the old romantic spark. How was I supposed to know she was doing it only because she was already sleeping with the instructor? I found that out later."

"Yes," Gadriel says, looking back at the screen, "I see that here. Well, that would certainly rack up another couple of the Big Ones — Envy and Wrath. One more and you get the set of steak knives."

I give him a look.

"Sorry," he says. "More EA humor."

He gets up from the desk and comes over to me, putting an arm around my shoulder. He has to reach up slightly to do so.

"Here's the thing, my boy," he says. "Now that I've read your full file, I see how we got here. Not exactly how you got *here* in AV — that's still a glitch I'll have to take up with the folks in Central Processing. But how you got into your current predicament.

"It seems your wife and her flyboy lover decided they'd be happier together with each other and without you. Your wife persuaded you to go up for a jump with her, with flyboy flying the plane. But she'd drugged your breakfast coffee, so you passed out shortly after you got on board.

"Flyboy's the expert, so he had sabotaged your chute — and your reserve chute too, by the way, so neither of them would open. With the plane briefly on autopilot, they pushed you out the door to plummet to your death. Sorry if that's too graphic. I'm just repeating what it says in the report.

"So then your wife jumps out and naturally her parachute opens perfectly and she lands safely on the ground. Where she finds you. Sadly, rather a mess. But of course, soon flyboy has landed back at the airport and is there to comfort and console her in her grief. Oh, and she gets the insurance money, of course."

I look at Gadriel, too stunned to say anything. He shrugs his shoulders and gives me a half-hearted smile, as if to say, "Hey, what are you gonna do?"

I shrug back at him. I guess this is out of my hands.

"Well, this has been fun," Gadriel says, again with a half-hearted smile. "Sorry again for the mixup. And sorry for the rest of it. But rules are rules. I don't write the script. I just watch the movie. Sometimes we're allowed to catch a falling sparrow. But sometimes we're not."

Great. Just great. I hear the whooshing sound of the wind again. Here I am, back in the sky. And here comes the ground — approaching fast, metric or otherwise.

I wonder if it will hurt?

# Suffer Little Children

*But Jesus said: Suffer little children and forbid them not*
*to come unto me, for of such is the kingdom of heaven.*
*— Matthew 19:14*

A PUFF OF WHITE SMOKE and it was done.

*Habemus papam!* With those traditional words from the longer declaration in Latin, the protodeacon of the College of Cardinals, standing in the *loggia*, or central balcony, of St. Peter's Basilic in the Vatican, gave news to the Roman Catholic faithful gathered in St. Peter's Square and to the world outside, "We have a pope!"

A new pope, that is to say. After all, with a few minor and relatively brief exceptions over the past 2,000 years (give or take) the world — particularly the Roman Catholic world — has never been without a pope. Sometimes two, if we are to believe the good people of 14th-century Avignon.

And so, upon the recent and not entirely unexpected death of his predecessor at a ripe old age, a new pope was inheriting the crossed keys of St. Peter as spiritual leader of more than a billion Catholics around the world. The position comes with eight official titles — none of them actually "pope." Although the most commonly known, it is, oddly enough, merely an informal, affectionate one, from the Italian "*papa*," for father. Officially, he had become Bishop of Rome, Vicar of Jesus Christ, Successor of the Prince of the Apostles, Supreme Pontiff of the Universal Church, Primate of Italy, Archbishop and Metropolitan of the Roman Province, Sovereign of the State of Vatican City and Servant of the Servants of God. Even the shorthand term "pontiff," which people sometimes use as a replacement, betrays an odd lingering connection to pre-Christian Roman times, from Latin "*pontifex maximus*," or greatest bridge builder, a pagan term for spiritual leader. Funny how some of the old paganism continues to bleed through. Since 2012, the pope's Twitter handle — with no apparent sense of irony — has even been @pontifex.

All in all, "pope" just seemed the easiest title to go with.

The papal conclave of cardinals (from the Latin *cum clave*, with key, because they were locked in together until by secret ballot they had elected the new pope) had been neither the shortest, nor certainly the longest, in the church's centuries-long history. Because real-world politics enter even the supposedly spiritual world of the church, these elections rarely if ever have concluded on the first or even second ballot. Some have taken many more.

Bernini's ornate 17th-century square, although housed within the walls of the Vatican itself, was for the purposes of crowd control, and by the terms of the Lateran Treaty of 1929, under the supervision of the Italian police. And they were doing their best to ensure the tens of thousands of faithful gathered there remained orderly. The crowd, and the cameras broadcasting the event even more widely, saw over the course of many days the black smoke, *fumata nera*, wafting from the special chimney on the Sistine Chapel roof signaling the burning (traditionally with wet straw, later with a chemical additive, to darken the smoke) of several rounds of inconclusive ballots. Finally, after what seemed a long wait but in the grand scheme of things was merely a blip, the pure white smoke, *fumata bianca*, rose aloft to signify that, by the grace of God and after much human machination, the cardinals had made their choice.

He took the papal name of Michael, which some Vatican observers saw as an allusion to the archangel Michael, who defeats Satan in the end-times *Book of Revelation*, and as a sign the new pope intended to stand up to evil. In this they were proven correct. That's exactly why he had chosen that name. The choice confounded the bookies, oddsmakers and most pundits, who had placed their bets heavily on either John Paul III or Pius XIII — though 13 being an unlucky number, especially for Catholics given the Last Supper, that had been given the longer odds. (Having twice previously seen a John Paul, the standup comics and late-night hosts, meanwhile, had been pushing for Pope George Ringo.)

But Michael it was, and his papal tenure began with little fanfare but also with little of the controversy that soon would follow. His first address to the faithful from that same *loggia* balcony, his traditional *Urbi et Orbi* address "to the city and the world" came with the usual blessings, the prayers for peace and the greetings in many languages. Clearly, the new pope was not about to rock the boat on his first day. That could wait.

At barely 50, he was the youngest pope the world had seen in many centuries. Italians, of course, had long dominated the post, and the world had since seen a German in Benedict XVI and an Argentine in Francis. But John Timothy McGuire, of Irish Catholic stock born and raised in Boston, Massachusetts, now Pope Michael, was making history as the first American ever to hold the job.

That alone had made choosing him an outside chance. As the longest-standing institution the world has ever known — at least as stolid and bureaucratic as any other enormous hierarchical entity — the Roman Catholic church was resistant to change. And many of his fellow cardinals saw McGuire as an outsider, an American interloper. But worse than that, as far too progressive for their liking — and therefore as far too dangerous to their comfortable *status quo*.

The fact that in the end he'd won the ballot was largely the result of a compromise between two main warring factions within the College of Cardinals — one staunchly conservative, the other at best half-heartedly centrist. Neither of them, despite some recent forward gains, was what you would call modern or progressive. Some insiders later admitted that, seeing the imminent failure of their respective chosen favorites, they'd voted in the end for McGuire in what they had hoped would be a spoiler move to prolong the process. Little did each faction know that the other side had also decided on the same strategy.

And so, by an ironic twist of fate — or of course as his supporters would say, by the hand of God secretly at work — the longest of long shots, the young upstart outsider, had in fact ascended to the throne of St. Peter. This made neither the traditionalists nor the centrists happy. But they had only themselves to blame.

θ θ θ

"So, Timmy, when are you going to do something about it?"

Several weeks had passed, a busy time filled with meetings, audiences, sacraments (the official investiture among them) and a surprising amount of paperwork. For most of that, the pope had a staff of secretaries and functionaries, like any large corporate bureaucracy, among the many priests who live and work in the Vatican. But still much of it required his personal attention, or at least his papal eyes and seal. He'd barely had time to catch his breath, to take in the surroundings — not to mention the monumental position — in which he found himself.

Now, finally having found a moment of relative calm in which to relax, Michael, dressed in the simplest black cassock, sat drinking the coffee his elderly priest assistant (valet, butler — call him what you will) had brought into the private papal apartment on the third floor of the Apostolic Palace. (Against his initial wishes, Michael had been persuaded, not wishing to cause a stir so early on, to wear the papal white cassock for his investiture. But at all other times he wore plain black — to show the world, he believed, he was still just a simple priest, albeit one with a higher calling.)

He was not alone. Lounging informally on an ornate couch nearby, looking incongruous in khakis and an old blazer, his collar open, tie stuffed hastily into his jacket pocket, sat another man of the same age, just 50, with slightly shaggy brown hair and scruffy beard flecked with grey, wearing glasses and also drinking coffee.

The man was Gregory Fletcher Flynn, a newspaper and magazine journalist. But this was no papal audience, nor was it a media interview. This was just two old friends and longtime intellectual jousting partners catching up over coffee. Neither of them, of course, would ever have believed it would be under these circumstances.

Although their lives had long since taken decidedly different paths, they had started out more or less the same — two young boys from a poor Boston neighborhood, just little Greg (quickly known as Fletch) and Tim thrown together as classmates at the same Catholic elementary and secondary schools. That early friendship solidified when coincidence (Fletch would say) or divine providence (Tim would say) had made them roommates for their first year in residence at Harvard — Fletch for political science and literature, Tim for poli-sci and economics. Along the way, Fletch's faith had long since lapsed as he became more immersed in the news and more disillusioned with the outside world, while Tim's had grown ever stronger. To the point where, after second year, Tim had felt a calling that took him away from Harvard to Boston's St. John's Seminary and along the path to holy orders.

But despite that, they'd stayed in touch and stayed friends — early friendships can form strong bonds. And over the decades as each of them advanced in their divergent careers, they'd kept up whenever they could get together their tradition of lengthy — sometimes heated but never disrespectful — discussions that in their serious moments usually ranged from politics to theology to economics and all the various ways they overlap and intersect.

So Fletch's question was entirely in keeping with the traditions of their long friendship, including the fact that Fletch was the only one who could get away with calling him Timmy, though he'd never think of embarrassing him with it in public.

"So, Timmy, when are you going to do something about it?"

"About what?" the new pope countered, though he suspected he already knew the answer.

"C'mon, Tim," the journalist replied. "And by the way, I guess I should get used to calling you Michael. Not gonna call you 'Your Holiness,' sorry.

"Anyway, we've talked about this for years. Sometimes it was the main thing we talked about. All those late-night discussions we'd have about all problems in the world — the injustices, the evil — and how we were going to try, even in our small ways, to correct them, to make the world a better place. You have your calling with the church and I have mine with journalism. You know I don't always agree with you, but you also know we're aiming for the same goal — helping people make informed choices for the greater good."

"And how best should we do that, Fletch?"

"Well, it seems to me you've found yourself in an ideal position to actually do something about solving some of the bigger ones. Within your church, anyway. And fixing those would go a long way toward benefiting the outside world and society as a whole.

"Such as?" (This was often how their discussions went, a kind of Socratic method of asking questions to which one already presumed an answer.)

"Well, to pick a few easy ones," Fletch said, "end the church's ban on women as priests. Though at this point, why any woman would want to join such a patriarchal and misogynistic institution is beyond me." The slight smile he added at the end was meant to take some of the sting out of that last remark, as Michael knew. "Allow priests to marry and end priestly celibacy, which has caused nothing but problems — and which you know as well as I do the church started enforcing in earnest only around the 12th century when it wanted to seize property that might otherwise have gone to a priest's widow or children."

"A gross simplification," the new pope said. "But I take your point."

"And there's the homophobia and abortion choice, of course."

"Of course," Michael said, smiling slightly himself. They'd gone over and over this ground many times in the past, and Michael knew what to expect.

"Easy, you say?" he said.

"Maybe not so easy to implement, I'll grant you," his old friend replied. "But you know they're easy in the sense of easily the right thing to do. Even you'd agree on that, as you always have. Unless you've suddenly changed your mind with your new lofty position?"

The new pope took a sip of his coffee, fast growing cold.

"No, my friend, I have not changed my mind — even in my new, as you call it, lofty position."

"Well, there you go. And if you'd feel better disarming your detractors with Scriptural warrant, you know that's easy enough to do too: Homosexuality was common in the time of Jesus, so he must certainly have been aware of it. It would have been all around him. And yet Jesus never even mentions it — and he certainly doesn't ever speak out against it.

"And if you want to bring Paul into it, there are some

scholars who say the 'affliction' Paul speaks of, the 'thorn in his flesh' despite which God loves him anyway, might have been homosexual yearnings Paul felt guilty about and was trying to suppress. So if Paul *were* homosexual and God can accept him anyway, where's the problem for anyone else?"

"A homosexual Paul might be a stretch of textual exegesis," Michael said, "but I'm glad to see you've been keeping up with your reading."

"As for women priests, sure, the 12 disciples were all men, but that probably has as much to do with symbolizing the 12 tribes of Israel as anything else. The Gospels are full of number symbolism. But outside of that inner circle, several of the closest followers of Jesus were women — Mary Magdalene, Martha, Mary the mother of John, Salome and others. In fact, doesn't at least one of the Gospels — Mark — tell us it was the women who first saw the empty tomb? And they had to persuade the boys, who didn't believe them at first."

"Again with the reading. Well done. It's good to see a journalist who's done at least a little research."

"Glad you agree," Fletch grinned.

Somewhere during this long exchange, the pope's assistant had discreetly shuffled in with a new carafe of hot coffee to replace old one. He'd been so quiet — and they so wrapped up in their discussion — that they'd hardly noticed until he was nearly out the door again. They took a break to refill their cups before launching back into it.

"Fletch, this is the same old argument we've been having since we were boys," the pontiff said. "You think the whole church — or most of it, anyway — is irredeemably corrupt. Which is why you walked away from it. And you think the only solution is to burn it to the ground. And I'm not even sure whether you want to rebuild it. That's about it, right?"

"Pretty much," Fletch agreed. "I mean, you can't spell 'Catholic' without spelling 'chaotic.' Oh, I'll grant you there are likely many fine people in the church — your good self included. And many of them undoubtedly do good work. But that's kinda like biker gangs: Sure, once a year they have a big toy drive to give some poor kids a better Christmas. But that hardly makes up for all the extortion, drug dealing, human trafficking and other crimes they commit during the rest of the year.

"In the same way, running a handful of homeless shelters and soup kitchens doesn't give the church a pass on its long history of misogyny, homophobia, shaming and corruption. OK, so the church does some good in the world. But as a whole, as an institution — let's face it, as a multi-billion-dollar transnational *corporation* — it's too damaged and corrupt and evil to be worth saving."

"Which is where you and I differ and part ways," Michael said. "You see, I believe in redemption. I'm in the redemption business, as you'd put it. Forgiveness and redemption are my stock in trade."

"Funny," the journalist quipped, "I thought it had more to do with snake oil." But his grin showed the scowling priest he was only teasing. Mostly, anyway.

"If we were back in our old Harvard dorm, I'd throw a pillow at you or something."

"I seem to remember a woman or two who shared one of your pillows back in those days. Remind me to ask you again sometime how difficult it must have been to take that vow of celibacy. You probably broke a few hearts."

If it were possible for a pope to look a little sheepish, he did so now.

"OK," said Fletch, getting them back on track, "let's get to the big one."

Michael, of course, knew exactly what he meant. This had been at the core of their many discussions over the decades.

Fletch put down his coffee, sat upright, and leaned forward on the couch.

"Look, Tim, you and I are Boston boys. We grew up under the corrupt reign of Cardinal Bernard Law. We know maybe better than anyone else how Law — there's an ironic name for you — and others in the church spent decades shuffling priests around from parish to parish. And they did it to cover up pedophilia — the sexual abuse of children, mostly boys — by these so-called 'men of God.' And it went on in Boston for decades.

"You and I were lucky," Fletch continued. "Personally, we escaped the worst. Neither of us was abused ourselves. I know I wasn't, and neither were you, right?"

Fletch looked inquiringly at his friend, who gave the smallest shake of his head.

"Right. So we personally were lucky, although I think both of us experienced at least the early stages of what they call 'grooming,' when a pedophile tries to gain your trust before he assaults you.

"Like I said, we both were lucky. But some of our friends weren't. You and I both know we have friends and schoolmates, guys we hung around with, went to mass with, who were victims, now survivors. Some of them got proper counseling and are doing OK, maybe. But some are still broken human beings — drugs, alcohol, failed marriages and relationships. Trust issues, self-esteem issues. And some, you know, couldn't deal with the trauma and took their own lives. They didn't survive."

"You don't have to remind me, Fletch. It breaks my heart."

"And so it should. The *Boston Phoenix*, that little weekly, had a bit of the story, and good for them. But it was the *Boston Globe* that picked up the ball and really ran with it in 2001. You remember their *Spotlight* series, turning over that rock and watching all the cockroaches scatter for the shadows. Hollywood even made a pretty good movie about it."

"Which you as a journalist admired."

"True. I do love seeing journalists do their job of comforting the afflicted and afflicting the comfortable.

"But was Bernard Law punished?" Fletch continued rhetorically. "Did the many victims get any sort of justice? Sure, there was an official academic report that uncovered thousands of victims spanning decades starting in the 1950s — they could go back only that far because from before that many of the abusers, and even many of their victims, were dead. And that helped bring the scandal to light. And sure, Law was forced to resign from the Boston archdiocese."

"Give some credit where it's due," the cleric said. "It was the U.S. Conference of Catholic Bishops that commissioned that investigation and its report from the John Jay College of Criminal Justice. At least they were trying to face up to the problem."

"Well, OK, points for that," Fletch conceded grudgingly. "And in that report, more than 4,000 priests were credibly accused of sexual abuse. There would have been almost double that, but by then most of them were already dead. And for only about 250 was there enough evidence to convict. And of those, only 100 actually went to prison.

"And true to form, Law skated away," Fletch said. "The archdiocese just shuffled him off for a little while to a convent in Maryland to get him out of the public eye. And then his buddy, Pope John Paul II, one of your predecessors in this fancy job, gave him a cushy spot at Santa Maria Maggiore in Rome, complete with a generous salary, a lavish apartment and very little actual work to do.

"And he even kept his rank as cardinal, which meant in 2005 he got to participate in the conclave that elected one of your other predecessors, Benedict XVI — and don't even get me started on that scoundrel Benedict and his role in the pedophilia coverup.

"Oh, and by the way along with the cushy Rome gig, ol' Bernie got himself Vatican citizenship. Which meant he was immune from prosecution in American or any other courts, since you like to pretend your little enclave of 120 acres or so and about 800 people, most of the them priests, smack in the middle of Rome, actually qualifies as its own independent country. What a joke!"

For a moment, Pope Michael sipped his coffee and said nothing, waiting for his friend to calm down from his impassioned — and sadly, Michael knew in his heart largely justified — diatribe.

"Are you done?" Michael asked.

"Not hardly," Fletch said with a smirk, showing he had, at least, brought his anger down a notch or two.

"Because of course you know even the thousands of likely Boston victims from the 1950s and onwards in that *John Jay Report* represent just the tip of the iceberg, just a tiny fraction of the thousands and thousands of innocent victims worldwide.

"And the church's sexual abuse of children has been going on for decades. In fact, centuries. Hell, even for the entire 2,000-year history of the church itself."

"How do you figure that, Fletch?" Michael asked gently, continuing the Socratic dialogue as they usually did.

By rights, Fletch should have felt foolish, even redundant, in lecturing a priest — the pope himself — on matters of theology and church history. But he was on a roll, and he wasn't going to let that stop him. Besides, these old friends had tossed this very football around many times before.

"OK, I'll remind you," said Fletch, laying out his facts as he might in pitching a story to an editor. "We know — or at least biblical scholars generally agree — that although the letters of Paul in the Bible come after the four Gospels by their placement in the book, Paul's writing of the letters actually predates the earliest of the Gospels. Mark likely dates from, say, the mid-60s to 70 — this is AD — Matthew and Luke from AD 80-something to 90 and John from AD 90-ish to 100 or so."

"With you so far," Michael said indulgingly.

"But Paul likely wrote his epistles sometime in the early 50s to late 60s AD. So, there might be some overlap with Mark, who might have known of at least some of his letters. But generally speaking, Paul is in his own little world, compared to the Gospels. He tells us nothing about the birth or even the daily life of Jesus. There's no biography. He's just interested in the teachings, and that in a pretty abstract way. And, by the way, Paul had nothing but condemnation for pedophiles.

"But here's the thing," Fletch continued: "You know as well as I do there are all sorts of other letters and writings and pseudo-Gospels that didn't make the final cut when your church fathers were putting together the Bible we know today as the Old and New Testaments."

"Yes, I am aware," Michael said with a little irony. "We did cover this in theological school."

"Yes, I know, but I'm trying to make a point: Among those documents of the early church, written perhaps as early as Paul's letters — maybe even before, probably at least not long after — is *Didache*, or the *Teaching*. It's basically a cheat sheet, the teachings of Jesus in point form. A bunch of 'thou shalts' and 'thou shalt nots.' Do this, don't do that. You know: 'Love God, love your neighbor; forgive sinners; turn the other cheek; don't murder; don't commit adultery.' The usual stuff."

"The usual stuff," Michael said. "I am familiar."

"You might even call it the church's first catechism."

"I suppose you might."

"Well, it's right there in *Didache* chapter 2, verse 2 — and forgive my lousy Greek pronunciation, I haven't studied it as long as you have: *ou paidofqorhseiv*. Now, depending on your translation, this has variously been given as 'you shall not commit pederasty' or 'thou shalt not commit sodomy' or 'thou shalt not corrupt boys' or — and points for inclusivity here — 'thou shalt not corrupt youth' or 'not molest children.' There's also 'you will not sodomize young boys' or 'you shall not seduce boys.' And in fact, given that most of these translators were still being a bit prudish and euphemistic, and given that this was written in the common Koine or attic Greek of daily life on the street, you could well put it more crudely to say it's a basic church teaching of: 'Don't fuck children.'"

If Fletch had hoped to get a rise out his debating partner with this crude remark, Michael wasn't going to take the bait. He just gave a small nod to continue.

"Anyway, you get the idea," Fletch said. "We don't tend to ban or condemn something that's hypothetical, that isn't actually already going on. There's nowhere in the Bible that warns, 'Thou shalt not fly.' Or, 'Thou shalt not walk on water' — since presumably Jesus was the only one going around doing that.

"So, obviously the 'corruption of youth' was already going on — maybe just by non-Christians and this was a way to say, 'We don't do that kind of thing,' the way Jews won't eat pork or shellfish. Or more likely, I think, it *was* going on. Maybe children, likely boys more often, *were* being sexually assaulted — by Christians generally, even by priests or whoever served as leaders in those early days of the church — and the other church leaders were trying to stamp it out."

"OK," said Michael, "let's say I concede your point. *Didache* or not, I'll certainly agree that, sadly, my church has a long and sorry history of the sexual abuse of children. We're not alone in that, but that's no excuse. We're faith leaders in a position of sacred trust and we're supposed to set a holy example. And I'll even agree, I'm ashamed to say, we've expended considerable effort in covering all that up. So, what would you have me do?"

"I'd have you do what you promised you would do," Fletch replied, "back when this was just an abstract hypothetical, if you ever found yourself in a position of real power within the church. Don't you see? This is your chance to actually put things right — or at least give it your best try."

"And what would that look like?"

"First off, you could start with a proper and sincere public apology."

"But Francis has already done that."

"Well, kinda sorta. He's apologized to a handful of victims, and that's a start. But I'd call that more papal bullshit than a real papal bull." Fletch smiled at his own wordplay, one he'd obviously been carrying around to use at the right moment.

"I'm talking about an actual papal bull or encyclical, or however you want to style it. You guys are big on confession — now's your chance. Stand up in that little balcony in front of the TV cameras and read it out to the world: You apologize on behalf of the church, and you promise to make full restitution. Real reparations. I'm talking actual money you pay to any and all victims who come forward. And to the families of all the victims who have died — many of them, as you well know, in shame and by suicide. Money won't absolve your guilt, but at least it may help victims and their families start to heal. And get proper counseling."

"Not to make this entirely about money," Michael said, "but do you have any idea how expensive that would be?"

"So what? Didn't Jesus say, 'Render unto Caesar?' You know this shouldn't be about the money. It should be about doing the right thing. Besides, the church is sitting on billions. Just in real estate alone, not to mention the priceless artworks of Michelangelo and Raphael and all those guys. Hell, you've probably got enough gold chalices and candlesticks to fund a small country — and I mean a *real* country, not your pretend one. Last time I looked, investment bankers put their best guess at the Vatican's overall wealth at somewhere between 10 and 15 billion dollars. I have no idea what that would be in lira. Just your investments in the Italian stock market alone are probably 1.6 billion, maybe 15% of the total listed shares. So don't tell me you couldn't liquidate that to pay the victims of your crimes.

"Because that's the thing that burns me, personally," Fletch said. "You — and by you, I mean the church and its leaders historically — have looked on all this sexual abuse as a sin. Which of course it is. And as you say, you're in the forgiveness business. And since it's a sin, you want to forgive it. But it's also a crime. And you don't have the authority to forgive crimes. That's a job for the courts, for the secular legal system. A few 'Hail Marys' and couple of 'Our Fathers' just won't cut it in the real world. And it's time you admit that."

"Is that all?" Michael's question was slightly mocking.

"Of course that's not all," Fletch replied, ignoring any sense of slight. "You have to root out the problem, get rid of the pedophile priests. They made children suffer, so make them suffer the consequences. Based on its sample, that *John Jay Report* from 2004 estimated the number of pedophiles among priests was somewhere around 4%. The Vatican has always claimed it's barely 1%, but that's self-serving at best and criminally negligent at worst. In jurisdictions where they've really cracked down on enforcement and reporting, with zero tolerance, the proportion is closer the 10% or more. Tell me, how many Catholic priests are there, worldwide?"

"Well, the number fluctuates, of course," Michael said. "We're generally losing clergy in Europe and North America but gaining in South America and Africa. In round numbers, I'd say maybe 400,000."

"So that means you have, what, as many as 40,000 pedophiles on the payroll? Quite a lot, wouldn't you say? Surely you must be the largest single employer of pedophiles in the world. Not a record I'd be proud of, if I were you," Fletch said. "And that's not even counting all the other priests and bishops and archbishops like our Boston friend who saw what was going on and looked the other way. Or worse, took steps to cover it all up.

"While I'm not in any way excusing the heinous crimes of those abusers, one might even feel a tinge of sorrow or empathy for them, for the actual pedophiles," Fletch said. "After all, at some level they're battling a mental illness — something wrong with the wiring or the chemistry in their brains that makes them feel sexual urges toward a child.

"But the others? All those other priests and bishops and archbishops and popes who did nothing to stop it, just kept sweeping it under the rug? That's a special kind of evil — a self-serving pride in their precious reputations and not wanting to lose their positions of authority and power. In some ways, that may be even worse. They can't even blame a mental illness. They're just morally corrupt. I believe you guys call those sins of commission *and* of omission."

Fletch paused. "I mean, after all, when Jesus says in Matthew

'Suffer little children to come unto me' he means 'let the children,' not 'make the children suffer.'"

Michael shot Fletch a look that, were they not fast friends, might have seemed close to withering disdain. But between them, it was more like an eyeroll — now a holy eyeroll, given Michael's new stature. Fletch had used this particular wordplay often before in their intellectual debates, so his friend was not surprised that he'd revived it. In their own way, each appreciated the sentiment and the cleverness of it.

"Let's say you're right," Michael said. "Do you expect me to just fire 40,000 priests?"

"Well," Fletch grinned, "it would make room for all those newly ordained women.

"But seriously," he continued. "You've been given the keys to the kingdom. You're the Vicar of Christ. You're God's representative on Earth. Hell, you're supposed to be infallible, at least on matters of doctrine and faith — as if infallibility is something you can just turn on or off like a light switch. But surely this qualifies. And really, if you call yourself a Christian, at some level isn't *everything* a matter of faith?

"So why not use your God-given authority? Stand on that balcony, issue that encyclical and command by papal decree that any priest who molested a child, and anyone else who helped in the coverup of those sins and crimes, shall report himself without delay to the proper legal authorities and submit himself to the appropriate criminal punishment. If they really think your authority is absolute, now's the time to put it to the test. Oh, and nuns, too — let's not forget about them."

There was a discreet knock at the door and the priest assistant entered the room.

"Your Holiness, I'm sorry to interrupt," the older man said with a small bow. "But you've gone past time for your next appointment. I had the cardinal wait as long as I could, but you'll get way behind on your schedule if we delay much longer."

"Yes, thank you, my son," Michael said. "Please tell him I'll be just a minute."

Turning back to his longtime friend, he said: "Fletch, always good to see you. We may come at things from different directions, but you always give me something to think about. And I appreciate that. And you've obviously given this a lot of serious and sincere thought. I appreciate that too. I will think and pray on our discussion, and I hope to see you again soon. But now, I'm afraid, I really must get back to my official duties. You know, those lofty ones."

The two old friends smiled, shook hands and hugged briefly.

From somewhere in the outer room, another priest appeared to usher Fletch out and, thankfully, guide him through the seeming labyrinth of the Apostolic Palace, after which eventually he found himself back outside in St. Peter's Square among all the regular tourists.

θ θ θ

Several more weeks went by. Fletch had to leave Rome on an assignment and unfortunately was not able to share another friendly coffee/sparring match with is old friend and former roommate. But the internet made information and reporting from a wide range of sources readily available, so he was able to keep current — as much as possible for so secretive an organization — on news coming out of the Vatican.

And so it came as perhaps less of a surprise to the journalist than to much of the world at large when word began to trickle out that the newly elected pope, scarcely a few months into his papacy, was expected to make a major announcement in the coming weeks or even days. Even more of a surprise to most, but less so to Fletch himself, was the rumored nature and content of the expected announcement.

*L'Osservatore Romano*, the official Vatican newspaper, was scant on any details and appropriately reserved in its coverage — which, pending an official papal announcement, was minimal at best. But *La Repubblica*, generally considered a more progressive and left-leaning Roman newspaper less likely to toe the Vatican line, offered slightly more detail, such as it could determine. Aided no doubt by its sources inside the Vatican, those both in favor of and opposed to the rumoured changes, the paper published something of a scoop to the effect that Pope Michael was set to announce — with full papal authority, no less — sweeping changes to the role and character of priests, including the ordination of women and an end to enforced celibacy. Also leniency on the matters of birth control and abortion choice.

And as if all these weren't controversial enough, the paper reported in a series of news stories and dueling opinion pieces a coming stringent crackdown on the church's long history of enabling and covering for pedophile priests. Lacking specific details but otherwise containing much of the same information, *La Repubblica* covered the same ground, though even more updated, as the *Boston's Globe*'s Pulitzer-winning *Spotlight* team had done in the early 2000s.

The news spread like wildfire in the Vatican rumor mill, and an institution prone to both secrecy and gossip found more than enough to feed its curiosity, even paranoia and insularism, as the expected day of the announcement loomed closer. Italian society, that of the wider church and of the world outside found itself fracturing and splintering along ideological and theological lines — the protectionists closing ranks, the progressives welcoming these expected changes and hoping for even more.

Working his own sources within his industry, Fletch was able to keep tabs as much as possible on the developments as the weeks went by. He did try twice to contact Michael directly. But he was firmly, if politely, rebuffed. Whether Fletch was the victim of a self-appointed priestly gatekeeper or whether Michael himself had decided it better to keep some distance for the moment, Fletch could not determine — and was never to find out. Looking back, he suspected Michael's assistant — so eager to deliver fresh coffee and possibly also listen at doors — likely had had a hand both at leaking what he'd overheard and then in keeping Fletch away from any further contact.

θ θ θ

On the day of the big announcement, preceded only by a terse and vaguely worded report in the Vatican newspaper, St. Peter's Square was almost as packed as it had been for the conclave that had elected Michael to the papal throne not so many months before. Once again, the Italian police were doing what they could to maintain order among the tens of thousands gathered there, once again with TV cameras on scaffolding, their lenses focused this time not on the traditional chimney but on the balcony where the pope was soon expected to speak.

Where normally in modern times the text of a papal encyclical would have been provided in advance to media outlets to aid in their analysis and reporting, the announcement on that day had been kept securely under wraps. Or at least officially so. But in fact most of the major news outlets — print, radio, TV and online — had already broken the news of the major changes likely to come. And since there had been no official Vatican denial, most observers knew at least in general terms what to expect. And had already made up their minds on whether or not they approved.

But assuming you know something, even from reliable sources, and knowing for certain are two very different things. And so when Pope Michael, dressed not in the formal papal white but once again in a simple priest's black cassock, emerged onto the small balcony overlooking the grand square, first a cheer of praise went up — though to be truthful, not from everyone — and then a respectful silence came gradually over the crowd. From his hotel room in another part of the world, in another time zone,

Fletch watched the event on TV as it was broadcast live to the world.

"My friends," the pope began in the informal manner that had quickly become his trademark, "my children, I come to you with a heavy heart and after much prayerful consideration."

Was he ill? some in the crowd wondered, was he about to resign? They waited for his next words.

"For too long, there has been a cancer infecting our beloved church. Despite all the good work we may do, the body of the church cannot be healthy, and it will not survive, until this cancer is removed. However painful that may be, we must do what is best and follow what we know in our hearts is the path of righteousness."

Another murmur rippled through the crowd.

"You know by now the cancer of which I speak," the pope said, his voice amplified and filling the square. "There are some of my brothers and even sisters in holy orders who have profaned their sacred calling by preying on — let me not be misunderstood and speak plainly — by raping and sexually abusing the little ones in their care. Children who trusted them, who by their very nature and by God's grace are innocent and blameless and worthy only of our love and protection. In this we have failed them, failed the teachings of our Lord and failed ourselves."

Michael paused to let his words sink in, before continuing. Fletch, watching a world away on TV, could hardly believe what he was hearing — even though he better than anyone had reason to know what most certainly was coming next.

"I speak to you now," the pope said, "in my full authority as Vicar of Christ, as God's representative on Earth and as Servant of the Servants of God. I invoke the full *magisterium* and infallibility of the office that by God's grace I now occupy. And I say this: I am sorry. We are sorry. The church herself is sorry. We have failed you.

"To all the victims of sexual abuse by clergy and by those who enabled them in any way, your pope, your servant, offers our humble, profound and sincere apology. We were wrong, and we will do everything in our considerable power to make amends, both spiritually and financially."

At this, the murmur of the crowd grew louder. Were they really hearing this? What did it mean? Was the church really going to sell off its treasures?

Sensing a shift in the mood, Michael spoke again: "My children, listen to me: There is much good, much kindness, much holiness in your hearts. This I know and I do not deny. And I am grateful for it. But you must also know we must confront this evil if we are to overcome it and once again become the church that our Lord and Savior wishes us to be."

Impressed, even amazed, by what he'd heard so far, Fletch wondered if Michael would follow through with what he hoped would come next. As Michael continued, he was not disappointed.

"But the cancer remains, and must be excised," Michael said. "And so I will speak directly now to my brothers and sisters in Christ who have taken their vow of holy orders: Those of you who are following the path of righteousness as best you can, you have my blessing and my thanks.

"But to those of you, to any of you, who have abused children in any way, but especially sexually, those who have perverted the words of our Lord and made children suffer, and those who for so long enabled such heinous acts to be kept secret — you I condemn with all the authority that is mine to wield. You have sinned in the eyes of God and of His church. But before there can be forgiveness, there must be accountability. For I have been reminded that your actions not only are sins, which are the province of the church, but also are crimes, over which the secular courts rightly have authority. And it is not our place to ignore that authority.

"And so, as your pope and spiritual leader, I implore you — no, I command you — to make a full confession of your sins before God, but also a full confession of your crimes to the police. Do so without reservation and without delay."

Fletch could hardly believe what he was hearing. And he could not have been more proud. Tim — he could even think of him now as Michael — was stepping up and following through in ways over all those years they had only dreamed of and hoped for. He turned back to the live broadcast.

"And now, my children," Michael was saying, "there is more we must do, more wounds we must heal. Among its many other sins and failings, our beloved church has had a sad and shameful history in its mistreatment of women. Beginning today —"

The sharp crack of the sniper's rifle that echoed through the St. Peter's Square took the crowd by such surprise and caused such immediate panic as they scattered that not everyone noticed the pope crumple into a heap as blood spread across his chest (the blood not as noticeable at a distance on the black cassock as it would have been on papal white). The cameras, of course, did catch the awful moment. And Fletch himself saw it live and in horrible clarity.

As the pope's handlers rushed to drag him inside to safety and then to a waiting ambulance, they knew there would be little hope. But they were in the business of hope — faith is the substance of things hoped for, Paul reminds us. And so they prayed as the ambulance took him away to hospital. The sniper had hit him in the chest, slightly off centre on his right side. Had Michael not turned slightly just a tiny moment before, the bullet would have pierced his heart directly, killing him in an instant. Coincidence, or the hand of God? Skeptics and believers kept the debate alive long after the event.

But the wound struck deep and too much of his blood was shed. Even as the ambulance arrived at the hospital, Michael had already lapsed into a coma from which he would never arise. And on the third day, he died. (Fletch above all others immediately noted the irony.)

The fatal shot likely had come from atop the north colonnade, though a later investigation had proven inconclusive. It was several hundred yards or metres away, but a distance quite within the range of a skilled marksman. And the shooter was never found.

Nor did investigators ever determine who the shooter was, whether the stereotypical "lone wolf" or an agent of those powerful forces within the Vatican itself who had viewed Michael as too radical, too dangerous to their complacent way of life. As someone who must be stopped. Whatever the case, the bullet had swiftly found its target.

From the rifle barrel, just a puff of white smoke and it was done.

# Joseph

HE WAS MY SON. He was my son.

Some might say differently. Would God say differently? God only knows. And God — I should of course say YWH or Yaweh — rarely speaks to a mere mortal like me.

True, I did not sow the seed. Did not spark the fire to bring that light into the world. Someone else had done that.

But he was my son. I was there at his birth — husband and father and midwife all in one. No one else was there to shepherd his birth into this world.

θ θ θ

They should have let him die when he was dead. Things might have been better. Different, certainly.

When David heard that Absalom was slain, he went up into his chamber over the gate and wept. "My son, my son, O Absalom my son, would God I had died for you!"

Indeed, would God I had died instead of my son. I am just an old man. He was still young, still so full of wisdom and promise.

They should have let him die when he was dead. Life might have been better. I know I would have been happier.

But then, what do I know? I'm only his father. (Well, not actually his father. But I raised him. That ought to count for something.)

I'm not sure who his father really was — or is — though I have been told and have no reason to doubt it. (Maryam, poor girl, has her own version. But we'll get to that later.)

His name was simple enough, a name with history: Yeshua ben Yoseph. Jesus, son of Joseph.

His followers would come to give him other names: *Rabbi*, teacher, which he was. But also *Christos*, *Messiah*, *Agnus Dei*. Which he was not.

They even called him the Son of God (a title, I'm relieved to say, he never had the audacity to assume for himself) and Son of Man (this he sometimes did use, but only as *ben-adam*, the lowly name we all give ourselves). Much later, they would come to call him a lot of other things, too — none of which, had he known, he would have approved of:

God of God, Light of Light, Very God of Very God. Begotten not made. Being of one substance with the Father, through whom all things were made —

Rubbish, all of it. Abomination. *To'eva*. Blasphemy. *Ne'atsah*. Superstitious claptrap. And he knew it. He was never any of these things. Nor to his credit did he ever claim to be. He knew better than that, knew better how to show respect to our God.

It was that troublemaker Paul. And Peter — spineless, though he struts like a cock — who wouldn't, or couldn't, stop him, despite their argument at Antioch. And legions of others who were to follow. James his brother did what he could to prevent the heresy, to keep the Law and abide by the prophets. As for Yeshua, he did his best.

But his best was not good enough.

θ θ θ

Sometimes in the evening, as the heat of the sun finally cools down (the psalmist says the sun shall not burn you by day — ha!) and the evening breeze wafts up, I liked to sit outside the door of my little house by the western wall of the city, as my wife inside tended to the children or to her spinning. I'd sit, watching the sun go down and the shadows lengthen, the quiet start of a new day.

At these times I liked to carve. Not an object nor an idol, of course — that would be *to'eva*, an abomination unto Yaweh. Just to whittle, really, carving patterns or something even less than patterns into an old stick or scrap of wood. I would spend all day reading words, reading the Law, writing or transcribing with pen and scroll, squinting at the letters and words until my eyes hurt. This work was different. It still needed my hands, but it was less demanding, a more forgiving material to work with. Or at least less taxing on the brain and the spirit. Didn't require me to think very much. And at the end, maybe something beautiful to look at, to touch and feel.

One such evening, long ago, I sit with my knife and a new piece of wood, part of an olive branch I had picked up off the ground on one of my walks. Yeshua, probably four or five (I don't remember) sits on the ground beside me. He has his own stick, much smaller. He's scratching in the dirt, practising (I smile to see) some of the letters and words I've begun to teach him. He is learning well.

"*Abba*," he says, "Papa."

"Yes?"

"You do this all the time, this carving of wood."

"Well, yes," I say. "Not all the time, but often."

"If you enjoy it so much," he says, "why did you not become a carpenter or a craftsman, a *tekton* like some of the other fathers?"

Already I see for my son the Aramaic tongue we speak at home, and the Hebrew I am teaching him for the Torah, will not be enough. Instead of Aramaic *naggara* or Hebrew *naggar* or even *kharash*, he is picking up *tekton* and other words in Greek from the merchants at the market where his mother takes him. Or perhaps overheard on the streets as he accompanies me to the Temple. And probably other words in Latin from the Roman soldiers and other travellers. Who knows? He is a smart boy, eager to learn.

"Yes, Yeshua," I say, "I enjoy this quiet time working with my hands. I like the smoothness of the wood, the trueness of the knife."

"So let's you and I be carpenters together, Father," my little boy says. "We will make boxes for the spice merchants and footstools for their servants and fancy thrones for all the kings.

"My mother says I am special and will do wondrous things," the boy continues, growing ever more excited. "I will find us the best wood — olivewood from the Mount of Olives and cedars from Lebanon and cypress from Parthia.

"And if it is not the best wood for the finest craftsmen, I will pray to Yaweh and he will hear my prayer and heed it and he shall make it whole and wonderful in his eyes. And if a board is too short for our purposes, or has too many knots and blemishes, I shall pray to Yahweh for a miracle and he shall make the board longer and without blemish. And people will come from all around Judea to see our marvelous craftsmanship. And we shall be the finest carpenters in all Jerusalem."

By this time, he was smiling and giggling and dancing about with joy, my lovely Yeshua. And I was happy to see my son — usually so serious, even at his age — look more like a happy little boy.

But why must mothers fill their children's heads with dreams of greatness? Of course we all want greatness for our children, but one must also learn humility and patience for the trials of life. Maryam, my sweet Mary, was always doing this, always filling his head with dreams and grandeur. I think she was still so afraid for him, so afraid and angry for the violation of his conception, that she made up stories in her head to make herself feel better.

That may be all well for herself, but I wish she wouldn't put such fantasies on the boy. But what was I to do? Clearly she loves him and he loves her, as I love them both. I can't just turn my face from them.

And so I say: "Yes, my son, I'm sure we would make wonderful carpenters together. But God has given me a higher purpose, a mind for the Law and a knowledge of words. He expects me to use that gift. To ignore that would be an insult to my Creator. Must I not do what I feel called upon to do?

"Do you understand, my son?"

"Yes, Papa, I understand. But I still think being a carpenter would be more fun than sitting all day as a *hakham*, hunched over a desk. When I grow up and become a man, maybe I'll be a carpenter instead."

"Yes," I laugh, rubbing my hand in his curly hair. "As smart as you are, you may be what you choose. Or what Yahweh chooses for you.

"Come, sit on my knee, we'll watch this beautiful sunset together."

And so we do, my little boy — my growing boy — curled in my lap with my arms around him as we watched one day draw to a close and another begin.

And it was good.

θ θ θ

Her cry wakes me in the night season. She sleeps on, but I take no rest.

Again she is having the nightmare, struggling against her unknown attacker. Crying, whimpering like an animal in pain. She holds her arms up, outstretched as if being held down, shaking her head. Her beautiful brown hair, long and loose, half-covering her delicate face. Her eyes — in the daytime deep, liquid pools, dark yet kind — are squeezed tight, her face a grimace.

Her body shifts, her legs twitch as she cries out. Perhaps in the dream she is trying to run away, to escape her defiler.

I do not know what to do, whether to wake her or leave her sleep. If I wake her, the nightmare will end, if only briefly, but she will awake in terror, remembering the pain of it. Sometimes it is better to leave her alone. A moment longer and the dream may pass and she will return to a peaceful rest. And then perhaps she will not even remember she has had this nightmare again.

But still it grips her, this night terror. Grips her as surely as he must have gripped her and held her down in his assault on that horrible day. An assault that has left her scarred and scared and that took from her something sacred.

Again amid the whimpering and tiny moans that in her head, in her dreams and memory, must surely be shouts of rage, she cries out in anger with one intelligible word. It is a name: "Pantera!"

And then she is silent. The nightmare seems to have passed.

Without ever waking, she falls back into a more restful sleep. Watching over her, I wish better dreams for her. Perhaps she dreams now of spinning and weaving, of her past life as a virgin in the Temple, weaving veils and raiment for the priests and elders.

I let her sleep, and hope myself to slumber.

θ θ θ

She was so young when first I met her.

I was much older than she, but still not so old a man myself. My wife, Michal, had succumbed to a fever, leaving me a widower with two young sons, James and Simeon, and a daughter, named for her mother.

One day, not quite a year after her death, one of the Temple Levites, sent by the high priest and the Sanhedrin, approached me as I was packing away my scrolls and writing tools at the close of day.

"Joseph, you are a wise and kind man," he said, after introducing himself as Kohath. "You walk in the way of our God and are known to be a righteous man."

I thanked him for his compliment and waited for the favor such flattery was sure to foretell.

"It is not just I," the young Levite assured me, "Shimon ben Boethus, our high priest you know also as Cantheras, asked among the Sanhedrin — where your friend Nicodemus speaks well of you. He also asked other elders for the names of righteous, unmarried men. Sadly, there were not as many as you might think.

"Plenty, of course, not yet married and some, like yourself, recently widowed," Kohath went on. "But among those even fewer whom we could consider blameless and godly. From those names, the priests and council drew by lot, and you were chosen."

I waited to hear him tell me that for which I was chosen.

"It has been almost a year," he said, "since Yaweh in his wisdom took your wife from you. We have seen that you have properly mourned and honored her, and shown respect for the blessing of her memory. And we are glad for that.

"But it is not good that a man should be without a wife," he continued. "Especially a man still young like yourself, a man with a young family in need of care and attention."

"My boys are old enough to begin looking after themselves," I said, "and I have a neighbor — a widow herself — who looks after my young Michal while I am away at my Temple duties."

"Yes, your neighbor Sara is kind to do that," he said. "But she is old and herself sick, and may not be long for this world. She is not a help meet for your needs as a vigorous man. You need a young woman to be your new wife, to raise your children and perhaps add to your family.

"For as the psalmist says, 'Like as the arrows in the hand of the giant, even so are the children of one's youth. Happy is the man that has his quiver full of them.'"

Here, Kohath looked at me and smiled. Was it perhaps mere coincidence that I had been transcribing that very psalm onto a new scroll this very day? Did he know that? Was it some divine hand at work? Or was it just that some priest, knowing the conversation that was to come, had assigned me that work as a prompt to my feelings? That might be something they would do.

"I sense you are leading me down a path of your choosing," I said to him. "Tell what the council wishes me to do."

"The Sanhedrin of course wishes you to be happy," he said, his words smooth as butter. "But yes, there is something you could do that would benefit us all."

I looked at him with a careful smile.

"There is a girl," he said, "a young woman, one of the Temple virgins, whose name is Maryam, sometimes known as Mary. Her mother, Anna, had lost her husband and did not have the means to care for her. Anna brought her to us when she was but three years old. She has lived among the other Temple virgins — learning to spin, sew, weave and care for the veils and vestments for the Temple priests, to bake the showbread and prepare the incense — for lo, more than a dozen years. She will reach 16 years by the next moon."

"What is that to me?" I asked, although I thought I knew where this was leading.

"The high priest and elders feel you should take her to you to be your wife."

"She is young to be wife to a man of my years," I said. "Surely there should be a younger man to whom she could be betrothed?"

"There are younger men, I agree," Kohath said. "But none of your unblemished stature in our community. There are special circumstances at play, which the priests and council feel require a man of good standing such as yourself."

"Special circumstances?"

"You must understand, Joseph, she is a good girl, a blameless girl. She has served her God and preserved her virginity, kept herself pure, all of her life."

"Yes," I said. "And?"

"And then she was defiled," Kohath said. "It was dusk, only some weeks ago. She was coming back from the well bearing water for her Temple sisters. A drunken man came out of the shadows in a narrow passageway, accosted her, threw her to the ground and violated her. She cried out, but there was no one nearby to hear her. Her sisters found her later when they came looking for her. The wife of one of the elders examined and cared for her and heard her story of the attack."

"And you believe her?" I asked.

"The signs are clear," he replied. "The stains of blood tell the story."

"So you wish her to be my wife to save her from shame?"

"The Law is clear," Kohath said. "She was a virgin, she was not betrothed to any man. She did not bring this shame upon herself. The sin is not hers, but that of the man who defiled her."

"Then surely you should be speaking with him to make this right," I said. "The Law is clear on that also. He must pay her father a fine and marry her himself."

"But as I have said," Kohath answered, "she is a daughter of the Temple and has no father. Her mother also is dead and she has no other family."

"What about her attacker? Do you know who he is?"

"Yes, we do know," Kohath said. "But we are powerless to act against him. Maryam recognized him, for he and some of his fellow soldiers are known to gather near the Temple when they have had too much to drink — which is often — and harass the Jews walking by. And in any case in his cups he has since been heard bragging about his so-called conquest. He is a Phoenecian-born solder named Abdes Pantera who has been made a Roman citizen and serves in a cohort of archers. He is a powerful and important soldier who has risen to the rank of signifer, the standard-bearer of his troop. When Rome made him a citizen, he took the full name Tiberius Julius Abdes Pantera.

"Our Law states that Pantera should pay 50 shekels, or 30 pieces of Roman silver, as a bride price. And the council did discuss appealing to the *ethnarch*, the governor, Herod Archelaus, to appeal to his sense justice. But he does not recognize our Laws anymore. Only those of Rome.

"We in Judea are under Roman rule, as you know," Kohath went on. "There are limits to how much we can push back or stand up to our oppressors. Tensions are already high. It was felt unwise at this time to draw attention to ourselves.

"But what to do with Maryam?" Kohath asked. "Naturally, she can no longer continue living with the other virgins at the Temple. That would not be right in the eyes of YWH. Some members of the Sanhedrin were of a mind to put her away privately. But others felt she deserved no such punishment. And so it was decided to find her an honorable man to be her husband. And that man is to be you, Yoseph ben Yacob."

θ θ θ

The wedding, of necessity, was small. The priests and elders did not want to draw any attention. And afterward I took her immediately into my home and family. Because she was still young, still withdrawn and afraid, I had resolved, beautiful though she was, not to know her until the time seemed right. And that time was not yet. She took to her duties of cooking and cleaning and caring for the children with grace and goodwill, and I was grateful for her shy smile and quiet charm.

And yet by the passage of three moons, my Maryam could no longer hide that she was with child. Everyone naturally assumed the coming child was mine and so I did nothing to correct that impression. But of course I knew the child was not of my seed, since I have never lain with her, not even on our wedding night. I had kept her pure — at least so far as I was able to.

And yet Maryam began always referring to "our child" and "the child Yaweh has given us," so it became less clear to me whether she actually knew that I could not have been the father. Perhaps in her innocence she was completely unaware of the ways of the world and the natural way in which a new child is brought into this world. She began speaking to the child, even as it began growing in her womb, telling the child it was special, "a gift from God" and "a child like no other."

And so a boy was born — at our home, much earlier and more quickly than expected, no time even to summon a midwife. I cut the cord myself and placed him in the first thing I could find for a cradle, a feeding trough with some hay from one of the household animals. She sang to him often in his infancy. And even by the time he was just old enough to listen (though not yet even understand), she would fill his head with the same words, calling him her "gift from God," her "miracle child." Perhaps I should have done more to put a stop to it when it began. As he grew older, she continued with such talk, to the point where he would even say it himself. Children love to parrot back the words their parents tell them. At first it might just have seemed sweet. But I began to worry that he himself was beginning to believe it too.

Maryam, though still sweet and innocent as a dove, did not help matters. One evening I had gone with my older boys to gather olives on the mountainside. Little Yeshua, perhaps six, had tagged along, wanting to help, and because he liked to emulate his older brothers. Maryam and my girl Michal, fast becoming a

—94—

young woman herself, remained at home. It was warm and the sun had not yet fully set, a perfect time to harvest a small amount for our needs.

A few other men had come for olives as we had, some also with their boys of various ages, and soon my little Yeshua had found some other boys his own age to play with. The other fathers and I kept half an eye on them as we picked the ripest olives for our baskets. I could see a little way off the younger children trying to climb one of the smaller olive trees. Even at his young age, my Yeshua was already learning well to climb trees, and liked to hang, half upside-down, from the lowest branches, swaying slightly and laughing his innocent laugh. This he was doing with some of the other boys, no doubt imagining themselves much higher off the ground than they actually were, as if among the clouds.

I went back to my work until there was a small cry and one of the other fathers looked up from farther off.

"My boy, Zenon!" he cried, dropping his basket, scattering the olives as he ran toward the little tree.

I, being much closer and perhaps faster of foot, got there first. A small boy lay on the ground, not moving, the other young boys gathered around him, looking down. My Yeshua was kneeling beside the boy, one hand on his tiny chest, another on his forehead, speaking softly.

"Come, Zenon," my little Yeshua said. "Come back to us. We would miss you."

As Yeshua said this, the boy on the ground gave a small cough and a tiny gasp. He opened his eyes, sat up and began to cry. I was reminded of the cry my baby Yeshua gave when first he came into this world from his mother's womb. By now my other boys and others from nearby by were coming to look.

His father arrived, out of breath and pushing his way through the gathering crowd.

"Let me through!" he shouted, and to my Yeshua he said: "What are you doing? Get away from him!"

Yeshua stood up, looking bewildered that the man should shout at him. For a moment, it looked like he too might cry. But his face got solemn and he came over to my side, clutching my leg and saying not another word.

"Zenon slipped off the branch and fell," said one of the boys.

"He was not moving," said another.

"But Yeshua spoke to him and he came back to life!" said a third, joining in.

Some in the crowd gasped, for to say such a thing was either to blaspheme against Yaweh — or it would have to be the hand of Yaweh at work. Some began to murmur one to another, some even calling it a miracle.

"Don't be foolish, boys," I said, loud enough that the crowd too could hear, and to silence them. "Zenon fell but a short distance and had the breath knocked out of him, but only for a moment. Nothing more than that. Active little boys do this all the time when they fall. See? Now he stands before you, only a little frightened. That is all."

And indeed, the little boy had stopped crying and was standing next to his father, who had crouched down beside him and was holding him close.

"My son, my boy!" he said. "You worried me, but I am glad you are well. Let us get you home to your mother."

Whereupon he turned to me and to Yeshua still beside me. "I am sorry I yelled at you, little child," he said. "I was frightened for my own little boy, and I lost my head." To both of us, he said: "Please forgive me."

"There is nothing to forgive," I said kindly. "It is natural for a father to worry about his son." Yeshua looked up at him and smiled.

"I forgive you," he said.

They turned away and walked slowly down the hillside. I gathered up my other boys, with our baskets of olives, and we too walked down the hillside and back to our home.

θ θ θ

On the walk home, James and Simeon, carrying their baskets, walked a little ahead. Yeshua I held by the hand, his shorter legs making him not as fast as his older brothers. He was quiet most of the way, saying little. But as our home came in sight, he ran ahead, excited to speak with his mother.

"*Imma!*" he shouted in his childlike voice, "Mama!"

Hearing his voice, Maryam came to the doorway to greet him, sweeping him up into her arms.

"And how is my little boy?" she said, smiling. "Did you help your father and brothers with their work among the olive trees?"

"I did, Mama," he said. "But I did much more than that! Little Zenon fell from a tree and was asleep, but I called to him and he woke up again. Some of the others said it was a miracle!"

"A miracle?" she replied. "My little Yeshua? And so it must have been."

"It was nothing of the kind," I said to her, rather too sharply perhaps, as my sons and I joined them. "The boy was climbing a tree and fell from no higher than his own height. He was merely winded for a moment. Don't give our boy foolish ideas.

"Yeshua is thoughtful and kind," I continued, "and it is good that he was worried for his friend. As his father, I am proud that he shows such care for others. But it was nothing like a miracle, just an ordinary accident such as small boys will have all the time. Just ask James or Simeon — I'm sure they would say the same."

"Oh, what's the harm?" Maryam replied. "If our Yeshua says he did something special, why not let him believe it was so? Now, go and wash your hands, all of you, and prepare for your meal."

As an old man now, looking back, I believe that might have been the real start of it — Maryam filling his head with foolish ideas, indulging his love of storytelling, making him feel more important than he should have been. As Yeshua grew older, he did grow in wisdom as well as stature. And his compassion grew only deeper and more profound, for which I am proud and grateful. But I fear some of seed planted that day also grew, watered and tended by Maryam and later by others who joined them, with talk of miracles and signs and prophecy and portents, that made my little boy seem bigger than he was.

θ θ θ

Years went by, my little boy grew and would soon become a man. In his 12th year, after the barley was ripened in the month of Nisan, at the time of the *Pesach*, the Passover, we went as an extended family — my older sons, now grown, with their wives and small children, my brothers and their wives and children also — and with other families not our kinsmen, to the Temple to pray and offer our sacrifice. With that done, we would come back home to prepare our own modest *seder* meal. Along the crowded, narrow streets leading to the Temple, young Yeshua would sometimes walk with me and the other men of our various ages, or sometimes lag behind to walk with Maryam and the other women who followed. He seemed comfortable with either group.

We came to the Temple and joined the large crowd milling about outside as we awaited our turn to give our offering to the priests. The smell of blood from the *korbanot*, the sacrifices, and pungent smoke from the burnt offerings hung heavily in the air. At their tables, the moneychangers — in later years, Yeshua would come to have harsh words with them — were doing a brisk business taking coins from visitors and giving them shekels and half-shekels that would not defile the Temple so they could purchase pigeons or doves for their own sacrifices or to pay the Temple tax.

"Stay together with the family," I said to my children and the others as the crowd grew and pressed upon us. "Do not be separated from our group." I looked for Maryam and Michel to keep them close. The crowd continued to grow as more and more people came to fulfil their duty to Yaweh.

And so finally it came our turn to offer our young lamb, the *korban Pesach*, to the priests for sacrificial blessing. As the eldest and the patriarch, I gave our offering and prayers on behalf of my family, paid the yearly half-shekel Temple tax for each of the older men, and prepared to return home for our meal. I joined the others waiting outside the Temple, the men standing apart as a group, the women and children a little way off. We had to push our way gently through the crowd as we set off down from the hill and back through the city.

I spoke with my sons James and Simeon as we walked, listening as they told me about their homes and wives and their new children. They had each moved away on their own, and the Passover was our time to gather each year as a family. I did not see Yeshua among us, and believed he must be following behind with Maryam and Michel and the other women and small children. Once at home, the women continued busily preparing the meal, and the children who were old enough went outside to play before the sun went down and the new day would start.

And so it was not until we called the children in and gathered for the meal that we noticed Yeshua was not with us.

"Was he not with you and the other women when we left the Temple?" I asked Maryam.

"No," she replied, her voice rising in fear, "I thought he was with you and our other sons."

"He was not with us," said James, with Simeon nodding in agreement. "We thought he was with you and Michel."

Trying to remain calm, I went out into courtyard we share with other houses, looking for him, even calling out his name. He was not there.

"I will follow our path back to the Temple," I said. "Perhaps he has just stopped to visit a neighbor."

"Please find him, Joseph!" Maryam cried. "He is my little boy!"

I set off walking briskly, half-running. Soon the sun would set and it would grow dark. I saw no sign of him along the way and soon arrived again at the Temple. Pushing my way through the crowd, I made my way again to the priests. Among them I saw Kohath the Levite, one of the priests' helpers, and the man who so long ago had approached me about the young Maryam.

"Kohath, my friend!" I shouted. "I must speak with you!"

He must have heard some desperation in my voice, for he looked up and quickly hurried over. But he was smiling.

"Yoseph ben Yacob," he said soothingly. "I have been expecting you. You seek Yeshua, your young son. Be not afraid. He is here with us and the Temple priests. Come, I will take you to him."

He led me to a side chamber, away and apart from the tabernacle where only the priests may enter. And there was Yeshua sitting with three elder priests and some of my fellow scribes, reading a scroll. He looked up when I said his name.

"Yeshua," I said, chiding him. "Have you been here the whole time?"

"I recognize you," said one of the priests. "You are Joseph, one of our scribes. Kohath here speaks highly of you. Is this your son?"

"And yes," said one of the other priests. "The boy has been with us, discussing the Law and the prophets. You have taught him well, Joseph. He reads well and asks many good questions."

"I am honored that you would say so," I replied. "I hope my son has not been disrespectful. I thank you for looking after him, but now we must be getting home."

With that, I took his hand and led him away, not saying a word.

Outside the Temple and back on the street, I turned to him, anger and fear mixing in my voice.

"Yeshua! You should have stayed with your family, not lingered at the Temple. I was worried when I could not find you. And your mother is distraught with fear."

"But why did you need to look for me?" Yeshua said dismissively, as if the answer should be obvious. "Did you not know I must be about my father's business?"

"I am your father," I said, "and I did not tell you to stay behind at the Temple."

"Not you, my earthly father," he replied. "I must do the work of my father who is in heaven. Our father, I should say. For he is father of us all."

I looked at him, not knowing quite what to think. He was still a boy and yet possessed of so much insight. But also I was still angry at his lack of respect for my feelings, and those of his mother.

"Yeshua," I said more gently. "I am glad you show deference to Yaweh our God. And I'm sure you will continue to grow in wisdom. But you are still a child and not yet a man ready to stand on his own. You also know the commandments, and one is that you must honor your father and your mother. You truly had us worried with fear and grief."

"I am sorry, Father," my young boy said, bowing his head. "I did not mean to concern you, nor my mother. I will apologize to her as I now apologize to you. But you must know, I hear my heavenly father calling me to his service. And that I must obey."

And so my young son, almost a man but still enough of a boy that he would take my hand, walked with me, hand in hand, back to our home.

θ θ θ

More years went by and soon enough my little boy, my son, did indeed grow into a man. For a time, he took the pledge of a Nazarite like Samson of old — vowing celibacy, abstaining from wine, letting his hair grow long before shaving it all off and burning it with the rest of a burnt offering when his period of abstinence was done. But even after he was no longer fully a Nazarite, he chose to continue with his celibacy. I have never understood why, but I accepted his choice.

For a time, Maryam fell ill, so even into early adulthood, Yeshua remained with us to help nurse her back to health. By his mid-20s he had moved away from home and lived for a time in the wilderness near the Jordan with the Essenes and his cousin John, who baptized him in the river. Later, Yeshua settled in *Kfar Nahum*, which some call Capernaum, a fishing village on the Lake of Gennesaret — which the Galileans call the Sea of Galilee, even though its water has no salt.

His sister, Michel, had married and moved away with her husband, a merchant. And so Maryam and I were alone, all our fledgling children having left the nest. I still had my scribal work to keep me busy. But Maryam, I could tell, was restless with only me for company. Despite our love — which, though never passionate had always been warm and respectful — I knew she was lonely and unhappy. Sometimes in the night, her dark dreams would return and I would wake up to feel her thrashing beside me, still in her sleep but gasping and fending off her ghostly attacker. I still do not know whether it was better to awaken her, but usually I let her try to sleep on until the terror has passed.

One day, some years after both Michel and Yeshua had moved away, Maryam told me at our evening meal that she wished to visit Yeshua at Capernaum. I do not know how or when, but she had already spoken with Michel and had arranged that she could travel with Michel's husband, who took his goods with camels and asses to Capernaum and Bethsaida and some of the other villages by the lake in Galilee. Michel's husband is a good man, so I was glad Maryam would travel safely with him and be among family.

I was frankly surprised my Maryam would show such determination and independence. But perhaps I underestimate her and should not have been so surprised, especially remembering her devotion and the special bond she had with Yeshua. She said she would be setting off in a few days' time and she might stay as long as a month or two. As it was, she stayed away several years, leaving me alone in Jerusalem.

I did not see her again until my son — our son — was dead.

I missed her, of course, but I did not mind so much. I could take care of myself, and I was glad that she seemed happy where she was. I would get word sometimes from my sons James or Simeon, or from Michel or her husband after one of his trips, telling me how Maryam and Yeshua were faring. Sometimes, old friends would ask after her and I would say truthfully that she had gone to visit our son. Those who knew me less well sometimes assumed I was a widower. I confess I did not usually bother to correct them.

θ θ θ

Before long, I no longer had to rely on my other children to bring me occasional news of Yeshua and of his mother. There were always travellers to Jerusalem, whether merchants with their wares or foreigners passing through or Jews come to pray at the Temple and bring their offerings to the priests. And soon, many of these travellers brought news of Yeshua's activities — some called them exploits, some even spoke of miracles — throughout Judea and beyond.

Though not formally trained, his knowledge of the Law and the prophets was deep and extensive. I had taught him as well as I could, and he had taken my teaching much further. Many times after that Passover when he was 12, he had gone back — this time first asking my blessing. Many times as he grew up, we would walk together to the Temple in the morning, Yeshua asking me questions and (I know) comparing the answers I gave him to those he would hear from the priests and Levites and other scribes at the Temple. I would set to my duties as a scribe and he would often spend hours in their company. He took delight in asking them questions, sometimes even challenging their answers, especially if he found them to be, in his opinion, overly strict or unforgiving. I imagine he later had similar discussions among the Essenes.

And so by the time he had begun to dwell in Capernaum he

had become an unofficial *rabbi*, a teacher widely respected for his gentle wisdom. He had begun to preach, and had gathered around him a small group of followers — some of them just simple fishermen from Capernaum and the nearby villages. One was even reported to be a tax collector working for Rome and so generally considered no friend of Jews. But Yeshua, it was said, did not judge, strove to be friend to poor and rich, Jew and Gentile alike, was friendly and accepting even to prostitutes and other outcasts.

It warmed my heart to hear such news, to know that the sweet little boy I had tried to raise to be wise and open-hearted and kind had grown into such a man. And that should be enough, as I had tried to teach him. What was the need of signs or miracles or magic tricks? The path of righteousness does not rely on these.

θ θ θ

Maryam his mother often travelled with Yeshua and his close followers, I learned. And there was another Maryam they called *Magdala*, "the tower," likely to distinguish her from his mother. But was it simply that she was tall? Or was it more, perhaps that she was to Yeshua a tower of strength? In which case I wondered again if he were keeping to his Nazarite vow of celibacy. I had heard they had been at a wedding at Cana in Galilee. Was it his own wedding? Had he married this Magdala? If so, why had I not been told, not least even been asked to attend? Had Yeshua grown so disrespectful of his own father? (Or at least the only real father he had ever known.)

At that wedding feast some said he had — as the old Greeks say of Dionysus, or Bacchus of the Romans — turned water into wine. Of course he had not, just as Dionysus or Bacchus had not. How could a mere man perform such a miracle? And even if it were Yaweh working through him, why would Yahweh concern himself to use his godly powers for such a trifling matter as a lack of wine?

As the number of his followers grew, others later said Yeshua performed such signs or miracles as those of the heathens and their gods. The ungodly, those not of Yaweh. They said he did not just turn water into wine, but also healed the sick, made the blind to see and the lame to walk. Like Dionysus, Osiris, even Pythagoras of long ago, they said he performed marvelous works.

Even raising the dead. I thought back to Yeshua's childhood and the little boy Zenon who had fallen out of an olive tree. Some called it a miracle then, and Maryam had helped our little boy indulge in that belief. Did she still believe that? Did he? Were these tales of Yeshua raising the dead merely repeated accounts of that incident from long ago, accounts that grew in importance with each retelling? Or did his followers truly believe he had done so again?

Blasphemy, *ne'atsah*. All of it. One should not ascribe to oneself the power reserved to Yaweh alone. I cannot believe my Yeshua would say such things of himself. His friends and followers were another matter. They seemed to delight in extolling and magnifying their claims about him — claims I trust he would never make on his own behalf.

A message truer to his own I was able to hear from a trusted source. My Temple friend Nicodemus, a respected member of the Sanhedrin, the inner council of elders, had himself been travelling and was among those who heard Yeshua speak from a hilltop in Galilee to a small gathering of followers and curious onlookers. (His most ardent followers, of course, would later say the crowd of listeners was much larger. They were always exaggerating his achievements for their own purposes.)

Nicodemus, who had been in his earlier years a Temple scribe like me, was able to write down some of the things Yeshua had said that day and relate them to me on his return to Jerusalem.

"Blessed are the poor in spirit," Yeshua had said and Nicodemus had written down, "for theirs is the kingdom of heaven.

"Blessed are the meek, for they will inherit the Earth. Blessed are the merciful, for they will be shown mercy. Blessed are the pure in heart, for they will see God."

In these words I could hear the voice of my son, and the longing for compassion and true justice I had always tried to instill in him. It was clear the foundation of his message was one of love and tolerance.

With the listeners sometimes talking among themselves, Nicodemus was not able to hear and write down everything Yeshua had said, but there was one more he did manage to hear:

"Blessed are the peacemakers, for they will be called the sons of God."

*That* I could imagine my Yeshua saying, remembering his remark at age 12 at the Temple that Yaweh is father of us all. He would not have called himself the son of God — not exclusively, but only in the sense that we are all sons (or daughters) of God. For that misunderstanding and misrepresentation, we must blame Simon who was called Peter and his other followers who called themselves disciples of Yeshua. And Paul, who in his letters well understood Yeshua's important message of love, but who nevertheless tried to elevate him to the level of *Christos*, of

*Messiah*, of divine saviour — after his death forcing Yeshua into kingly robes and a role he had never wished to take upon himself.

θ θ θ

More years went by, and I was to hear more news of Yeshua and his travels and teachings. In some, his teachings seemed pure and simple and righteous. He taught others as I had taught him. But other stories grew more fantastical with each telling: Yeshua calmed a storm on the ocean. He drew a net full of fish where there had been none. He walked on water. Each tale seemed to grant him greater powers, a level of divinity almost equal to that of Yaweh himself. I do not believe Yeshua was saying these of himself. I do believe his followers were happy to make claims on his behalf and those claims soon grew beyond his ability to control them.

And so came again the time of the Passover, and I learned from James that Yeshua was once again in Jerusalem with some of his followers to observe the feast. He did not make any effort to contact me, certainly did not come back to his old home to visit. I saw him one day on the steps of the Temple, preaching to a small crowd that had gathered to listen. Among those with him I could see a woman I took to be the Magdala — tall enough, I suppose, but not strikingly enough that I would call her a tower. I could also see my own Maryam, who like Yeshua had made no effort to see me, certainly not to be with me. It was as if to her I was already dead. Perhaps she thought I was. I held back, choosing not to dispel that illusion. But partly hidden by a pillar, I moved closer so I could hear Yeshua speak.

Turning his attention and scorn to the moneychangers, who were doing their usual brisk business of selling pigeons and doves for sacrifice and changing drachmas and other foreign coins into shekels for the transactions, he said: "It is written: 'My house shall be called a house of prayer.' But you have made it a den of thieves!"

Saying this, he reached over to the nearest table and in one motion swept as much as he could of its contents onto the ground. Birds in their cages fell onto the paving stones, some cages breaking open and allowing the birds to fly away free. Coins of all kinds scattered on the ground and many bystanders scrambled to scoop them up. The merchant stood up and began shouting angrily, soon followed by other nearby merchants, even though their tables had not been disturbed. With good reason, perhaps they feared they would be next. I could see Roman soldiers, alerted by the noise and turmoil, drawing their swords and approaching to quickly put down any disturbance. I feared for my son and wife, that they would be arrested.

Looking over again to where Yeshua and his followers had been, I saw only the confusion of the crowd and the stricken moneychanger desperately trying to rescue his wares. Doubtless fearing the same risk of arrest, Yeshua, the two Maryams and the others had quickly departed. I could not see them anywhere. But I knew the high priest Caiaphas and the other priests and elders would not be happy with his actions. Nor would the Roman authorities governing Judea, who feared any acts of unrest that might lead to an uprising among the people.

θ θ θ

Retribution came swiftly over the next few days — so swiftly that there was nothing I could do to stop it, not that I had much power in my hands to do so. Given more time, I might have been able to urge the high priest toward clemency. But soon it was out of his hands also. Rome, in the person of its local governor, Pontius Pilate, had brought down its imperial fist.

Betrayed at Gethsemane by one of his own disciples, Yeshua was arrested, swiftly and briefly tried before Pilate on a false and absurd charge of sedition against the Empire and sentenced as a common criminal to death by crucifixion. By such a brutal, tortuous death they intended to make an example of him.

In the brief period before the trial and sentencing, I had tried for permission to see Yeshua in his jail cell, but was denied. Also denied were my attempts to speak directly to Pilate, to seek clemency, or at least to have Yeshua's supposed crime adjudicated in a Jewish court, where I had hoped for greater justice and mercy.

But it was not to be. Whipped and scourged, weak from hunger and thirst, Yeshua had to carry his own cross piece to the hill of Golgotha, outside the walls of the city. There he was crucified, and there he died. Standing afar off, I could see my Maryam with Magdala and some other women near the cross, the only ones brave enough to stand watch over his suffering. Simon Peter and the other disciples had fled and gone into hiding, fearing for their own arrest. The women who stood by had tears in their eyes. There were tears in mine also.

He was my son. And now he was gone.

θ θ θ

After his death but while he still hung on the cross, I went again to Pilate and this time was granted an audience. I had told

Pilate's guard only that my name was Joseph and that I wished to speak with the governor to procure the body of the crucified Yeshua. I did not tell anyone I was his father. Nicodemus had come with me also. As we stood in the courtyard of the governor's palace waiting, the soldier entered and called my name. Turning to Nicodemus, I entreated him to go to the market and buy a linen shroud and spices, that we might prepare the body.

I thanked him and as he left, said to him in our Aramaic tongue, *Alaha menookh* — meaning "Godspeed," or "go with God."

The soldier, overhearing but not knowing Aramaic, misunderstood and announced me to Pilate as "Joseph, of Arimathea," that being a small village outside Jerusalem. I saw no need to correct his error. Pilate would not know who I was. To him, I did not matter. I was not about to lie, but neither did I feel obliged to give him the whole truth.

"You, Jew," Pilate said to me dismissively, "why do you bother me about this common criminal? Who is he to you?"

"I wish only to give him a proper burial after the precepts of my Jewish faith," I replied, only partly answering his question. "If you would grant me possession of his body, I will bury it in a tomb hewn out of rock that belongs to my family. I will bear any necessary costs."

"I have already washed my hands of this matter," Pilate said, again dismissively. "Do with it as you will. Go, and trouble me no more."

And so with the sun soon to go down and the Sabbath fast approaching, Nicodemus came with me to Golgotha and we took Yeshua's body down from the cross. Nicodemus had brought his mule and a cart to carry the body to the cave.

And so we wrapped my son in the linen shroud, anointing him with oil and spices and placed his body in the tomb where the bones of my first wife already lay. Alas, I could not prevent Yeshua's death. But at least in death I could grant him peace.

θ θ θ

Nightfall was coming soon, and with it the Sabbath. After together rolling a large stone across the entrance to the tomb to protect it, Nicodemus and I had gone separately to our homes. I spent the evening in prayer to begin my period of mourning.

I do not know how they learned of it — they must have been watching us take the body at Golgotha and followed us back to the sepulchre where we placed it. Would they know I was Yeshua's father? Unless Maryam was with them, there was no reason they should. And Maryam herself did know about the tomb, since I had purchased it and moved my first wife's ossuary there after she had gone away. At any rate, somehow some of the followers of Yeshua must have learned of where his body lay.

And when the Sabbath was past, I had gone back to the sepulchre some hours after the rising of the sun to pray again for my son. The stone, which had taken two of us great effort to put in place, was rolled back, leaving the entrance open. His body was gone.

Who would do such a thing? And why? Why show such disrespect to the dead?

All too soon, I was to find out. Rumors flew, and his followers told stories. And before long, many in Jerusalem and even beyond had heard the tale of Yeshua the Nazarite, the preacher from Galilee, who was crucified but had risen from the dead.

His followers told the story, told of the empty tomb, of the death and supposed resurrection of their teacher and spiritual leader. With each telling, it became more elaborate. Each version added more detail, more wonderment to make the story more fanciful and amazing.

It was of course not true. He had died a horrible, needless death. He was buried — I buried him — and that was the end of it. It should have been enough that he was man who preached a message of peace and love and acceptance and forgiveness. And for that the Romans killed him to silence that message, which they feared as dangerous. It should have been enough for which he could be honored and remembered.

I have no proof, no way of knowing for sure, but I know in my heart and soul what must have happened. Sometime after the Sabbath, in the dark of the night, his followers had come to the tomb, rolled away the stone guarding the entrance and taken the body. What they did with it, I do not know. I hope at least they buried it somewhere else and gave it the respect it deserved.

But for their purposes, it was not enough that his teachings were pure and noble. They wanted more. They wanted a message they could sell to Jew and Gentile alike. For that, they felt they needed a miracle. They need a resurrection.

They were wrong. But there's nothing I can do about that now. I'm just an old man.

Yeshua was not a god, nor did he ever claim to be one. He was neither miracle worker nor magician. He was a teacher who preached a message based on love. He was a sweet boy who had grown to become a good and decent man.

He was my son.

# The Adventure
## of the Sunken Parsley

THE MONTH OF JUNE 1899 was remarkable for two reasons. The first was an unusual, and unseasonable, spell of extremely warm weather, which did much to lift my spirits after a particularly damp and dreary spring. Accustomed as I was, from my military service in Afghanistan, to the heat of the tropical sun, I was experiencing less discomfort than most of my fellow Londoners, the majority of whom must have found the stifling heat rather oppressive. The second unusual feature was the curious affair which involved my friend Sherlock Holmes with the Abernetty family of Boston.

One morning we sat, Holmes and I, in our rooms in Baker Street, engrossed in our own private pursuits. I was enjoying a book of sea stories, while Holmes played meandering notes upon his violin. He then began to play a melody which I was certain I had heard before, although I could not place it.

"What is that tune, Holmes?" I asked, "I am sure it is familiar."

"And so it should be, Watson," replied Holmes, laying down this violin and beginning to fill his cherrywood pipe, "for you heard it only a few evenings ago."

It was then that recognition dawned. "Of course!" I said, "It is the theme from the variations by Mr. Elgar, which we heard the other evening at St. James' Hall."

"Under the admirable baton of Herr Richter," continued my companion. "Your astuteness outdoes itself today, Watson. But you are not correct in calling it the *theme*. You should rather call it the *Enigma*, for that is what Elgar himself calls it. Exercise your mind a little further, Watson. Have you discovered the enigma yet?"

There are times when sharing rooms with the world's greatest detective genius can be trying indeed, and this was one of them. What may have been mere child's play for my friend to deduce required a much greater effort on my part. He, in turn, seemed to derive some pleasure in observing my groping about the intellectual dark.

"Surely," I replied, "the enigma refers, as Elgar himself says, to his friends 'pictured within.'"

"A commendable beginning, Watson," said Holmes. "But observe what the composer has said: 'The Enigma I will not explain — its "dark saying" must be left unguessed.' Further, he said, 'through the over the whole set another and larger theme "goes," but is not played ... the principle theme never appears.'

"Even by this terminology he gives the answer away," Holmes said. "It's really quite elementary, old fellow —"

But he was interrupted in his explanation by the entrance of our landlady, Mrs. Hudson, to announce that we had a visitor. There next rushed into the room, at her very heels, an elderly gentleman whose evident noble bearing was much belied by his agitated state.

"Thank God I've got you, Mr. Holmes, "you must help me!"

"Do come in, my good sir," said Holmes in his imperturbable manner, "and enlighten us as to what business brings you to our door."

Our visitor made an effort to regain his composure, and began:

"My name is Sir Miles Wagner, a Member of Parliament, as you may know. But it is not I, but my household, that needs your aid. My sister has been murdered and her husband's life was also almost forfeit. I went out unexpectedly on business early this morning, and returned home to find the police and Scotland Yard had overrun my house and had arrested the maid as a suspect. You must come and help me, Mr. Holmes. The police are certain it was the serving girl, but she has been with me for so long, and served me so faithfully, that I know it cannot be she."

"One moment," interjected Holmes. "Have you no other servants in the house?"

"I have a butler," replied our visitor, "who has been in my service for years, and his wife, who acts as my cook and housekeeper. It is their custom to have this day of the week off, when they visit relatives in the country. Since there is no one then to prepare a meal, I customarily dine at my club."

We hailed a four-wheeler, and in the moment we were hastening toward the home of Sir Miles. On the way, we learned further that it was Sir Miles' sister, Mrs. Sylvia Abernetty, and her husband, Mr. Charles Abernetty, who had been the victims of the crime. Mr. Abernetty had been able to combine the interest of his business — he was the director of a prosperous American importing firm based in Massachusetts — with the desire of his wife to return to her home in England, in order to pay a visit to her elder brother. It was a visit which, it would seem, had ended in tragedy.

"But I fear that it is I who was the intended victim," continued Sir Miles, fretfully. "A man in my political position makes many enemies, and more than once I have had threats made on my life.

I had dismissed them as the ravings of lunatic minds, but now…" His voice trailed off into awkward silence, which was soon broken by our arrival at our destination.

We entered the drawing room to find Inspector Lestrade questioning the maid, a mere slip of a girl who nevertheless seemed unintimidated by his gruff manner. He looked up to see us enter and joined us by the doorway.

"Ah, Mr. Sherlock Holmes and Dr. Watson, come to meddle as usual in police business," he began. "Well, you needn't have trouble yourselves, for we've found the murderer — and without any of your fancy theories, I might add. I've seen few cases as clear-cut as this one. Sir Miles has told us of the threats he has received from his political enemies, and it's obvious that this girl has been hired to do the dirty work for them."

"We seem not to be the only ones with theories, Inspector," replied Homes. "But where is the body of the deceased lady?"

"It has already been taken to the morgue. Fortunately, Mr. Albernetty has survived the attempt on his life and is resting in his room. No doubt his testimony will make for a strong case against the maid."

Holmes seemed not to hear the last part of Lestrade's comment, so angered was he that the victim's body had been removed before he had had a chance to examine it.

"I fail to see, Watson," said he under his breath, "how I can be expected to shed any light on this case when Lestrade has made such a mess of the evidence." Then to Lestrade he said:

"I suppose that you would have no objection if I were to have a few words with the girl?"

Lestrade grumbled his permission and went off to speak to another of his men, whereupon Holmes went over to the young maid, who was being guarded by a police constable.

"I've come to help you if I can," began Holmes. "Tell me what happened this morning."

"Well, sir," she faltered, and then gathered the courage to go on, "I had gone out to do some errands for Mrs. Albernetty, and when I came back I found them here in the drawing room. Mr. Albernetty was coughing and choking and half dead, sir, and all pale and sick-looking. I brought him some water, sir, and then helped him to recover."

"Am I to assume that Mrs. Albernetty was already dead when you entered the room?"

"Yes, sir."

"Then what did you do?"

"I called for the police, sir," she replied, "and then for a doctor."

Holmes then asked her how long her errands had taken, and was told about an hour, and whether she enjoyed her services with Sir Miles, and was told emphatically, it seemed to me, that she did.

He next took out his pocket lens, and I beheld the now-familiar sight of my friend, like some tall, lean bloodhound, clamber around the room, now looking at the door frames, now the window sills, and finally turning his attention to the silver tea service which sat on the low table.

"A fine English tea setting we have here," he remarked, "buttered scones and tea, and an assortment of marmalades and jams. Well, it would seem that the Abernettys will not be having jam today, at any rate. Halloa! What we have here?"

With this exclamation, Holmes stooped down and spent a moment in scrutinizing the butter dish with the aid of his powerful lens. In a moment, he begun to examine the teapot itself, spooning a small quantity of the soggy tea leaves on to his pocket handkerchief. He peered at them and turned once again to the girl.

"Did you make this tea?"

"No, sir," she replied. "Mr. Abernetty said he would do that himself. He had just made it before I returned."

Lestrade broke in. "You've no need to try to fancy your theories on the teapot, Mr. Holmes," he said, with a trace of arrogance in his voice. "You aren't the only one who can make observations, and I can see enough to know that there's been poison put into the pot itself. And who better to put it there than the maid, I say. I should not at all be surprised to find that she has put poison into the entire canister of tea."

Holmes seemed to pay no attention to Lestrade's superior tone, but instead turned to me and remarked, "Remind me, Watson, to produce a monograph on the subject of tea and tea brewing. It has a number of aspects which make it quite remarkable, and invaluable to the study of crime. There is as much to be gained from the close scrutiny of tea leaves as there is from the ashes of the various tobaccos.

"This tea, you will notice by its rather pungent aroma, is of the blend known as Lapsang souchong. I also see, by the arrangement of the articles on the tray, that Mr. Abernetty is left-handed — which may or may not be of import — and that this pot of tea has been once reheated."

"How can you tell that, Holmes?" I asked.

"By observing," was his reply, "what is, I believe, properly called the 'agony' of the leaves. An apt metaphor under the circumstances, you will agree. I also see, by his expression, that Inspector Lestrade had failed to notice this last factor."

Lestrade struggled to retain his air of smugness. "Even if that were true, Mr. Holmes," he said impatiently, "I do not see of what possible importance it could be. It is clear to me that the girl has put a deadly poison into the teapot. Most likely, she is a member of the political gang which has threatened Sir Miles."

"A fine line of reasoning that is, Lestrade," continued Holmes in a sarcastic tone, "that of all the opportunities presented to her, she should choose a time when her employer was not even at home, incriminate herself so clearly, as you put it, rescue one of her intended victims and immediately call the police, as many law-abiding citizens would do. It has been my experience, Inspector, that murderers are more intent on breaking the law than on preserving it."

Lestrade seemed momentarily lost for words and lapsed into silence.

Holmes turned to the girl and questioned her.

"You said earlier that Albernetty had made the tea just before you entered the room to discover the deceased lady and her husband. How came you to know this — did you see the tea being made?"

"No, sir," said the girl, "but Mr. Albernetty said as much himself afterward, and besides, when I first found them, in my excitement I spilt some of the tea on my hand, and it was still very hot."

"Capital!" exclaimed Holmes, "You could learn a thing or two from this remarkable girl, Watson."

Sir Miles Wagner had remained unobtrusive and silent throughout the proceedings thus far, and it was obvious to my medical eye that he was still in his mild state of shock. I said as much discreetly to Holmes, who nevertheless felt the need to ask him some questions.

"Tell me, Sir Miles," he began, "have you often received these threats which you have mentioned?"

"Several times in the past, Mr. Holmes," he replied, "and most recently just the other day."

"And I don't suppose that you have kept any of these threatening letters?" continued Holmes. "No? Well that is a pity, as they undoubtedly would have furnished a clue to the identity of the murderer. Did you by any chance happen to mention this latest letter to your sister and her husband?"

"I believe I might have," Sir Miles answered, "but, as I said, I paid little attention to it at the time. I wish now that I had, and my poor sister's life might have been spared."

"I'm afraid you are most likely mistaken about that, Sir Miles," said my companion. "And now, Watson, I should very much like to have a few words with Mr. Albernetty himself, the intended victim of Lestrade's murderer. Shall we go to his room?"

This turned out to be unnecessary, since at that moment, Albernetty entered the room, looking a trifle pale but otherwise not unhealthy, considering the recent circumstances. He was a robust man of middle age, and it was doubtless his good health which had helped him to recover so rapidly from the effects of the poison which had proven fatal to his wife.

"Well, Inspector," were his first words, "you seem to be taking your time in arresting the wretched girl." And to Holmes, he said:

"Who are you?"

"I am Sherlock Holmes, and have been asked by your wife's brother to find the person who murdered your wife and very nearly yourself."

"Well, surely," said Albernetty impatiently, "any fool can see that the girl put poison into the tea, intending that Sir Miles, and perhaps all of us, drink it. When she came home to find that her deadly scheme had not completely worked and that I was still barely alive, she tried to cover herself by pretending to aid me. Given another chance, she would probably do us all in."

"That is certainly the theory to which our friend the Inspector would subscribe," replied Holmes. "But there are a number of points which I should like to clear up. First, why was the maid sent out this morning?"

"My wife was fond of making embroidery work," Abernetty replied. "I believe she sent the girl to the shop for some colored thread and other articles."

"Embroidery, indeed. And while she was out," said Holmes, gesturing to the silver tea service which sat on the nearby table, "you laid this lovely tea setting. But why this blend of tea? I should have thought Lapsang souchong was a tea more suited to the late afternoon or the evening."

"I wouldn't know that, I'm afraid," Abernetty replied. "We Americans are not as particular as you English about our tea. And besides, it was my wife's favorite."

"It is a pity," said Holmes, thoughtfully, "that she was not more fond of one of the less pungent blends, such as jasmine or an oolong, for the aroma of the Lapsang very nearly — though not entirely — masks the odor of poison. Tell me, Mr. Abernetty, do you enjoy butter on your scones?"

This last remark was made in the most casual manner, as Holmes calmly took out his pipe and lit it. I must confess that I could see no significance in the question, but I know my friend well enough to know that his questions were rarely, if ever, unimportant. The effect that it had on Abernetty was immediate.

"This is an outrage!" he cried. "My health is not well, and I have better things to do than to stand here and answer your idiotic questions."

"I'm afraid I must ask you to leave, Mr. Holmes,' said Lestrade. "You are upsetting Mr. Albernetty with questions which have nothing to do with the case."

"Very well, Lestrade,' said Holmes. "In that case, I shall be more direct. Tell me, Albernetty, what finally made you decide to murder your wife? Was it because of your new mistress?"

At this, Albernetty uttered a cry and lunged at Holmes, whose mastery of *baritsu*, the Japanese form of wrestling, made it a simple matter for him to parry the attack. In an instant, he had the attacker in an unbreakable hold.

"Tut, tut, my good fellow," said Holmes, effortlessly, "it was a simple task to deduce that you were carrying on an illicit affair. Your pocket handkerchief proclaims as much. In addition, I note that, although you are left-handed, your necktie has been tied for you by a right-handed person, facing you. Possibly your wife, but I should think it more likely the action of a playful mistress. There are other factors which led me to my deduction, but these will suffice. You really ought to be more careful in your grooming habits, if you wish to be discreet."

Holmes then released the man into the hands of a police constable.

"You've had some outlandish theories in your time, Mr. Holmes,' said Lestrade, chuckling, "and I must admit that you have often been proven right. But here you've gone too far with your deductions. You saw yourself that the entire teapot was filled with poison, and that Abernetty must have drunk just as much as his wife. It was only luck and a healthy constitution which helped him to survive."

"That, Lestrade," said Sherlock Holmes, with a slight bow in the direction of the still-guarded Abernetty "is where I must salute the cleverness of the man's scheme. You will no doubt find, Inspector, that Albernetty has built up an almost complete immunity to the poison he used to kill his wife by taking a series of small doses over an extended period of time. A drink of the poisoned tea which killed his wife was not harmful to himself, though it may well indeed made him slightly ill, thus making it all the more easy for him to feign his narrow escape from death. By himself posing as one of the victims, he was able to divert suspicion onto the young maid. You will recall events of the Camberwell poisoning — which is, in many respects, similar.

"Without examining the threatening letter which Sir Miles received, I will not say whether Albernetty himself sent it or whether it was genuine and he merely took advantage of the situation to divert suspicion onto some mysterious political enemies."

"You can prove nothing, Holmes," said the captive vehemently. "It is all conjecture."

"It may indeed be, Mr. Albernetty," said Lestrade, "but we shall be wanting a few more words with you down at Scotland Yard. But I've not forgotten the girl, Mr. Holmes, and she'll come along to Scotland Yard also."

The Inspector then led them both away under the watchful guard of his constables, and Sherlock Holmes and I returned to Baker Street. Shortly afterward, I spent some time at my surgery tending to my patients. This took me the rest of the afternoon and I did not rejoin Holmes until shortly after dinner.

Although the day itself had been quite warm, the evening brought a chill to the air, and I for one was grateful to be once again comfortably sitting in our rooms beside a cheerful fire. Holmes sat in his customary armchair, silently smoking his pipe. He then reached up to the mantelpiece and removed a letter which had been affixed to it by his jackknife.

"It may interest you to know, Watson, that I received this note late this afternoon, from our friend Lestrade. Abernetty has finally confessed to the murder of his wife and the young maid has been set free."

"Your powers never cease to amaze me, Holmes," I replied, "How did you know it was he?"

"Elementary, Watson," my friend replied. "Albernetty, having served the poisoned tea to his wife shortly after the maid had left, doubtless derived malicious pleasure in watching that poor woman die, slowly and horrible, before his very eyes. But it was essential to his well-laid plot that it should seem as though they had just sat down to tea when the maid returned, so she could appear to have arrived just in time to save Albernetty. That is why he reheated the teapot before her return."

"Do you mean to say," I asked, "that you managed to deduce all of that merely by reading the teapot leaves?"

"My dear fellow," said Holmes, drily, "you make me sound like some sort of fortune teller. The position of the handle of Albernetty's teacup led me to conclude that he was left-handed. This was further confirmed when I saw the man himself and noticed the unmistakable groove in the second finger of his left hand and also a telltale ink stain — both the result of a fountain pen. This belied the right-handed nature of the knot in his necktie. From there, the inference of a mistress was not difficult. My mention of it to Albernetty was perhaps a trifle theatrical, but you know well my occasional flair for the dramatic, and it produced the desired effect. There were other factors, but I will admit the truth of the matter was first brought to my notice by the depth to which the parsley had sunk into the butter."

"But this is magic, Holmes! How can that have told you?"

"I was certain," he explained, "by my examination of the window sills, that there has been no forced entry into the room. And so the murderer must have been the girl, as Lestrade thought, or Albernetty himself. A girl who has just committed murder is not likely to send immediately for police without first removing the more obvious incriminating evidence against her. Since both parties were in agreement that it was Albernetty who had laid out the tea, he must have done so as soon as she had left and not later, as she claimed."

"But, the girl — did she have any part of the plan?" I asked.

"Only as an unwitting pawn in Albernetty's clever scheme to draw attention from himself and lay the blame on an innocent servant."

"But the butter," I cried. "I still do not understand what you mean by that."

"That," replied my friend, filling his pipe once more with shag from the Persian slipper, "is because you see, Watson, but you do not observe.

"Only this morning, you remarked to me that the weather of late has been unseasonably warm. For the parsley to have sunk as deeply as it had into the butter could only have meant that it had been removed from the larder — and the tea things laid — much earlier than we had been led by Albernetty to believe. Unfortunately, the girl's statement seemed to support that conclusion, as it was meant to do. At any rate, the entire affair is somehow reminiscent of an earlier Boston tea party, in which Lapsang souchong also played an integral role."

Having said this, Holmes lapsed once more into silence. After a few moments, he again picked up his violin and began to play the same lovely tune with which we had begun our day.

"Well," I remarked, after he had played for some time, "you may have explained the identity of the murderer, but I confess that I am still no closer in guessing to the identity of Mr. Elgar's *Enigma* theme.

"Do not guess, Watson," scolded Holmes. "You know my methods: Apply them. Really, the answer is so absurdly simple that I am surprised no one else has discovered it. You of all people, Watson, should have been able to discern it."

Holmes resumed his playing and left me puzzling in silence. At length, he paused and said:

"Perhaps Elgar is right, Watson. The enigma I will not explain. Its dark saying must be left unguessed. Music, unlike murder, seems to benefit from a little mystery."

# The Case
# of the Heir Presumptive

IN MY RECOUNTING THE MANY ADVENTURES and cases which it has been my great fortune to share with my close friend and associate, Mr. Sherlock Holmes, I have often remarked that in all instances, it was the peculiar nature of the case itself, rather than any possible personal or financial gain, which made it of interest to my friend. Nor did he engage himself on these affairs out of any desire for publicity or recognition. On the contrary, I have known few men who have shunned the limelight of public renown as did Sherlock Holmes. The very fact of his growing reputation as the world's greatest consulting detective — due largely, I will admit, to my own efforts and the many accounts of his cases which I was able to bring before the public — this public acclaim was a continual anathema to him.

He ought, perhaps, to have been more grateful for my published accounts, since they brought him an increased number of the "singular problems of some interest" upon which he thrived. Nevertheless he shunned the public eye, and preferred to conduct his life as privately as he could. On numerous occasions, he would allow Scotland Yard officials to claim credit for solving a case, even though they could not have done so without his intervention.

As readers who are familiar with his exploits will know, Holmes was particularly reticent regarding details of his early life. So much so that even I, who could be considered his closest of friends, knew very little indeed about his childhood, and of those years prior to our introduction to one another and our subsequent friendship when we shared lodgings at 221B Baker Street. It was to come, then, as a considerable surprise that I should be given a glimpse which would raise as many questions as it answered.

Although the facts as I am about to relate them are true, at least insofar as I have no reason to question their veracity, they are quite beyond anything I might have imagined possible. But the old saying that "truth is stranger than fiction" may well apply in this case. Certainly, many of the other events which I was to share with my remarkable friend were in their own way no less fantastic. What makes this story unique is the manner in which it is so closely concerned with Holmes himself, and with details of his heritage hitherto unknown to me.

Indeed, so delicate is the nature of this report, that I had considered not committing it to paper at all. The knowledge might well then have died with me, since I felt certain that no further revelation would be forthcoming from Holmes himself. After considerable thought, however, I have decided that it is in some way my duty, as Holmes' chronicler, to include these facts, that a fuller picture of the man may be portrayed. As a manner of compromise, I shall include this completed chronicle among the many other of my private papers, to be kept in the vaults of the bank of Cox and Co., at Charing Cross, and there to be held until a period of at least 50 years after my death. After this time, it is to be supposed that the principals in this unusual drama will, as I, surely be gone. At this time, perhaps the world will be afforded, as I was those many years ago in 1897, a deeper insight into the complex character of my dearest and closest companion.

The day upon which this remarkable chain of events was to be revealed to me began in a most unpromising manner as a rather dull and rainy morning in the early spring. Much against his usual practice of rising late in the morning, Holmes was awake and gone when I roused myself for a breakfast of rashers and eggs, this being somewhat of a specialty of our landlady, Mrs. Hudson. I do not know what business it might have been that would lead my friend's uncharacteristic early morning activity, although I suspect it might have been connected in some way with the case upon which he was engaged at the time, involving the unexplained disappearance of Mr. James Phillimore, the details of which I may someday also relate.

Having completed my breakfast and stoked the fire, for it was a damp and chilling morning, I settled myself into my accustomed armchair, having decided to pass the remainder of the morning perusing a book of wildlife prints, drawn by the talented Mr. Audubon.

I had not long been reading, when there came a quiet knock at the door. It was Mrs. Hudson, announcing that there was a visitor to see Mr. Holmes.

"Send him in," I said, "and he may await Holmes' return by the comfort of the fire."

In my long association with Sherlock Holmes, I have seen a great number of individuals cross the threshold of our Baker Street rooms, and they have been of all types. Some have been noblemen, and some commoners. Some have been rich, and some poor. Many have been victims of some sort of injustice, and most have in some way required the services of my remarkable friend. But there was no way of knowing beforehand what sort of person it might be who would enter next. Following the example set by

Holmes, I had resolved to discover, by observation, as much as I could of the visitor, and what it was that might bring him to see Holmes.

In the event, however, there was little need to speculate, for I recognized the man from the moment he entered the room. Tall and distinguished, though now somewhat stooped with age, a shock of fine silvery hair atop lively grey eyes that still sparkled with vitality, despite their 70-odd years, the figure of Dr. Moore Agar was one which would still command respect from all who knew him. I had never met the distinguished Harley Street physician, but knew well his reputation as one of the finest medical men in the city.

"Dr. Agar, what a great pleasure," I said, rising from my chair. "Do come in and make yourself comfortable by the fire. I am Dr. John Watson, Mr. Holmes' associate."

"The pleasure is indeed mine, Dr. Watson," he replied, shaking my hand warmly. "I am glad that we have at last met, for young Sherlock has told me much about you," This having been said, he sat down in the armchair opposite me, right next to the fire.

I confess that I do not know which was a greater surprise to me — that Dr. Agar should have known Holmes at all, or that he should refer to him as "young Sherlock."

Granted, there was a difference in their ages of some 30 years, but the remark betokened an easy, almost avuncular familiarity, which I would have thought quite foreign to Holmes' basic nature. It was all the more remarkable in light of the fact that I have never before heard Holmes mention any association with the man who now sat across from me, warming his hands by the fire.

Not wishing to convey any of my surprise to my guest, I simply said:

"As you can see, sir, Holmes is not here at present, but may shortly return. In the meantime, you are most welcome to wait. It is too early in the day to offer you a glass of brandy, but perhaps you would care for something else?"

"Very kind of you, Dr. Watson. I should actually prefer tea, if I may. I find it suits me better, at my age." With this, he smiled, and lapsed into silence.

I was just getting up to ring for tea, when the door opened and Holmes entered. It was evident that he had been standing in the rain, for his garments were quite wet. Pausing only to take off his cap and cloak and hang them by the door, he strode across the room and extended his hand to our visitor.

"My dear Dr. Agar," he said "What an unexpected surprise. I trust that you have not been waiting long?"

"Not at all," he replied. "Dr. Watson has been most kind."

"I was about to ring for tea," I said.

"A splendid idea, Watson," said Holmes, "but I have anticipated you, I met the good Mrs. Hudson on the stair as I returned. When she said I had a visitor, I asked her to prepare a tea service for us. I had no idea the visitor would be you, my friend," he said, turning again to Dr. Agar.

Holmes appeared in unusually high spirits, which often meant that work on some case or other was going particularly well.

"Have you uncovered anything further in the business of James Phillimore, Holmes?" I asked.

"An interesting little case, Watson," he replied. "Despite having spent a fruitless morning, which involved long periods of standing in the rain, I am confident that I shall have the answer by later today."

The ability of our landlady to produce refreshments at a moment's notice was merely one of her many sterling qualities. Accordingly, it was at this juncture that she knocked in the door and entered the room, bearing tray with the makings of a substantial 11 o'clock tea. After a few moments spent serving ourselves, Holmes resumed the conversation by turning to our guest.

"What brings you to Baker Street, Doctor? Surely you must be kept busy enough at your surgery?"

"More than enough indeed, for a man of my age," he replied. "In fact, I have all but retired from medical practice, and now continue to serve only a small handful of my former patients. It is that, in a somewhat roundabout way, which has brought me here, for I have something which belongs to you. Perhaps I should explain."

"Please do, for it intrigues me," said Holmes, settling himself into his worn armchair and filling his favorite pipe. I, for my part, was content to sit in silence and to listen. I was not then to know that what I was about to hear would shake the very foundations of my comfortable beliefs.

"As I said," Dr. Agar continued, "I have few remaining patients. But one of those whom I have continued to treat has been my patient for many, many years. He has also become, over the course of time, a very close friend. I shall not tell you His Lordship's name, for it is of no concern to you, but suffice it to say that his word is beyond reproach. His family is a very wealthy one, as well as very old. He has long since inherited the title, and with it a considerable fortune in family treasures.

"Despite my greatest efforts, his health is quickly leaving him, and I should be very surprised if he were to survive the week. Knowing that he had not much longer to live, he summoned me yesterday to his bedside, where I had ordered him to rest. Rousing himself by great effort, he bade me accompany him to the room where much of his family wealth is housed. The room is, in fact, one of the finest private museums of art in the country, and I have often admired the many beautiful pieces contained there.

"As a special token of our friendship, and of the many years during which I have administered to his illness, he said that I should choose any object, of whatever value, to be a memento of his affection for me. I need hardly mention that all of the objects in the collection are priceless articles of exquisite manufacture. It was only at the insistence of my friend that I agreed to accept his kind gift. At length, I chose a very fine 12th-century goblet, said to be from the court of Eleanor of Aquitaine. But there also was something else that caught my eye. When I expressed an interest in it, my friend insisted that I take it too. I felt it only proper that I should now return it to its rightful owner."

So saying, he reached into his coat and removed a small bundle from his pocket. It was wrapped in chamois leather, which he opened to disclose a smallish gold object. I could see that it was engraved with some sort of crest, or coat of arms. Holding it almost reverently, he passed it over to Holmes.

I should mention that, throughout his narrative, Holmes had adopted his customary listening pose, with his eyes shut, his chin resting on his chest and his fingers held in a steeple in front of him. Only an occasional wisp of smoke from the cherrywood pipe he held in his mouth betrayed the fact that he was not actually asleep. Quite the contrary, it was at moments such as this that I knew Holmes was engaged in the most intense concentration, focusing all of his listening powers on our visitor's tale.

When he had opened his eyes and taken the object in his hand, Holmes regarded it with keen attention, staring at it as if transfixed.

"It would appear to be genuine," Homes said softly, as he turned the object over in his hands, examining both sides of it with great care. He took out his pocket lens and gave the object closer scrutiny.

"There can be little doubt of its authenticity," replied the doctor. "Every piece in the collection is *bona fide*."

"But what is it, Holmes?" I asked.

Both men had been so intent upon their private conversation that they seemed to have forgotten my presence in the room. When I spoke, Holmes actually gave a small start of surprise.

"Forgive me, Watson," he said "I had not meant to exclude

you, my friend. You may observe for yourself." He then handed the small gold object over to me. Sinking back into his armchair, he again closed his eyes, arched his fingers in front of his chest, puffed meditatively upon his pipe and was lost in thought.

I could see that what I held in my hands was some sort of signet or seal, used when making an official wax impression upon a document. The carving of the crest itself was quite detailed, and the workmanship was excellent. Even the side which did not bear a crest was ornate. It appeared to be of great value.

I will readily admit that the subject of heraldry is not one about which I know a great deal. But even with my limited knowledge, I was willing to hazard a guess that the coat of arms was not an English one.

"Are these arms from France, Holmes?" I asked.

Holmes languidly opened his eyes and regarded me for a moment in silence. At length, he replied:

"They might, of course, be of Norman origin. But you are in fact quite correct when you say France. You have in your hands, Watson, the private seal of Louis XVI, of the House of Bourbon, King of France."

"But that's impossible, Holmes!" I cried. "Louis XVI was executed more than a hundred years ago, in Revolutionary France. His family was killed and his palace ransacked. How could this have survived?"

"How, indeed?" was my friend's cryptic reply. He said nothing further for a long time, but remained motionless, his eyes closed.

At great length, he rose from this chair, taking the seal, which was once again wrapped in its protective covering, from the table where I had placed it. Crossing the room to where the desk was, he locked the package in one of its many small drawers.

For the latter part of the visit, Dr. Moor Agar had remained silent and introspective, quite unsurprised by Holmes' taciturn nature. He now stood up as Holmes approached him, and they shook hands.

"I must thank you, my dear friend," said Holmes, "for bringing this to my attention. It does help to clear up a matter which has troubled me. But now, I am afraid, I must dash off. At this stage, delay could mean a man's life. Would you care to join Watson and me for dinner this evening? Perhaps we could go to Simpson's on the Strand."

But our visitor begged leave to decline. After a few more words, Homes was out the door and gone. Dr. Agar and I spent some time discussing our common medical interests. I found him to be keen and perceptive in his observations and quite well informed of the latest developments in the medical field. Instructive as this conversation was, however, I was unable to gain any further insight as to what appeared to be the relationship of the long standing between Holmes and the doctor.

At length, he too excused himself from my company, since he was expecting a patient in his surgery. Bidding him farewell at the door, I said it had been a great pleasure to have met him, and expressed the hope that we should meet again soon.

Holmes did not return to Baker Street until later that evening, and I had spent the remainder of the day quietly reading. My reading was often interrupted when my thoughts drifted back to the events of the morning.

What connection, I wondered, could there be between a deposed French monarch, a Harley Street physician and the man with whom I had shared lodgings for so many years? I began to realize how little I actually knew about the early life of Sherlock Holmes. I had assumed that he came from gentry stock, perhaps the younger son of a gentleman farmer (his brother, Mycroft, was seven years his senior). He had gone to university, although I did not know which one. Aside from this, and his passing mention of a family connection to the French artist Vernet, I knew next to nothing of his family, nor of his background.

Upon his return, Holmes joined me as we sat once again by a cheery fire. I was grateful for the warming glow, which did much to combat the dampness of the foggy night air which hung about the city like a mantle of deep velvet.

We settled down, each in his own chair, I with a small drink from the tantalus, and Holmes with a freshly filled cherrywood pipe. After some quiet minutes of contemplation, Holmes broke the silence and spoke:

"Watson, your reading public seems quite enthralled by the accounts of my cases which you have seen fit to publish — although I must say, my dear fellow, that you do delight in placing far too much emphasis upon the almost romantic nature of the crimes, to the detriment of the true value of the cases, which lies in the instructive method by which the solution is deduced.

"Be that as it may, you may nevertheless find it useful someday to lay before your readers the means by which I was able to arrive at a solution to the curious disappearance of Mr. James Phillimore. My conclusion was reached only this afternoon, after many weeks of patient investigation. There are still one or two trifling matters to be cleared up, but I am satisfied with the case as it now rests. For the moment, I will leave you with this thought: Under what circumstances would a man find it in his best interests to vanish completely? Answer that, and the rest will surely follow."

"I am glad you were able to bring that business to a successful conclusion, Holmes," I replied. "But I must confess that I am at present far more intrigued by the business this morning of our visit from Dr. Agar, and of the valuable object he brought to you. What did he mean when he said that he was returning it to its rightful owner? I had no idea that you were interested in the collection of antiques."

"In a general sense, my friend, I am not. This particular object, however, is of special significance to me. It has been in my family for a hundred years. Some 10 years ago, it vanished and I had given it up for lost. Now, I am glad to see it returned. I keep it merely as a reminder of where I have been."

"I'm afraid I do not understand what you mean."

"Watson, my dear fellow, perhaps I owe you an explanation. You have been a stout friend these many years. I could not have wished for a more reliable and helpful companion. It is not right that I should withhold the truth from you. Perhaps it will help you to understand better why I am the man you see before you. I must ask, however, that you treat this matter with the confidentiality you might give one of your patients.

"How much do you know of the final days of the French Revolution?"

"Not a great deal," I answered, "except that the villains responsible executed their king, without benefit of trial."

"Do not judge them too harshly, my dear Watson. For although regicide is an act to be deplored, it may also be said that Louis had betrayed his sovereign trust and become a despicable ruler. At any rate, there are valid arguments on both sides, and we would do well to avoid a lengthy discussion of them at the moment."

"But, Holmes, I still do not see what connection all of this has to do with you, or Dr. Agar."

Holmes regarded me thoughtfully for a few moments, as he refilled his pipe. After it was lit, he said:

"Allow me to tell you a story: Louis XVI, King of France, was executed in January of 1793 — his wife, Marie Antoinette, shortly thereafter. Of his immediate family, there remained only two small children — a boy of eight and his younger sister. It was decided that the children were too young for so brutal a punishment as the guillotine, and they were kept instead in prison. The small girl did not survive very long. In 1795, the news was put out that the boy, the Dauphin, heir to his father's throne, had also died. Later — at the restoration of the monarchy — the line of descent was traced through the brother of Louis XVI, since the true heir was presumed dead.

"The truth is that Dauphin did not die, but was smuggled out of prison and out of the country. This was accomplished by an Englishmen of French descent, a Royalist sympathizer named Agar, who accompanied him. The young Dauphin, now a boy of 11 years, was brought in secret to England, to the country home of a squire named Holmes, who was the husband of Agar's sister. The boy, Louis, was adopted into the family, and took the surname Holmes. His new father loved him as a son, and the boy grew to manhood and inherited the squire's estate. It was not, to be sure, a kingdom, but the boy has seen enough of injustice. He had no wish to lay claim to the throne of France.

"In time, he married and produced a son, whom he named Siger Holmes. That son likewise grew up and married. His wife bore him two sons, delivered by the son of a man who had brought the Dauphin to this country, the same Dr. Agar who was here this morning. Those two sons are my brother Mycroft and myself. So, you see, our two families, Holmes and Agar, have had a long association."

"But, this is outstanding, Holmes!" I cried. "Do you mean to tell me that you are the great-grandson of Louis XVI?"

"In a word, yes," Holmes replied softly. "But you must realize, my good friend, that I am English. Although my ancestry is French, I was born here, in this country, and it is here that I belong. Like my father before me, and his father before him, I have no wish to claim for myself the French throne. I wish only to see a world where justice is served and order upheld. I feel that I can do that far better from this room on Baker Street than from a throne room in Paris.

"Besides," he continued, "you must realize that I have very little concrete proof of my claim. At the restoration, there were many pretenders to the throne, some of whom seemed to have had a valid claim. The royal seal, which was returned to me this morning, remains as one of the few reminders of my heritage. Since neither Mycroft nor I intend to marry, nor to have children, the direct line of descent will die out with us, and the world will never know. Believe me, my dear Watson, this is how it should be. It is how I wish it to be."

Holmes lapsed into a profound silence, staring into the fire, the dying embers of which were the only illumination in the room. Saying only, "Goodnight, Watson," he later got up and went off to his bedroom. I was left to my own thoughts, as I sat by the fire and contemplated that most remarkable man, whom I had known as Sherlock Holmes.

As I sat quietly thinking, many aspects of my friend's curious nature were made more clear to me. His devotion to our Queen (which proclaimed itself, among other ways, by the patriotic initials of Victoria Regina which he had inscribed in bullet pocks while engaged in eccentric indoor target practice) and yet his refusal to accept a knighthood for services he had rendered; his relentless pursuit of justice for all, regardless of their social station; most important, his reluctance to speak of his childhood and ancestry, and his constant desire to avoid public recognition. All of this spoke of a man who wished to leave his past behind him, and who felt somehow that he must atone for past injustice, without drawing undue attention to himself.

My respect for my friend, already deep and strong, increased manyfold that evening, and I resolved to continue helping him in the work which he had chosen for himself. Happily, we were to have many more years together, and many other adventures.

The strain of the past few weeks of constant work, as well as that of his revelation to me, took its toll on Holmes. It was only after a few days later that Dr. Moore Agar returned for a visit, and ordered my friend to surrender himself to complete rest.

Accordingly, we went to the seacoast of Cornwall. It was there that Homes and I became involved in the case which I have elsewhere referred to as the *Adventures of the Devil's Foot* — in some respects, the strangest which we had ever been called upon to handle.

But strange as it was, it cannot compare to the remarkable insight which I have been given into the private life of my friend, Sherlock Holmes, whom I shall always consider to be the best and the wisest man whom I have ever known.

# The Adventure
# of the Hertfordshire Horror

OVER THE MANY YEARS WHICH I HAVE taken up my pen
to recount the singular adventures of my friend Mr. Sherlock
Holmes, I have on several occasions remarked on the apparent
disdain he felt for the company of women. Indeed, several of his
comments on the subject were tinged with the utmost asperity, an
attitude bordering almost on contempt. It is true that in his blacker
moments he was wont to dismiss the entire sex as burdensome,
an encumbrance on his ability to solve the little problems which
so engaged his faculties. But as for me, I secretly thought that, his
outward protestations to the contrary, Holmes inwardly harbored
a greater affection for the fair sex than he allowed the outside
world to see. I, being his closest companion and confident, was in
a better position to judge my friend's true attitude, in those rare
moments when it did reveal itself.

Such was the case on a dreary evening in the late May of 1894.
As in so many of those other adventures I have elsewhere recorded,
the events which were to develop into such a remarkable test of
my friend's powers of detection began simply enough. We were
seated, Holmes and I, in our customary chairs in the sitting room
of our old Baker Street quarters, to which I had lately returned
at my friend's invitation, having sold my Kensington practice. A
cheery fire was burning in the grate, helping to take the chill out
of the air after a gentle rain.

Since wrapping up the final details of our encounter with
murderous Colonel Sebastian Moran, Holmes had had little in the
way of work to occupy his mind. Now, sitting in front of the fire
in his favorite armchair, Holmes gazed pensively off into space,
as he smoked another of the numerous pipes of tobacco he had
consumed since our last meal.

"My mind shall atrophy from lack of exertion, Watson,"
Holmes said in the tone mixing disgust with impatience. "Ah!
Unless I miss my guess, perhaps the very remedy I seek is about
to pass through our door. I fancy I perceive the sounds of Mrs.
Hudson showing a visitor up the stairs. And by the weight of
their footsteps, I should judge our visitor to be a young woman —
certainly one not yet having arrived at middle age.

As if in answer to his prediction, our faithful housekeeper gave
a small knock at the door and, on hearing Holmes bid them enter,

ushered in a lovely young woman, whose expression bespoke great agitation and not inconsiderable fear.

"I'm sorry to trouble you, Mr. Holmes," she began somewhat hesitantly, "but there is a matter of great urgency for which I require your assistance. I will pay you whatever you require."

"Tut," replied Holmes, holding up his hand to forbid her from saying any more. "We shall have no more talk of money at this juncture, for although I can see that your means are far from modest, money is of little import to me.

"Pray, please be seated and warm yourself by the fire," continued Holmes, "for I know you have come here straight from a journey of some miles, both by carriage and by train. Your country trap being open to the elements must freeze the blood on such a damp night as this. I perceive the urgency of your business, which has bought you in such haste from your country home north of London."

"Indeed I have, Mr. Holmes," the young woman said. "But, how — ?"

"My methods are simple," Holmes interjected, answering her question before she had time to pose it, "and based entirely on observation and deduction.

"The hem of your long dress is spattered with mud in a manner suggesting an open horse-drawn trap, and of a color found most abundantly in the environs of Hertfordshire. Furthermore, your dress has buttons up the front, but some of the buttons are askew, meaning you were agitated and dressed hurriedly, with little thought to your appearance. Judging, however by the quality of your attire, which is quite fashionable, and likewise by the attention you pay to your hair, I should venture to conclude that under normal circumstances your appearance is of quite concern to you.

"Finally, the ticket stub you still hold in your right hand proclaims clearly that your manner of conveyance to the city, since it bears the markings of one of the suburban lines that ends at the King's Cross station. That your face is flushed and your breath short merely adds corroborative details to my conjectures. Moreover, I see by the new diamond ring on your left hand — which, although charming, is of modest size and clearly not a family heirloom — that you have recently become engaged to a man whose social standing does not match your own. As you can see, my deductions are quite elementary."

As he spoke, Holmes had led our guest to his chair, nearest the fire, and, having seated her, helped her to remove a knitted shawl from her shoulders.

During this time also, our estimable landlady had returned bearing a serving of fresh tea, which Holmes poured for each of us. As I had in similar encounters in the past, I marvelled silently at the gracious and reassuring manner which belied the coldness he so often professed to feel.

"My name is Mary Willoughby," our guest said. "And I must ask you for help in solving the dreadful murder of my uncle, Carson Willoughby, of Twin Oaks Manor, Hertfordshire."

"You say he was murdered," said Holmes in a quiet voice. "But can you be sure?"

"Oh yes, quite sure, Mr. Holmes,' said she, stifling a small sob and dabbing her eye with a dainty pocket handkerchief.

"He was shot in his bedroom late last night or very early this morning, apparently through a window, which he had opened to clear the room of a smoky fire. The police even believe they found the man who did it. They have arrested my fiancé, James Whitmore, and charged him with murder. But I cannot believe that he could do it, Mr. Holmes. I just cannot."

With this, the unfortunate woman dissolved into a fit of tears which lasted several moments, during which time both Holmes and I struggled awkwardly, but to little avail, to comfort her.

When at length she had regained her composure, she related the details surrounding the death of her wealthy uncle, who had become her legal guardian several years before, upon the death of her parents. The evidence against her fiancé was quite damning, and it seemed to me that the police had very good reason to have arrested him.

It seems Miss Willoughby's uncle did not approve of the young man, who had aspirations of becoming a writer, which profession the uncle thought an unsuitable one. Only two nights before the murder, her suitor had publicly fought with the old uncle, who had refused his consent in the marriage and threatened to alter his will, which is in her favor, should the two lovers persist in seeing one another.

Our guest thereupon disclosed other details of the events, some of which had been told to her by the police as they investigated the case: Carlson Willoughby had been shot with a revolver, at close range, through the open window of his second-storey bedroom. A revolver with the initials "J.W." scratched on the butt, and with one chamber discharged, had been discovered in the young man's house. Without question, the bullet in the man's body had been fired from this very revolver. As further proof, there were marks of a ladder on the ground beneath the window. Young Whitmore admits it is his own. Bearing fresh traces of similar soil, it was found in a garage shed behind his house. On the strength of this evidence, the investigating police officer had placed James Whitmore under arrest in the village jail.

"And that is why I came to you, Mr. Holmes," said our visitor at the conclusion of her narrative. "I need you to clear the name of my beloved James."

Sherlock Holmes drew silently in his pipe for several moments, his eyes closed and his hands steepled in front of him in a customary meditative pose.

"Your case does possess some small points of interest," he said at last.

"Doubtless young Mr. Whitmore denies that he is the murderer?"

"He does, Mr. Holmes," Miss Willoughby replied. "He does not even own a gun, so he has no idea where this one might have come from. The police found it in the top drawer of a bureau in the front hall of his house, where anyone might easily have planted it. As to the ladder, it is indeed his, but he swears that he has had no cause to use it in the past four weeks, since last he made repairs to a small section of the roof over his verandah."

My heart went out to this lovely woman, who in her gentle manner and appearance reminded me of my own dear wife, also named Mary, so recently departed from me.

"You clearly believe him to be innocent," said Holmes. "Do you have reason to suspect anyone else of wishing murder on your uncle?"

"I have no proof whatsoever, Mr. Holmes," replied our prospective client, "but only my own intuition. There is a wealthy nobleman landowner whose estate borders on my uncle's own grounds. This man, John Earnscliffe, the seventh Baron Dowson, has made it plain that he favors my attention, though I have done nothing to encourage him. I find him repulsive and I have been quick to discourage his advances in the severest manner possible. Yet still he persists.

"I would not be surprised if this loathsome gentleman were the true villain in this horrible crime. With my uncle dead, and my beloved incarcerated, the baron would surely redouble his efforts to win me over."

"Your plight intrigues me," said Holmes with a gentle smile. "And I have learned to put some trust in feminine intuition. I fancy that in good Dr. Watson and I would find a short sojourn in the countryside most refreshing.

"It is late," continued Holmes, "and, you are no doubt tired from your ordeal. You may spend the night here, in Mrs. Hudson's spare bedroom, and we three will get a fresh start first thing in the morning. "And now I wish you a goodnight. Rest assured that if your fiancé is innocent, we shall not let him suffer for this crime."

With this, Holmes summoned Mrs. Hudson and sent the young

woman off to sleep. Presently I too retired to my own room. But, my friend stayed up well into the night, smoking his pipe and staring pensively into the fire.

In periods of idleness, Sherlock Holmes was not an early riser. But when involved in a case, I have known him to exist on scant hours of sleep for weeks at a stretch. True to form, we had risen at the crack of dawn the next day and, after a hearty breakfast, had taken an early train from King's Cross to the small Hertfordshire village outside of which Mary Willoughby lived, in her uncle's country home.

On first arriving at Twin Oaks Manor, Holmes went immediately to the dead man's bedroom. His quick inspection of the room might have appeared cursory to an outside observer, but I had gained enough experience of my friend's methods to know that no significant detail had escaped his careful eye.

"There is little more to be gained here, Watson," Holmes said shortly. "Come, let us examine the grounds."

When we went outside, Holmes went to the front of the bedroom window. Pulling out his pocket lens, he spent several minutes in the closest scrutiny of the garden soil directly beneath the window.

"Ah!" he said at length, the slightest gleam of satisfaction in his eye. "Just as I suspected. There's more here than some might suspect, Watson. Fortunately, last night's rain was not hard enough to wash away all of the evidence this garden has to show us."

At that moment, a young man about 30 years of age, with an official bearing and an honest, intelligent face, walked briskly up the gravel path that led around to the side of the house where we stood.

"Good morning, sirs," the man said. "I am Detective Inspector John Redmond, of the Hertfordshire constabulary. And who might you be?"

"I am Sherlock Holmes of London," replied Holmes, with a curt nod of his head, "And this is my associate, Dr. John Watson. Young Miss Willoughby has engaged our services in the matter of her uncle's death."

"Indeed, Mr. Holmes," replied the policeman. "It is an honor to meet so great a detective as yourself. My friend and colleague, Inspector Stanley Hopkins of Scotland Yard, speaks highly of your accomplishments in criminal matters. But I fear that your talents will find little to challenge them here, sir. For although it pains me to admit that such an honest-seeming gentleman as James Whitmore could be capable of such a crime, the evidence against him is quite convincing."

"But merely circumstantial, you would agree?" said Holmes.

"I agree, Mr. Holmes," the policeman replied. "There are several points which still trouble me. But until a more likely suspect emerges, I am obliged to consider Mr. Whitmore the guilty party. But I have no objection to your conducting a private investigation. I should find it most instructive to observe."

So, with Inspector Redmond's blessing, Holmes continued his careful search of the area around the window.

At times such as these, Sherlock Holmes resembles a sort of lanky bloodhound, his body bent close to the ground, his face peering intently through a thick magnifying glass. Occasionally he would emit a small grunt of satisfaction or disgust, depending on what object or circumstance caught his eye.

Moving slowly up the gravel side path back toward the main gate, Holmes spent some minutes examining a small clump of bushes on the side of the path farthest from the house. At one point, I could see him carefully pick up a small object from the ground underneath the bushes. This he placed in an envelope which he had extracted from his coat pocket.

Shortly, he asked the inspector if he might speak briefly with the suspected man. Redmond consented readily and soon we found ourselves at the police station, sitting in a small cell with a very dejected James Whitmore before us.

"I swear to you, Mr. Holmes, I did not kill Carson Willoughby." Whitmore's manner was both earnest and pleading. "Although I make no secret of the fact that I did not like him, nor he me, I did not hate him enough to kill him."

"Do you deny that the gun is yours?"

"I own no firearms, Mr. Holmes," Whitmore replied. "Obviously the lethal revolver was planted in my house by someone who wishes to do me harm, someone who roughly scratched my initials in the handle to make the connection more obvious."

"And what of the ladder, Mr. Whitmore?" asked Holmes.

"I do have a ladder, but I have not used it in four weeks at least. I cannot explain how it came to bear the soil of Mr. Willoughby's garden."

As the young man spoke, Holmes reached into the pocket of his travelling cloak and pulled out his well-worn cherrywood pipe and pouch of tobacco. Rummaging further in his pockets, Holmes appeared to be looking for something else.

"Excuse me, Mr. Whitmore," said Holmes casually. "Could you spare me a match?"

"I'm sorry, Mr. Holmes, but I never smoke, so I am not in the habit of carrying anything of the kind."

"Well," said Holmes, "here, I seem to have found my own. These are the very best Swedish safety matches, recently developed by Rudolph Christian Boettger and Johan Edvard Lundstrom. You would find that they are a vast improvement over the frictional sulphur matches earlier developed by John Walker. I picked these up during my recent travels through the Scandinavian countries. They are invaluable to those of us fond of tobacco's pleasures."

After lighting his pipe, Holmes stood up and took Whitmore's hand. "Never fear, my good man," he said. "I think we shall be able to convince your Inspector Redmond that he has been somewhat hasty in his zeal to settle the case."

With that, Holmes and I began a short walk back to the Willoughby estate, after Homes had requested that Redmond meet us there later in the afternoon.

"Holmes," I said, as we walked back through the village. "I believe the young man is telling the truth. I cannot see him as the murderous type."

"It is a capital mistake to reply entirely on one's instinct or emotions, Watson," my friend remonstrated, "for appearances can sometimes be deceiving. But in this case you are quite correct, although I prefer to base my conclusions on observations and solid logic.

"Let me tell you a little story, Watson, concerning the American president named Abraham Lincoln. Someone once asked Mr. Lincoln how long a man's legs should be, to which he shrewdly replied that they should be just long enough to reach the ground."

"I am afraid I don't quite understand, Holmes. What bearing has this on the case before us?"

"In good time," he replied cryptically. "Here we are at the village store. Wait for me a moment while I go inside."

Less than a minute later, Holmes emerged from the little shop. He had a small smile on his face, the kind I knew he got when his deductions had been confirmed. He rubbed his hands together briefly as we set off for the house.

"Yes, my dear Watson, this case is coming together nicely. There is but one more detail to be confirmed."

Upon our arrival at the house, it was a distraught Mary Willoughby who greeted us at the door.

"Oh, Mr. Holmes, what shall I do?" she asked. "That horrible Baron Dowson came by the house while you were away. He pretended to express his condolences, but immediately tried to force his attentions, claiming that with my uncle and fiancé both gone, now more than ever I needed him to look after me."

"The scoundrel!" I shouted, "Taking advantage of a woman's sorrow like that."

"He is a bold one, this baron," said Holmes. "But perhaps it would be best if I spoke with him. Watson, you would be of better help by staying here with Miss Willoughby. I shall return within the hour."

It was slightly more than an hour later when Holmes actually returned, but he seemed preoccupied and in a foul temper. Shortly afterward, Inspector Redmond arrived. Holmes led him around to the side of the house.

"Tell me, Inspector," Holmes asked. "What do you make of those marks in the garden soil under the window?"

"They appear to be made by two upright sticks or poles, Mr. Holmes, such as a ladder. The soil on the feet of Whitmore's ladder confirms that."

"Perhaps so. Is there anywhere nearby where a bulky object might be concealed?"

"There is a disused well in a nearby part of the yard, Mr. Holmes," the inspector replied. "I have not bothered to search it, since nothing appears to be missing."

"If you would indulge me, Inspector Redmond," Holmes said graciously, "I should like to have a look down that well."

After being shown the old well and deciding that the hole was too small to admit a grown man, even one as wiry and nimble as Sherlock Holmes, we engaged the services of one of the village boys, a small lad of about 12 years, who consented to be lowered into the well at the end of a rope and carrying a lantern. Just before the boy was to be lowered, Holmes went over and whispered something in his ear. The boy looked somewhat startled, but nodded in agreement.

Carefully, we lowered him down into the well. A few moments later, he tugged on the rope, which was a signal for us to return him to the surface. To my utter amazement, and to that of the inspector and Miss Willoughby, the young lad carried with him a pair of long, sturdy stilts!

"Good Lord!" cried the police detective," who on earth could have expected this?"

"I did," replied Holmes.

"But why?"

"Because the marks on the garden soil were made by two perpendicular poles. The feet of a ladder, which is on a slope, would have made depressions slanting toward the wall."

"Obviously," continued Holmes, "the murderer got to the high window by standing on stilts."

"But there are no tracks anywhere else," said the policeman.

"There are some tracks on the gravel pathway, but they are

very faint. Nevertheless, the evidence is there, if you know where to look for it."

"I admit, Mr. Holmes, that this new discovery weakens the case against Mr. Whitmore, but there is still considerable evidence that seems to convict him."

"I also offer you this, Inspector," said Holmes, pulling a small envelope out of his coat pocket. "This is a cigar ash, which I found on the ground by the bushes near the window. As Watson can tell you, I have made quite a study of the ashes of the various tobaccos, and I am able easily to identify several hundred brands at a glance. Evidently our murderer stood hidden in the bushes, smoking a cigar, either waiting for Carson Willoughby to enter his bedroom or trying to screw up sufficient courage to perform the deadly act of murder.

"I know from my questioning this afternoon that James Whitmore does not smoke. But this particular type of ash, you will discover, comes from a very special brand of cigar that old Baron Dowson has manufactured especially for him by a tobacconist and delivered to the village store. I was unable to get a confession out of the baron this afternoon when I went round to call, for he is a crafty sort. But I have no doubt that he's the man you're after."

"I thank you for your advice, Mr. Holmes." said Inspector Redmond. "Your evidence is suggestive, but we shall see that the inquest jury has to say in this matter."

Holmes and I returned to London by evening train, after endeavoring to assure Mary Willoughby that all would be well. Two days later, however, she sent us a telegram, urgently requesting us to return to the village. Swayed by the evidence of the initialed revolver and by Whitmore's public argument with the old man, the inquest jury had brought a verdict against Whitmore and sent him to trial for the murder of Carson Willoughby.

"This will never do, Watson," cried Holmes angrily throwing down the telegram. "An innocent man's life is at stake. I'm afraid drastic measures are called for."

We returned to the village the next afternoon, in time for the burial of Carson Willoughby. As we stood at the edge of the small gathering, Holmes pointed out to me a corpulent bully of a man with a smug, reddish face. This was none other than the baron himself, come to gloat over the death of a girl's guardian.

Later that night, Holmes retired to his room with a small valise which he had brought with him from London. When Holmes emerged two hours later, it was a different man who presented himself to me. His very likeness had changed to that of a wizened old man with a grey, shrivelled face. A few tufts of stray hair projected from the sides of his bald head.

When he entered the sitting room, Mary Willoughby gave a small scream and her face turned white with fear. "My God!" she cried. "It is my Uncle Carson!"

"Do not be alarmed, Miss Willoughby," said the reassuring voice of Sherlock Holmes. "By means of a few tricks of theatrical makeup, I have taken on the appearance of your late uncle. I assure you that the deception is necessary if we are to apprehend his true killer."

With that, Holmes bade me accompany him to the side gate of the baron's estate, which was separated from the Willoughby's property by a low, stone wall. With us were Inspector Redmond and two of his officers, whom Holmes had persuaded to come along.

Holmes had brought with him the stilts which had earlier been recovered from the well. Mounting these with an athletic grace, he began walking toward the baron's bedroom, all the while calling out his name in a ghostly, sepulchral voice.

"Baron Dowson," cried Holmes eerily, "it is I, Carson Willoughby. As you came for me, I have come for you!"

Holmes continued shouting in this chilling vein for several minutes as he approached the house. Through the bedroom window, I could clearly see the baron's face as he looked out, first in disbelief, then in horror. As the ghastly apparition got closer and closer, the old man let out a horrible scream of fear and ran toward the door of the room.

The policemen and I rushed into the house, up the stairs and into the baron's bedroom. He darted over to us and grabbed me by the lapels.

His face was white, his brow was covered in sweat and his hands shook uncontrollably. "Save me!" he cried frantically. "My God! He has come for me as I came for him!"

Baron Dowson collapsed with fear and began babbling out loud, confessing fully to the murder of Carson Willoughby. He himself had walked up to the other man's window using stilts and shot him with his revolver. This he later marked with James Whitmore's initials and placed in the young man's house where the police would easily find it. He had also smeared soil from the garden onto Whitmore's ladder.

By these actions, he had hoped to remove both his rival and Mary Willoughby's uncle, leaving him free to gain possession of the young woman and her money. His own resources were severely depleted by his gambling debts, and the prospect of acquiring the neighboring property, not to mention the beautiful heiress, had driven him to such a mad scheme.

Three weeks later, on a beautiful, sunny afternoon in June,

Holmes and I returned yet again to the small Hertfordshire village. This time the occasion was a happy one, the wedding of Miss Mary Willoughby and Mr. James Whitmore. Unaccustomed to such social affairs, Holmes seemed quite embarrassed to be treated as such an honored guest, but he allowed their thankful attention with good grace.

"That was quite the performance you gave, Holmes," I said to him as we stood apart from the crowd after the ceremony. "Shakespeare himself might have been impressed by your ghostly performance."

"Indeed, Watson," replied Holmes, allowing himself the slightest of smiles, "just last week, on the night before he was hanged, the baron himself congratulated me on my performance, albeit grudgingly. He said that in my case, what the law has gained the stage has lost. I took it as a great compliment, Watson — though I hardly think a change of vocation would suit me after all these years."

# The Strange Case
# of Mr. Erdman's Alibi

IT WAS A LONDON COCKTAIL PARTY that I first made the acquaintance of Mr. Irving J. Erdman. (That, at least, was the name by which he had introduced himself, although I never did find out what the "J" stood for. Perhaps the middle initial was there merely to prevent his other two names from jostling into one another. From certain aspects of his character I was subsequently to discover, I now suspect it was probably not his real name at all. He would have called it an *alias*.)

My detective friend Mr. Sherlock Holmes having long since retired to the Sussex Downs, where he kept bees and was writing a monograph on the subject, I often found myself somewhat at loose ends in London, missing the old days of our adventures together. Thus I would sometimes, more out of boredom than anything else, attend social events which otherwise would not have engaged me.

That two such different persons as Mr. Erdman and I had been invited to the same cocktail party to begin with serves only to demonstrate one of the vagaries of modern life I shall never be able to explain. I find such affairs unendingly tedious, and this one was no exception. Were it not for my meeting with this rather singular fellow, the whole event might by now have slipped my mind, as have all of the others.

Mr. Erdman was himself, at first — or even second — glance, hardly a memorable figure, being small and somewhat mousey in appearance, with horn-rimmed spectacles perched at an odd angle on the bridge of his nose. His suit was old-fashioned but well cared for, in a somewhat painstaking manner which suggested it was one of a very few and needed to serve several functions. He struck me as the sort of timid but likable fellow who might be a professor at one of our lesser colleges. It would not have surprised me to be told that he was indeed a professor, although I never learned his true vocation.

We were standing on that particular evening (I suppress an urge, as I am sure he would not, to call it "the night in question"), engaged in what passes for conversation at these affairs, when there was a rather loud noise which sounded to me like an automobile backfiring — a sound which since the automobile's replacement of the horse-drawn carriage had become much more frequent in the city. The conversation in the room seemed to come to a momentary halt, but resumed almost immediately. It had undoubtedly not occurred to anyone in the room that the sound was anything *but* that of an automobile backfiring. It's only in murder mysteries and penny dreadfuls, and not in real life, that the sound of a backfire sounds exactly like the sound of a gunshot (or, as is more usually the case, a gunshot sounding innocently like an automobile backfiring). In fact, the two are quite distinct, and while I make no claims to expertise on the subject, I daresay I would not mistake the one for the other, especially in such sedate surroundings.

This insignificant event, in a generally insignificant evening, might have passed entirely unnoticed had it not been for Mr. Erdman's remarkable response. Immediately after the noise was heard, he pulled out his watch (he was wearing, as might have been expected, a large silver pocket watch on the end of a fine silver chain. I can only imagine what he might have used as a fob). He seemed to take a careful note of the time, and even went as far as to write it down in a notebook he had produced from his inside breast pocket. He then glanced about the room, as if taking a mental inventory of the occupants. I believe it was at this point, if memory serves, that he asked me to confirm my name and occupation. When he ascertained that I was indeed *that* John H. Watson, the retired medical doctor and sometime chronicler of the exploits of Sherlock Holmes, he seemed particularly pleased, and appeared to make a special mark in his notebook.

I thought no more about it, and if he did, he said nothing. Although it struck me as somewhat curious at the time, the event, as I have said, would probably have slipped my mind. It was Mr. Erdman himself who brought it to my attention several weeks later.

We had happened to meet at the theatre (in the interval of a performance at His Majesty's — something with Beerbohm Tree, if I recall correctly). He was sitting several rows behind me, with an empty seat beside him. (I later found out that he invariably bought two tickets for any show he attended. Sometimes he would invite a friend, but more often than not he simply liked to have an empty seat beside him. It occurred to me that it was only the great expense which prevented him from buying three tickets and having an empty seat on each side. As it was, he had to content himself with feeling safe from one side at a time, at least.)

When I first caught sight of him in the theatre, I could not remember who he was (he had a forgettable face), but was filled with vague thoughts of recognition. I experienced that momentary feeling of panic, the "where have I met this fellow and how important is it that I remember who he is" syndrome. I remembered only in time to extend my hand as he approached. He did not take it — but whether this was from rudeness, distraction or trepidation of germs, I was not sure. (I now suspect the last of the three).

"Ah, Dr. Watson. Do you recall," he asked, "the cocktail party where we met?"

Since, as my friend Sherlock Holmes was often quick to remind me, I sometimes fail to notice details which he considers important, I was pleased to admit that I did.

"Do you remember," he continued, "a rather loud noise?"

I confessed that I did not.

"It was an automobile backfiring."

He seemed relieved, and I think he expected that I would be, also. "I thought at the time it might have been a gunshot, but it wasn't. It was an automobile backfiring. I checked." He seemed more relieved than ever. I am sure, if I had asked, that he could have told me the make and the model of the automobile, its age and, no doubt, several interesting facts regarding the driver. I began to wonder about this fellow. He chuckled, dryly.

(Professors seem unable to laugh, but only to chuckle dryly — except, as happens more often than one might expect, when they are drunk, at which point they begin loudly to declaim Shakespeare, or Chaucer. If they happen to have a PhD, this is done in the original dialect. If they happen to be professors of history, they may quote Bede, or aspects of British textile exporting in the 14th century.)

Again he chuckled his dry, professorial chuckle. "Still, one can never be sure," he said. "It may have been a gunshot. One can never be too careful. That's why I made a note of the time. I wanted to be able to account for my whereabouts."

The reason for his curious actions began slowly to dawn on me. Believing (or perhaps hoping) that he had heard a gunshot — no doubt of the murderous and fatal variety — he had taken great pains to establish his presence at a locale safely removed from the scene of the crime (for so he imagined it to be). My role, for which he had carefully made a note of my name, was to be that of a witness, one to corroborate his story, should that become necessary. He was, in a word, establishing an *alibi*. This also explained his relief in discovering that the sound had been, in fact, only that of an automobile backfiring. That everyone in the room at the time had already reached that obvious conclusion weeks ago, I felt too polite to point out. No doubt he had gone to great lengths to support his conclusion, and he took it all very earnestly.

I began to formulate a picture of his character, which seemed a trifle too absurd to be true. Hoping to prove myself incorrect, I said: "I noticed an empty seat beside you. It's a pity that your friend couldn't come, too."

"No," he replied, "I'm here by myself. I feel safer with an empty seat beside me."

I might have pointed to this as an unnecessary expense, but have already mentioned that I suspect it was only the expense which deterred him from purchasing two additional seats. I also question whether he had, in fact, that many friends. I expect that most people, as I was beginning to, found him altogether too peculiar. No doubt he compensated for this by alternating the side on which the empty seat was, thereby throwing any would-be assailant off his guard.

I began to conclude, silently to myself, that this Mr. Erdman must have read too many mystery novels: I could picture his library, rows upon rows of books, neatly arranged in alphabetical order (or perhaps chronological order, or some other system even more esoteric, such as in methods by which the victim had been dispatched). Hundreds of novels, by such authors as Wilkie Collins, Poe and — I flatter myself — perhaps even my own chronicles of the exploits of Sherlock Holmes. All these and more had become the models for his life.

As we continued speaking, I learned that Mr. Erdman had a mind crammed full of the most trivial facts on the widest variety of subjects. It was his contention that one might never know when one such particular fact would sway the balance in determining the guilt of the culprit and the innocence of the others. He seemed to feel that it might be his ability to distinguish an alligator — where others might have seen only a crocodile — or his obscure familiarity with the migratory habits of a variety of birds, that would trap the guilty party in an otherwise perfect crime. (Holmes, of course, had made knowledge of such minutiae his particular calling.)

But unlike the great detective, who used such knowledge to help others, Mr. Erdman's obsessive need always to have an alibi seemed all the more ridiculous to me, since it appeared obvious that he was, in fact, guilty of no crime. I have read that certain men have a compulsion to confess to crimes which they did not commit. His was the opposite obsession: a need to establish his innocence of crimes for which no one would possibly suspect him.

He appeared to have a paranoid fear (fixation, the analysts would call it) that someone (I had no idea who — nor, I suspect, did he) was intent on framing him for some nefarious crime which he did not, of course, commit. I also believe he felt that, despite his best efforts, he would, in the end, be unable to prove his innocence. All of his knowledge would fail him, since he would overlook the one, seemingly insignificant detail which would have been his salvation. (The fact, for instance, that the deadly box of poisonous chocolates, which he was supposed to have been sent through the mail, was tied with a particular kind of string, found only in southern Poland.)

When it came to parcels which he himself received in the mail, he had the most annoying habit of immediately dunking them in a bucket of water which he kept by his door for that very purpose. This was to safeguard against any parcel bombs he might receive. (He never did.) This curious obsession caused much surreptitious snickering amongst the employees of the book club to which he belonged, when it came (somehow) to their attention. Someone kindly took to wrapping his books first in plastic, which I am certain went a long way toward preventing a library full of mildewed mysteries.

Although there was no particular reason that Mr. Erdman and I should have seen a very great deal of one another (since we were so different, he and I), I must candidly admit I found him so fascinating that I often went out of my way to keep in touch with him, in a casual way. On occasion, we would go to the theatre together. And although he never said so, I suspect he was secretly glad of my company, even if only to defend him from imaginary attacks by phantom assailants. From one side, at least.

The longer I knew him, the more his paranoia grew (or the more I became aware of it, at any rate). It took on new facets. He began to wear disguises, leaving his house in the middle of the day to do some grocery shopping, dressed as an old man with a slight limp. He would return, later in the day, in the guise of the meter reader, or sometimes the postman, by which, perhaps, he assured that his parcels were not lethal. (I'm not certain that he ever considered poison-gummed stamps, although I expect he did, since he rarely sent out any mail.) He was very careful where he might place his fingertips, although he did not constantly wear gloves, since — as he once pointed out to me, when I was naive enough to ask — a total *lack* of fingerprints might in itself be suspicious.

He took to walking home by circuitous routes, lest he was being followed. He endeavored not to become a creature of habit. Idiosyncrasies, he reasoned, might prove his downfall: He squeezed the toothpaste sometimes from the middle of the tube, sometimes from the bottom, and he was not consistent in the way in which he placed his toilet paper on the holder. He felt all this, somehow, to be of deep significance.

I eventually lost touch with my friend Mr. Erdman. He seemed to have vanished. Or perhaps he just left London. It was just before this time that he entered what might be considered the final stage of his peculiar outlook. He began to conceive various words and phrases, all of them most notably cryptic, as might serve as his dying words. These, he was convinced, would puzzle those at his deathbed (undoubtedly for a long time), until someone would perceive that in his dying gasp lay some important clue. Perhaps he would cite a literary allusion to the Bard, or give a warning — "Beware the Jabberwock, my son!" Whatever it was, you could be sure it would be cryptic and fraught with significance.

Whatever he has decided upon for his last words, I shall have to wait along while yet to discover. At his rate of precaution against the ordinary, I expect he will live to a ripe old age, continuing all the while to establish alibis, adopt new aliases and create fresh disguises, thereby confounding any who would wish him harm.

# The Case of the Solitary Canary

IN PERUSING MY NOTEBOOKS for the early months on 1897, I see that my companion Sherlock Holmes and I had found ourselves involved in several interesting events, those criminal puzzles which Holmes was almost always able to bring to a satisfactory close. Rare indeed was a situation which, having at first presented itself — to anyone else, not least Scotland Yard or some smaller, local constabulary — as seemingly impossible, did not soon become easily resolved once the great detective had applied his methods of deductive reasoning. Methods which, even after lo, these many years together, I confess may still have baffled me. But to Holmes they inevitably produced a solution he was invariably wont to call "simplicity itself."

And so, I note in January of that year our contribution to the events I have elsewhere referred to as those of the Abbey Grange and in March our encounter with Dr. Moore Agar and then the mysterious incidents surrounding the Devil's Foot. Around the same time, Holmes, with some modest help from myself, was also able to assist the General Post Office with a minor scandal involving a blind telegraph operator, the curious events of which I might someday commit to paper.

But April dawned, bringing with it a glorious representation of the very best an English springtime has to offer — the welcome chirp of returning birds, the occasional soft rain and from that the flowering bud and lovely fragrance of lilacs and fresh apple blossoms, and of course the glorious Easter music after the sombre season of Lent to be heard from the choir at St. Paul's, surely among the finest such choirs in our great land. But amid all this wonder, Holmes found himself somewhat at a loss. It had been some weeks since the events of the Devil's Foot and no crimes nor puzzles had presented themselves to provide the kind of distractions which Holmes so desperately needs to keep his keen intellect firing, and to keep him away from some of his more destructive and deleterious pastimes. None, that is, apart from the postal matter which Holmes had resolved within a matter of mere days, and which it seemed he considered barely a trifle, hardly worthy of his time.

"My dear Watson," he had said, "surely having noticed that Upham is left-handed and that his family hails from Devon should have made the solution obvious even to such as yourself." (I admit that it had not.)

At other times, and for good reason, I might have found myself concerned for my good friend's well-being, since I better than most understood and had observed the dangers which too long a period of idleness might have presented had Holmes allowed himself to lapse into a slough of despond.

But as it came to pass, my fears soon proved to be unfounded. For a distraction — one of a seemingly pleasant, rather than criminal, variety thankfully soon presented itself. It was a Monday morning — Easter Monday, as it happened — and I had stayed abed somewhat later than usual, having dutifully gone the day before to the Easter Sunday morning service at St. Paul's and subsequently rather indulged myself in the fine dinner graciously prepared for us by our steadfast landlady, Mrs. Hudson.

Although sleeping late was not a habit to which I was accustomed, being generally more of a habitual early riser, one could never say the same of Sherlock Holmes. Not that he was inclined to sleep late of a morning, but rather that one could just never predict his sleeping schedule at all. There might well be days that he would barely rouse himself before noon — though generally that would be the result of his having stayed awake the night before and into the wee hours of the morning solving, or merely stewing over, some particularly troublesome puzzle. At other times, especially if the game were afoot, he would be up with the dawn and bustling himself — and often the both of us — out the door on some urgent business which could not wait. And yet other times I have known my friend to forgo sleep for days and days at a time, with an energy that never seemed to flag.

And so, I was pleased, if somewhat surprised, to find him that morning already wide awake, fully dressed and enjoying a pipe of his favourite tobacco from the Persian slipper on the mantlepiece. The remains of a breakfast long-since consumed — eggs, toast, jam and tea — gave evidence of the fact that he had been up and around already for a few hours at least.

"Good morning, Watson," Holmes said cheerfully. "I trust you slept well."

I acknowledged that indeed I had.

"Capital!" he said. "Since I could hear you stirring in your room as you dressed, I have already asked Mrs. Hudson to provide another breakfast for your enjoyment. And then, my good fellow, we must be on our way."

"On our way?" I asked. "To where?"

Waving a telegram paper in the air, Holmes replied: "Do you

fancy a short trip to the country? We have been invited down to the lovely county of Wiltshire, home of the ancient Stonehenge and the magnificent Salisbury Cathedral. Pack a bag for a stay of one or two nights. I believe that should suffice. And since this trip should be pleasurable, I warrant we would be safe enough that you needn't bring along your service revolver."

"Well," said I, "that does sound fine indeed. But to whom do we owe the pleasure of this gracious invitation?"

"You are familiar, of course, with the esteemed singer Molly Sloper?"

"Ah, yes," I exclaimed, "she sings like a canary!"

"Surely not, Watson," Holmes demurred. "With such a high voice, a canary would be a soprano, would it not? Or perhaps a treble — a boy in one of our fine cathedral or parish church choirs. The great Miss Sloper is a celebrated contralto, renowned for her rich, deeper vocal tones and dramatic delivery.

"At any rate, it is she who has invited us down to Ravenscroft, her beautiful home in the Wiltshire countryside outside of Salisbury. Her telegram arrived first thing this morning, and I have already sent a return reply."

Mrs. Hudson having arrived with another breakfast, which I dispatched forthwith, and Holmes having gone down to the street to secure a cab, I quickly packed a bag and joined him as our four-wheeler arrived.

"Waterloo Station in good time if you please, my good man," Holmes said to the cabbie, "for we have a train to catch."

The cabbie was indeed a good man and delivered us to the station in a timely fashion. Ever efficient, Holmes had previously secured us a private compartment in a coach on the London and South Western Railway line to Salisbury and had already sent ahead a further telegram noting the timing of the train's arrival and arranging for someone to pick us up at the station and thence on to Ravenscroft to meet our musical hostess.

His having travelled widely and also moved in circles much wider and more diverse than those to which I am accustomed, it should not necessarily have surprised me that Holmes should somehow not only know of the great Molly Sloper but also, it seemed, know her well enough to have been granted a personal invitation to her country retreat. Settling into our seats, I inquired of my friend how this had come to be.

"Ah, Watson," he explained, "some years ago when she was but a budding ingenue, I performed a minor service in recovering for her an emerald pendant given her by a musical admirer and which subsequently had gone missing. The impresario of that performance, an old friend, had engaged my services. It was but a simple matter to deduce that her costume fitter had purloined the emerald from its jewel case in her dressing room while the singer herself was performing. The impresario was relieved and Miss Sloper was grateful. I have followed her rising career and have kept in touch in the years since.

"The London musical scene being a small one, in relative terms, it should not surprise you that the same impresario is mounting the commemorative anniversary performance of Handel's *Messiah* this coming Saturday for which, as you know, you and I have been given tickets. And I know you are much looking forward to the event."

"Indeed I am, Holmes," I agreed. "I was pleased when you told us we had tickets. But I had no idea they were complimentary ones, nor that you had a personal connection to the star soloist. Although, given the number of famous people among your many acquaintances, I suppose it should not have surprised me."

"Well, it should be quite the event, Watson. To be held at St. Michael, Cornhill, a fine parish church near the Leadenhall Market. The Great London Fire of 1666 destroyed an earlier structure, but a newer one was soon built, its design traditionally attributed to Sir Christopher Wren, though I myself would dispute that. Nevertheless, it has fine acoustics and shall be a fitting venue for this performance.

"Someday, Watson," Holmes said, "I shall put pen to paper to elucidate my thoughts as to why the Christian church leaders have kept Easter as a moveable feast instead of more logically fixing it, as they have long since done with Christmas, extrapolating from the available information. It should be a matter of simple arithmetic to calculate from the birth of Jesus in the year zero to the time of his death on a Friday — what we now call Good Friday — on the eve of the Sabbath in the Jewish month of Nisan in that year. But alas, the Church continues to calculate the feast relative to the phases of the moon and the progression of the sun. Thus, in any given year, Easter Sunday (and so the Good Friday preceding it) is reckoned as being the first Sunday after the first full moon that has occurred after the vernal equinox. I'm sure your vicar could attempt to explain it, but it all seems to me rather pagan for an ostensibly Christian festival.

"At any rate, Easter this year happens to fall on April 18, whereas it had been March 25 in 1742, the year of the first performance of Handel's *Messiah*. So, the debut performance of Handel's great oratorio took place on April 13, 1742 — at a concert hall in Dublin, mind, not in a great church in London as we see today — well past the Paschal time of the year. And not, as is now more usual, a performance at Christmastime.

"The organizers of this year's performance had hoped to mount their production on the same date as Handel's, April 13th, but alas it was felt at this time inappropriate to hold the performance during the solemn season of Lent. And so, we can look forward to a commemorative performance of *Messiah* this Saturday, April the 24th — the closest Saturday that the Church calendar and a suitable available venue would allow."

By this time, the train had left the city proper and ventured its way past the outskirts and on to the pastoral countryside.

"The performance, it may interest you to know," Holmes continued, "will be unlike the large, splendid affairs you and I are used to seeing in London, and which have continued, and continued to expand, since the days of Handel himself and since his death in 1758.

"No, this performance, marking an anniversary of its first performance, shall attempt to hew more closely to Handel's own, striving for historical authenticity. The orchestra will be small, about 32, and without the elaborate extra winds, brass and timpani that Mozart's popular arrangement later added. Nor will we be seeing the huge chorus of a hundred or more singers — glorious as that can be — which we have come to expect of our annual London performances. Indeed, apart from Miss Sloper and three other soloists, the chorus itself shall comprise a mere 32 singers, drawn from St. Michael's choir and St. Paul's — 16 boy trebles singing the soprano lines, and 16 gentlemen lay clerks singing the other three parts: alto (male altos, of course, not female contraltos), tenor and bass."

"I shall perhaps miss some of the grandeur, Holmes," I admitted. "But it does sound intriguing to hear what Handel himself might have had in mind.

"And yet," I added, quickly doing the sum in my head, "this will be the 155th anniversary since 1742. It seems an odd number. Why was this special performance not considered to mark the sesquicentennial, the 150th? A nice, round number."

"My dear Watson," Holmes replied, "Need you ask? Quite simply because five years ago we did not have available to us the mature, polished voice of the great Miss Molly Sloper to be our contralto soloist."

As if that entirely settled the matter — which I suppose it did, since I could think of no sensible rejoinder — Holmes turned toward the window and was soon lost in his own thoughts as the gentle scenery passed by.

Presently, we arrived at the station of the lovely parish seat of Salisbury and Salisbury Cathedral, with its magnificent 14th-century church spire — at more than four hundred feet the tallest in our great Empire, and among the tallest in the world. Perhaps recognizing the great detective from his own impressive height, and his usual Inverness travelling cloak and pipe, a stooped old man standing beside a horse-drawn wagon stepped forward as we alighted from the train, doffed his cap, and spoked directly to us.

"I take it you are Mister Holmes, sir," the driver said. "Miss Sloper sends her compliments and asked me to take you and your companion along to Ravenscroft."

The old man lifted our bags into the back and climbed slowly and stiffly into the driver's seat as Holmes and I settled into rough seats behind. It was clear from its rustic look that our horse-drawn conveyance was likely more often used to deliver supplies and provisions from town, but its seating was nevertheless comfortable enough for our journey. And certainly I had endured far greater discomfort on the dangerous back roads and goat trails of Afghanistan than I would on the pleasant country lanes of Wiltshire. With the cathedral's magnificent spire soon receding behind us, presently we found ourselves turning through a stone gate and approaching a stately country house which — though of course much smaller — was in its own way as beautiful and magnificent as the cathedral we had left behind.

Ravenscroft Hall was a handsome structure of stone with newer (though still quite old) brick additions tastefully blended in with the original, smaller dwelling. In some wise it reminded me of a similar country house — that of Wisteria Lodge and the murder Holmes had solved there some five years previously. But a different vegetation, that of stout English ivy, framed and decorated much of the front face of our current destination.

Upon arrival and alighting from the wagon, our driver kindly said he would tend to our bags and we were greeted at the open door by a young maid or serving girl.

"Good afternoon, gentlemen," she said with slight curtsy as we entered. "Mr. Holmes, Dr. Watson, you are most welcome. My name is Rose. My mistress apologizes for not greeting you in person, but she is busy in the music room with her customary afternoon rehearsal. Your rooms are prepared at the top of the stairs — Perkins will have put your bags there, should you wish to freshen up from your journey. And although it is a bit early, Cook has taken the liberty of laying out an afternoon tea service in the parlor in case you are hungry. You may wait there at your comfort until Miss Sloper has finished. Thank you."

With this, having taken our coats, she disappeared down the hall and left us on our own.

Even I could surmise from our luggage which room was mine and which was for Holmes, and so presently, after brief ablutions, we found ourselves enjoying tea and a light repast in the parlor. Holmes had left the door ajar, and so coming from behind the music room door we were able to hear, at least faintly, the sound of Miss Sloper's rich, warm, contralto voice and a capable piano accompaniment.

"Hark, Watson!" Holmes said softly. "We have arrived at an opportune time. If you pay attention, you will note that Miss Sloper is singing those heart-cramping notes of melody from near the start of Part II of *Messiah*, the solo setting of a text from Isaiah, *He was despisèd*. Judging from the added ornamentation, I would say this is the *da capo* return to the opening statement. Such tender, sublime singing!"

And indeed it was. Ample evidence that Miss Sloper's renown was well deserved.

"We are, in a sense, hearing a moment of history, if you will," Holmes said. "It may interest you to know, Watson, that our Molly Sloper is by some generations removed a direct descendant of Susannah Maria Cibber, the same actress and singer for whom Handel expressly composed this aria for that first *Messiah* performance in 1742.

"Susannah Cibber," he went on to explain, "was originally Susannah Arne, the sister of the fine English composer Thomas Arne, from whose masque setting *Alfred* we get our robust anthem *Rule, Britannia!* Which is mostly neither here nor there, but still, an interesting family connection. At any rate, she went on to marry the actor and theatre manager Theophilus Cibber. Although helpful to her career, he was not, I'm sorry to report, a very admirable gentleman. He treated her badly and mishandled her finances to his own gain. She soon found herself in the arms of a more sympathetic companion, one John Sloper. The natural child of their union, Susannah Maria Sloper, born in 1739, also came to be known as Molly."

"I say, Holmes! Did you learn all this from our present-day Miss Sloper?"

"You know my methods, Watson," he said with a slight smile. "Some I did learn from Miss Sloper herself, but some is the result of my own diligent research in the British Library. Handel has been an area of interest of mine for some time, even before this *Messiah* anniversary was upcoming.

"At any rate," Holmes continued, "Miss Cibber's liaison with Sloper had caused somewhat of a scandal in proper London society — which is one of the reasons she had agreed to travel to Dublin to debut Handel's new and as-yet-unknown oratorio.

That notoriety, of course, had preceded her and there were some in Dublin society who felt her an inappropriate addition the program. Nevertheless, she was resolute to perform. Miss Cibber's voice was perhaps not as robust as our present Miss Sloper's — the historian Charles Burney says it was just "a thread" — but she was justly renowned for her dramatic delivery.

"In fact, it was upon first performing this self-same aria, *He was despisèd*, that Dr. Patrick Delany, the chancellor of St. Patrick's Cathedral in Dublin, was so moved that he broke all decorum, stood up and shouted, 'Woman, for this, be all thy sins forgiven!'"

At some point during Holmes's narration, the music had come to a close. I could barely hear some murmuring of conversation between singer and accompanist, perhaps some shuffling of paper, and soon they started up again, with a slow, waltz-like introduction.

"Ah," said Holmes, "We've moved closer to the beginning, I perceive. This is the alto aria from one of the lesser prophets, *But Who May Abide the Day of His Coming?* This lilting opening is quite lovely — but wait till we get to the fiery *Prestissimo*!

And indeed, only moments later, the piano accompaniment had become faster and quite agitated, as the singer began the warning declamation, "for he is like a refiner's fire." It was stirring stuff, and quite dramatic in its effect, with the singer leaping all up and down the scale. Fire, indeed. But quite soon, the music stopped abruptly. There was a brief discussion — the details of which I could not perceive, hearing merely the two voices talking — and the music started up again, back from the beginning of the faster section.

Rehearsing music, even I know, is much different from performing it. Rehearsal is for practice, for going over and over the difficult passages again and again until they become natural and seemingly effortless. Not being musically trained, I do not pretend to understand the details, but I imagine it must be like medicine or anything else: One reads, one studies and one learns by doing. We practise music in the same way we practise medicine. Certainly as a field doctor in Afghanistan I had to practise stitching up wounds and setting broken bones until I had gotten it right. And so it was with Miss Sloper, who seemed to be experimenting with tempo and pacing, emphasis and slight ornamentation, over and over again. And, it seemed to me, the piano accompaniment was becoming increasingly agitated — even more so than the music itself might suggest.

Until suddenly there was a crash of sound, a harsh, discordant clamour as of both hands being slammed down on many keys all at once. I thought I heard a voice — slightly muffled in the faraway room, deep, possibly male but also possibly that of the contralto — shout what sounded like "*Frantic!?*" as both an exclamation and a question.

I looked over to Holmes and could tell by his puzzled expression that he had heard the same thing as I. Whereupon we heard the clanging down of the piano lid, the opening and slamming of the music room door and footsteps stomping down the hallway toward the side exit. As he passed the open doorway of the parlor, from my vantage point I had caught a brief glimpse of a young man with tousled hair as he receded quickly from view.

A moment later, the music room door opened and the great Molly Sloper herself came out of there and entered the parlor. She had her hair up and wore a simple frock dress — evidently her "working attire" for rehearsing, a far cry from any elegant gown she might wear for a performance. Her initial scowl turned to a warm smile upon seeing Holmes.

"Ah, good afternoon, Mr. Holmes. So nice to see you, and so good of you to come," she said, extending a dainty hand, to which Holmes gave a brief, gentlemanly kiss. "And you must be Dr. Watson," she said to me, not proffering her hand, but favouring me with a slight smile and nod.

"You must forgive Mr. Lambe," she continued. "He is a good pianist, and even himself a capable enough singer, and I am happy to have him staying at my home this week to make rehearsing here more convenient. But he is young and at times impetuous and rather opinionated when it comes to matters of musical interpretation. Although I am not unwilling at times to listen to the ideas of others, I do expect my accompanist to know his place. I have been singing these Handel arias, and many others, for many years. And I believe the critics have spoken warmly of my interpretation and delivery.

"Indeed they have," said Holmes warmly, "including none other than the great George Bernard Shaw — who if I recall correctly, described your *He was despisèd* as "beautifully mournful and heartfelt."

"How good of you to remember that, Mr. Holmes," the diva replied, with perhaps the slightest blush. "And now, it is my custom to have a brief nap after my rehearsal. Mr. Lambe's perfunctory exit has cut today's somewhat short. But never mind. I am in need of rest. We dine early, at 7. Until then, I shall leave you to your own devices. My girl, Rose, can see to any needs you may have. Good afternoon, gentlemen."

And with that, the great Miss Sloper left the room and ascended the stairs, I presume to her own bedroom.

The tea service was fine, but I was looking forward to a proper meal. And there's nothing better for building up a healthy appetite than a good walk in the fresh air. I prescribed the very thing to Holmes and myself, and he agreed. So off we went to explore the grounds of Ravenscroft Hall and the surrounding Wiltshire countryside, our conversation bouncing among several topics, for Holmes is knowledgeable in so many areas. We covered some of the history of Salisbury Cathedral, completed in 1258, a fine example of early English Gothic architecture and home to its own unique Sarum rite, a local version of what we generally call Gregorian chant. Holmes also regaled me with interesting facts and anecdotes about Handel and his *Messiah,* and on occasion identified rare trees or plants which had caught his eye along the way. Our walk was invigorating and the time passed quickly. Later, we were back at the hall with time to wash up and prepare for our meal — which, we had already been told and I was glad to hear, did not require formal dinner attire.

Our dinner was pleasant, a combination of some dishes as fine as one might find in any of the best London restaurants, mixed with simpler, fresh, hearty fare of the countryside. And the conversation was lively, engaging and — as always, when Holmes is at table — informative. As one might expect, musical connections were much in evidence. We learned from our hostess that her stately country retreat, which she had purchased some years ago as a respite from the spotlight of her growing fame, took its name from an English composer a century before Handel, one Thomas Ravenscroft (1588-1635). Holmes added that Ravenscroft's tenure as a church musician provided yet another link to our magnificent St. Paul's back in London. A composer known for his church music as well as for the lovesick secular round *Downderry Down,* Ravenscroft had also made some effort to gather and preserve old folk tunes, Holmes had learned in his wide reading. And so it is Ravenscroft whom we should thank that we know of the charming, if perhaps morbid, children's nursery rhyme *Three Blind Mice.*

Miss Sloper's somewhat truculent accompanist, William Lambe, had joined us for dinner and seemed to be in a slightly better mood, or at least calmed down, though he remained quiet and withdrawn much of the evening. Holmes, by contrast, seemed uncharacteristically ebullient, making an effort to draw Lambe into the conversation.

"Mr. Lambe," Holmes said at one point as the staff were removing the remains of the main courses, "I understand that in addition to your role as accompanist to Miss Sloper, you are employed at Salisbury Cathedral?"

"That I am, sir," Lambe replied. "I am a lay clerk — one of the gentlemen of the choir."

"A tenor, perhaps?" Holmes said with a slightly quizzical smile.

I detected in Lambe's response some hint of defensiveness, tinged with pride.

"No sir," Lambe replied. "I am a countertenor — or a male alto, as you would say. One of only two in the section, for we are a rare breed."

"Rare indeed," Holmes agreed. "I thought you might be, from the timbre and wide range even of your speaking voice. I have not yet had the pleasure of hearing your choir, for I find that London quite occupies my time, but I'm sure it is a fine one. Have you sung there long?"

"Some four years among the gentlemen," Lambe replied. "But before that, since boyhood as a treble, rising to the rank first of senior prefect, and then as head boy, before my voice changed, as I was turning 16."

"Much to be proud of, then," said Holmes. Then changing the subject slightly, he said: "We already know of the famous Miss Sloper's family connection to Susannah Cibber, and thus to the very first performance of Handel's great *Messiah*. But my research tells me, Mr. Lambe, that you yourself can also provide a connection to that historic event. I know from having perused the original program of that debut performance in Dublin that in addition to the male altos in the choir, there were two countertenors among the soloist — a Michael Ward and one Joseph Lambe. A relative of yours, perhaps?"

"Well spotted, Mr. Holmes," Lambe replied. "Yes, my great-uncle, plus a few more generations. I would have to count them to know how many. But yes. I too am proud of my connection to Handel's great masterpiece."

"Too proud sometimes, I think," Molly Sloper chimed in. Her smile was sweet, but I thought I detected some tension beneath it. "Mr. Lambe is strongly of the opinion that there should be more male altos, and fewer female contraltos, in any *Messiah* performance, to follow the example of Handel's original. He said as much again just this afternoon."

"Miss Sloper," Lambe said a bit tartly. "You are, I will admit, a fine and accomplished singer. And especially through your family connection to Miss Cibber, you may well claim the right to sing *He was despisèd*, as she so movingly did. Handel, after all, wrote that aria with her in mind. But you must acknowledge that Handel also composed the florid "refiner's fire" section of *But Who May Abide*, which we rehearsed this afternoon, not for a contralto, but for a male alto. So if anyone should be singing it, it should be a countertenor, not a contralto. And for God's sake, there's not one shred of evidence that he ever gave it to a bass."

"And of course our Mr. Lambe thinks that should be he himself," Miss Sloper said. "I'm sorry, William, but I believe the audience has come to hear me, and not you."

Before Lambe could reply, and perhaps risk being even more rude, Holmes slid in with soothing tones to defuse the tension.

"If I may say," Holmes began smoothly with some flattery, "at least on historical principles, and with all due respect to our lovely hostess, Mr. Lambe does make a valid point. For a performance by the Italian male alto Gaetano Guadagni, Handel did take what had been a simple recitative and expanded the piece, adding the impressive "refiner's fire" section, the better to show off Guadagni's talents. But that did not come until a 1750 performance in London. So if we were to be strictly accurate in re-creating the 1742 performance, we should drop that aria, and neither Miss Sloper nor Mr. Lambe would be performing it.

"But of course," he said, turning his charm to our hostess, "we should not want our London audience to be deprived of hearing the lovely Miss Sloper do it justice."

Miss Sloper returned his smile, but there was a moment of awkward silence. Then Mr. Lambe rose from the table and spoke.

"Excuse me, Miss Sloper," he said somewhat stiffly. "Dinner was welcome and I'm grateful to have been included, and to have met our interesting guests. But I'm rather tired, and I should like to turn in early for the night. If you will allow me, I shall be in my room. Thank you again."

And with that, he up and left the table and ascended the stairs.

The servants then arrived with the sweets course and a choice of tea, coffee or light sherry. As we busied ourselves with that, Holmes continued where he had left off.

"It's quite interesting, you know, that while male altos have continued to flourish in our many cathedral and parish choirs of men and boys, they have all but disappeared from the concert stage, whether in *Messiah* or any other works where they might once have been found — other oratorios and indeed many operas, for example. After Dublin, Handel mounted yearly productions of his *Messiah* in London through the 1740s and '50s to raise funds for a children's hospital. And some of those included male altos in the chorus and even among the soloists.

"But as those productions got bigger, with larger orchestras and more singers, ironically the number of male altos declined, replaced increasingly by female contraltos such as Miss Sloper and others. I believe even by the time of Handel's death in 1758, the countertenor had all but vanished from the *Messiah* stage."

"I say, Holmes," said I, "you seem to have put considerable thought into this."

"What can I say, Watson?" he replied. "When a subject interests me, I do tend to delve into research. I have spent many happy hours at the British Library reading about the subject from some of the original sources and reports of the day.

"You will recall," he continued, "I have mentioned pursuing a monograph on the polyphonic motets of Lassus, an even earlier composer. But meantime I am, in fact, nearly finished a slight monograph on this very subject, *On the Disappearance of the Countertenor Voice in the Operas and Oratorios of G.F. Handel by the late 18th Century.* The coming performance by Miss Sloper had inspired me to explore the subject more deeply. I do find it quite fascinating. I'm sorry Mr. Lambe is not here to continue our discussion."

After breakfast the next morning, I set off for another pleasant walk along country lanes to aid in my digestion. Leaving Ravenscroft Hall, I passed Perkins the driver, already hard at work in the stable mucking out the horse stalls. A light rain had begun to fall, not enough to prevent my being outdoors, though I did make my walk shorter than my previous had been. My return found me with Holmes once again enjoying tea in the parlor. Holmes had been up early and had already gone for a longer walk on his own, as was sometimes his custom. So as I returned to sit in the parlor, Holmes had already been there some time, seemingly lost in his own thoughts, looking out the window and smoking his pipe. I knew enough of my friend not to disturb him in such moments, and so I too kept to myself.

As I arrived, I had seen Miss Sloper and Mr. Lambe enter the music room for their morning rehearsal. Rose had set the tea service on a parlor table, closing the door behind her as she left. With the doors to both rooms closed, the sound was slightly more faint and muffled than it had been the previous afternoon, but soon I could hear Miss Sloper warming up the scales and arpeggios, with Mr. Lambe providing discreet support on the piano.

Before long, they began again rehearsing in earnest, beginning first with some of the deceptively simple recitative movements — *Behold, a virgin shall conceive* and *Then shall the eyes of the blind be opened* — before returning to Miss Sloper's signature aria, *He was despisèd.* Even with the sound dampened through doorways, it seemed, if that were possible, even more beautiful and heartfelt than it had yesterday. All must have been well with that movement, for soon they had returned to the other lengthy alto aria also from the day before, *But who may abide*, with its fiery "refiner's fire" in the second section.

But as before, this aria seemed — to my untrained ear, at least — to be giving both singer and accompanist considerable difficulty. The opening slow waltz was languid and lovely and seemed to go well enough. But in the faster section, accompanist and singer could not seem to agree, with Mr. Lambe playing the piano part at a faster tempo, or with greater intensity, than Miss Sloper was inclined to sing it. Several times they would start, then stop, then start again either at the beginning or where they had left off. But no sooner had they resumed then they would break off again. More than once I heard a shout of exasperation from Miss Sloper that would bring the music to an abrupt halt. And once I heard Mr. Lambe, as the day before, pound his hands on the piano keys in frustration. I half expected again to hear the slam of a door and the sound of his footsteps stalking away.

But this time that did not happen. Perhaps with the performance another day closer, both musicians realized they had better stick with their work. After a pause, the two returned to their rehearsal and all once again seemed well. The sound of the crashing keys had caught the attention of Holmes, who had perked up and looked in the direction of the music room, as if expecting something more to happen. But as the music resumed, he closed his eyes and seemed to drift off.

They began again with the slow opening, which went swimmingly. But soon the "refiner's fire" was once more causing agitation, and not just musically. There was more starting and stopping, some raised voices and harsh words. Suddenly there was a dull thud, as of perhaps a large book, or several books, falling to the floor. And someone — Mr. Lambe, Miss Sloper, it was hard to tell which — let out a muffled groan.

There followed a momentary silence. I looked over and saw Holmes at full attention, as if ready to pounce. But then we heard the voice of Mr. Lambe — rather louder than necessary, it seemed to me, but perhaps he felt a need to explain himself, saying, "I'm so sorry, Miss Sloper. Terribly clumsy of me. Shall we start again?"

And soon the music resumed with the slow opening — the piano first, and the alto voice joining in with "*But who may abide the day of his coming?*" And when they came to the *Prestissimo* section, singer and pianist seemed to have resolved their differences in Mr. Lambe's favour. This "refiner's fire" was as sprightly, and indeed as fiery, as I had ever heard it — with trills and ornaments wherever the music would allow. It was more wild than refined, and ending with a showy cadenza that took the singer to the very top of the alto range. In fact, the singer went through the whole aria twice more, each time with the full repeat which is written into the music, before finally finishing. It seemed to me that Miss Sloper was preparing to make this yet another signature aria, impressive as it was. The vocal fireworks had certainly caught the attention of Holmes, who was listening intently.

After a moment of silence, I heard the music room door open and Mr. Lambe saying, "Thank you so much, Miss Sloper, for a wonderful session. You sound especially fine this morning. I look forward to working with you again this afternoon. Good morning." I heard the sound of the door closing and Mr. Lambe walking quietly up the stairs.

Miss Sloper seemed to be remaining in the music room by herself and we heard no more sounds. But that was not in itself so unusual. Perhaps she was making notes to herself in the score, or reading over passages to commit them to memory. I can't do this myself, but I do know trained musicians are able to look at a page of music without making any sound, or just quietly humming to themselves, all while hearing the entire score in their heads as if being fully performed.

And so it was not until as lunchtime approached that anyone thought it odd that we had not seen nor heard from Miss Sloper for nearly two hours, at which point Holmes and I were just returning from another stroll outside, the rain having recently let up. The serving girl Rose had gone to Miss Sloper's bedroom to ask her a question about the menu. Not finding her there, Rose had thought to look in the music room. Opening the door, she let out a small gasp and was met with a shocking sight.

"Mr. Holmes! Dr. Watson!" she shouted. "Come quickly!"

Rushing to her side, we came to the music room itself — an ample, bright room with high ceilings and large windows looking out over the back garden. Near the centre and off to one side stood a beautiful grand piano of dark wood, perhaps mahogany. The name plate above the keys proclaimed it as a Bechstein, one of the finer and more expensive brands, as befit a singer of Miss Sloper's stature and reputation. The piano lid remained down, but with the front hinged part open to expose the strings nearest the keys. The cover for the keys was open, ready for the player. There were some music books piled haphazardly on the lid, and in the centre on a felt pad, a white marble bust of a bewigged figure I took to be one of the great composers. All this I took in at a glance, as I'm sure Holmes did also.

I could see the body of Miss Sloper lying on the floor beside the piano. She looked quite lifeless. I quickly went to her, knelt down and felt her wrist and then her neck for a pulse. But there was none. She was no longer alive. I could see a slight gash on the side of her head, but only a small amount of blood. Evidently she had not bled to death, but it seemed the blow itself must have killed her. Looking up, I could see the edge of the piano lid, with its pointed corner. Although wooden, it might well have been sharp enough to inflict a fatal wound if she had perhaps fainted and struck her head against it as she fell.

I said as much to Holmes, after pronouncing that there was nothing I could do for her. Holmes merely knelt down and felt her forehead with his hand, before standing up and examining the corner of the piano lid with the magnifying glass which he always carries in his pocket.

The girl's shouts had roused the rest of the household, and soon Rose was joined by the cook, Perkins the driver and Mr. Lambe, each coming from different parts of the house and crowding by the doorway to look at the body.

"Ladies and gentlemen," Holmes said brusquely. "Please, I must ask you to leave the area so as not to disturb us. Watson needs to oversee the body and I must examine the area. Mr. Perkins, if you would be so kind as to take the wagon into town and return with the local constable, I should ask the rest of you to go quietly about your business and leave the room to us until the police arrive. But please, stay in the house and do not go far." And with that, the others left, leaving Holmes and me alone with the body.

"Well, Watson," Holmes said, "what do you make of it?"

"As I said, Holmes," I replied, "Miss Sloper has evidently died from a blow to the head. It's possible she fainted — or I suppose perhaps stumbled — and hit her head on the sharp edge of the piano lid, here." I pointed to the corner of the lid, but was careful not to touch it.

"Possible, I suppose," Holmes allowed. "But there is some blood on the side of her head near her right temple, and even with my magnifying lens I can detect no signs of blood on that corner of the piano lid, as you might expect there would be. And when do you think this accident — if it were in fact an accident — took place? Just moments before the serving girl found the body, or some longer time before that?"

As Holmes had done already, I felt Miss Sloper's forehead, and then her cheek. Both were cool to the touch.

"Without my medical kit it is more difficult to determine," I said. "But her body has already begun to cool, so likely she had already been dead for at least a short while before the girl Rose discovered her body. And yet *rigor mortis*, the stiffening that comes with death, has not yet set in. As you know, that generally begins to happen within two to four hours *post mortem*. So suppose I would say she died sometime within the past two hours. After all, it was only about two hours ago that we last heard her singing."

"Was it?" said Holmes quizzically. "I suppose perhaps it was. Stand here, Watson, and do not move for a moment."

I have elsewhere related how the behavior of my friend at the scene of a crime — for so he must have believed it to be — resembles that of a bloodhound on the trail of a scent. Or perhaps a hunting beagle tracking a fleeing fox, though without the beagle's baying or yelping. Instead, with only the occasional small grunt or quizzical hum to himself, Holmes looked intently about the room, often pulling out his lens to look more closely at one aspect or another. He looked again at the wound at Miss Sloper's temple, then intently again at the edge of the piano lid where I believe she might have struck her head. He then peered at the pile of books on top of the piano and carefully picked up the marble bust of the composer, examining its underside and paying particular attention to one of the bottom corners. Then, striding across the room on his long legs, he tested the windows overlooking the garden, assuring himself that they were securely fastened.

"Excuse me a moment, Watson," he said. "I will be right back."

With that, he left and went down the hallway to the side door. Presently I saw him through those same windows as he reappeared in the back garden, checking them from the outside near the latches and then stooping down to look at the ground beneath them. I saw him give a slight smile, and soon he was back at my side in the music room.

"It is as I feared, Watson," he said. "Miss Sloper did not die by accident, though that is certainly the impression her killer wished to convey. Make no mistake, this was a crime — though I'd wager it was a crime of passion, done in the heat of the moment, rather than one long in the planning. And then the killer had to improvise hastily in an attempt to cover it up."

"But who would do such a thing?" I asked. "And why?"

"The very questions behind every murder, Watson," Holmes replied.

"But you shall soon have your answer," he continued, "for I see Perkins the driver has returned with the police constable from Salisbury."

And indeed in they came from the stable side of the house, Holmes walking into the central hall to greet them as they arrived.

"Ah, Constable Thomas Bell," Holmes said, extending his hand. "I had not thought we would meet again so soon, but it is good of you to come." And gesturing to me, he said, "And this is my companion, Dr. Watson."

While I know that Holmes knows many people, it seemed unlikely to me that he should already be acquainted with a local constable in a small city so far from London. Especially since I do not recall our having a previous case in this area. But in the next moment, Holmes provided the answer.

"I had walked into town early this morning, Watson, before you had roused," he explained, as if anticipating my query. "Constable Bell here was kind and quite capable enough to provide answers to a few of my questions — questions which I fear have turned out to be all too prescient."

Holmes then took him into the music room, where I could see him gesturing to the body, pointing to various objects and areas of the room and conferring quietly with the constable. Although hardened both by battle and by my long years as a physician, I saw no need for my presence again in the room with body. If Holmes had need of my opinion, he would surely ask for it. For the moment, I was content to stay in the central hall, contemplating the sad loss of a fine talent. The arrival of the constable had spurred the others to return, and soon the entire remaining household was gathered outside the door to the music room.

Coming out of the room, the policeman asked each of them in turn their whereabouts that morning. The cook, of course, had spent the entire time in the kitchen and scullery, first making breakfast and then preparing lunch. Perkins had been in the stable tending to the horses. Mr. Lambe said that after leaving Miss Sloper in the music room, he had gone upstairs to his room, where Rose the maid had brought him tea and a light breakfast, which he consumed there. She confirmed that, adding that she had returned later to his room to retrieve the breakfast tray, and had had a brief conversation with him at that time. Other than that, Rose had busied herself tidying up around the house, mostly at the stairs and in the front hall. She further confirmed that during that time she had not seen anyone enter nor leave the music room.

"I thank you for you co-operation," Constable Bell said. "I may wish to speak with each of you further, and may require you to come later to the station to make a formal statement.

"But in the meantime," he continued, after a quick glance at Holmes, "my immediate concern is to speak directly with you, Mr. Lambe."

Lambe, who had been looking down, nervously wringing his hands, looked up with startled expression.

The policeman took a step toward the young pianist and put a hand firmly on his shoulder.

"Mr. William Lambe," he said solemnly, "I am placing under arrest for the murder of Miss Mary Sloper. And I shall be taking you back to the station house for questioning. Now, come along quietly and there won't be any trouble."

I half expected perhaps an outburst, some protestation of innocence from the young man. But whatever anger or spite may once have been in him, had doubtless prompted him to a sudden act of violence, was since gone. He looked instead only sad and dejected, a man of sorrow, as the constable led him away and Perkins agreed to drive the two of them back into town.

The rest of the day had seemed a bit of a flurry: The coroner had come to take the body to the morgue for further examination and preparation. The young Rose, a trifle shaken by the ordeal but nevertheless firm of resolve, had taken charge of the household, cleaned up the music room and packed up Lambe's clothing and personal effects. Holmes and I likewise had packed our things and prepared to depart. Perkins, having returned, was once more pressed into service to ferry us into Salisbury — first to the police station to provide more details as we knew them (Holmes had spent longer speaking with Constable Bell than I had needed to) and from thence to the railway station for the train back to London.

By early evening, Holmes and I were back home at our Baker Street digs, having finished the light supper the admirable Mrs. Hudson had prepared for us on short notice. Holmes had lit his after-dinner pipe and was once again lost in his own thoughts.

"Holmes," I said, "I heard only some of your conversation with young Constable Bell at the station. I'm still puzzled by your connection to him, and how it was seemed so easily to have concluded that, first of all, Miss Sloper had been murdered, and that Lambe was indeed her killer. It may have seemed obvious to you, but I fail to see how you reached that conclusion so swiftly."

"Ah, do not berate yourself, Watson," he replied, "for I had at my disposal a great deal more information that you had. And as I have often said, while it is foolhardy to theorize without facts, when one has sufficient data, the solution will usually present itself in good time.

"Let us begin with that first afternoon of our arrival, when we from the parlor heard Miss Sloper and her accompanist rehearsing.

You will recall there was a brief *contretemps* and a raised voice before the pianist abruptly and angrily left the room."

"I do recall that," said I. "I thought I heard him — or possibly her — shout the word 'frantic.' I assumed that to be a reference to the musical tempo being too fast for the singer or player. I'm not sure which."

"Close, Watson," Holmes said, "but not quite right. I was closer to the partly opened door, and in any case I'll wager my hearing might be a trifle more keen than yours from all the gunfire and cannon fire you've had to endure in the war. No, what you heard was definitely the pianist, shouting the word 'Authentic?!'

"I'll admit I gathered this in part by hindsight," Holmes continued, "once we learned that his name is Lambe. It was perhaps a coincidence, but since we later learned he is indeed a countertenor descended from one of the countertenor soloists of Handel's original *Messiah*, it seemed pertinent. You'll recall that their altercation came during their rehearsal of the "refiner's fire" portion of the aria *But who may abide?* Which, you'll remember from our dinner conversation that evening, Mr. Lambe strongly believes should be sung only by a countertenor such as himself. He felt that for Miss Sloper to sing it was not 'authentic' to Handel's wishes."

"But surely that shouldn't be enough to suspect him of murder?"

"Quite right, not on its own, Watson," Holmes answered. "But that, combined with Mr. Lambe's tense behavior at dinner, was enough to make me concerned for Miss Sloper, if only for the sake of her emotional well-being. Hence my long walk into town early this morning and my conversation with young Constable Bell. Although Mr. Lambe has no official police record, he is known about town for being sometimes quarrelsome to the point of violence, and quick to take offence. That, of course, added to my suspicions."

"But still, Holmes," I said, "at this morning's rehearsal I'll admit it sounded fractious at first. There was that dull thud — perhaps someone by accident or in frustration dropped some books on the floor. But later and by the end all seemed well again. Miss Sloper's singing went on for quite some time and it all seemed smoothed over. Even the "refiner's fire" section was once again sprightly and energetic. And we heard Mr. Lambe's departure from the room. He sounded quite complimentary and gracious."

"Of course he was, Watson," Holmes said. "He took pains to speak loudly enough that we would hear, and believe he was speaking to Miss Sloper. But he was in fact complimenting his own singing."

"I say, what?" I was amazed.

Holmes smiled one of his enigmatic smiles.

"I put it to you this way, Watson," the great detective said. "You have pieced it together exactly as Mr. Lambe had hoped you would — you or indeed anyone else of the household who might have been within earshot, for he would not have known who else might be nearby. Although Mr. Lambe's anger had long festered, the crime itself was the result of a momentary outburst, immediately regretted. But once having been done, there was nothing Mr. Lambe could do but try hastily to cover it up and hope for the best. From the evidence — and in fact from Mr. Lambe's own eventual confession to the police — here's what actually happened this morning:

"Their rehearsal began as usual and went along without incident," Holmes explained. "But the troublesome aria — which Mr. Lambe seems to regard as his own personal property — was causing tremendous friction between them. Mr. Lambe resented Miss Sloper performing it at all, and in any case took umbrage at her musical interpretation. You will recall the many stops and starts, the raised voices, the harsh words

"Then the thud. It was not the books, though Mr. Lambe had later misaligned them on the piano lid to make it look as though they had fallen and been sloppily replaced. No, that sound was indeed the sound of the unfortunate Miss Sloper falling to the ground, by which time she might already have been dead. It was the blow to the head that killed her. Almost instantly, I imagine."

"From the sharp corner of the piano lid?" I asked.

"No, Watson," Holmes answered, "although again that is probably what Mr. Lambe had hoped it would look like. You will recall seeing the marble bust sitting on top of the piano. In a moment of desperate frustration, Mr. Lambe had picked it up — ironically, it is a bust of the composer Handel himself. Perhaps Mr. Lambe meant at first only to gesture with it, or to appeal to the spirit of the great composer. But in his anger, he hit Miss Sloper on the side of the head with it, thus causing her fatal wound. He had tried to wipe off the blood with his handkerchief, but I noticed there were traces of blood on the sharp corner of the base still there when I examined it. We later found blood on the handkerchief in his pocket. In his confusion, he had neglected to get rid of it."

"But that can't be, Holmes!" I said. "You say we heard her body fall to the floor. But after that — for quite some time after that — we again heard her singing. She sang through the entire aria twice more, with Mr. Lambe accompanying her on the piano. And then he complimented her and graciously departed, leaving her in the room alone."

"Exactly as we were meant to believe," Holmes said.

"But first, let me dispense with some other details. When the serving girl first found the body and called to us, her shouts brought the others from various parts of the house. And I could hear them as they variously arrived — the cook from the kitchen at the far side of the dining room; Perkins from the stable, tracking in mud from his shoes as he came; and Mr. Lambe down the stairs from his bedroom above. None of them was close enough nor had enough time to have killed Miss Sloper, having come and gone, without being seen. Because of the rain that morning, Perkins in any case would have tracked mud in both directions, not just the one. From examining the windows from the inside and from outside in the garden, where the damp earth had not been disturbed, I had already concluded that no one had come into the music room from the outside. And the girl, you'll recall, had been in and around the front hall most of the morning. She surely would have noticed anyone entering or leaving, or anything else amiss."

"But why did you suspect only Mr. Lambe, and not the cook or Perkins or the girl, Rose?" I asked.

"The blow to the head that killed Miss Sloper would have taken considerable force to inflict," Holmes said. "Perkins the driver is old and becoming arthritic, and the cook and the maid have neither the strength nor the stature to have done so. Besides, even assuming they had motive, they are more likely to have poisoned Miss Sloper's food than to have done her any physical harm.

"Mr. Lambe, on the other hand, has both the strength and the volatile emotional temperament to have assaulted her in a fit of rage."

"Well, obviously you are right," I said, "especially since he has now confessed to the crime. But I still don't understand the timing. You say the noise we heard that morning was the sound of her body slumping to the floor after the fatal blow. But clearly, we could hear her singing for quite some time after that. How do you explain that, Holmes?"

"Now, Watson," he replied, "you know I deplore criminal behavior in all its forms, and murder is especially vile. But I do confess to a grudging admiration when a criminal shows signs of being inventive or clever in the execution of the crime. Such is the case here.

"As I said, Mr. Lambe had struck Miss Sloper in a momentary

fit of rage, which he immediately regretted. He has said, and I believe him, that he never intended to kill her, nor even seriously harm her. But there he was, standing over her body on the floor. What was he to do? He should, of course, have immediately called for help in the hope that she might still be alive.

"But he panicked, and his first thoughts were for self-preservation. And this is where he was clever — or rather, devious."

"How so?"

"He knew we were in the next room listening, and would have heard at least some of what had transpired. And he had no way of knowing who else from the household might have also been within earshot," Holmes said. "He could not, obviously, be in two places at once and thereby establish a solid alibi for the time of her death. His best hope, he felt, was to attempt to confuse us as to when her death had occurred. He wanted at least to make it seem as though she were alive longer than she actually was."

"I still don't understand," I said.

"The singing, Watson," Holmes answered. "You said you heard the sound of a thud, or thump. You took it to be a pile of books, as Mr. Lambe hoped you would. But then you thought you heard Miss Sloper resume her singing. So obviously you believed she must still be alive."

"And she was not?"

"Sadly, no," Holmes said. "The great singer had already taken her last breath. The singer we heard was Mr. Lambe, both singing and playing the piano at the same time. He was attempting to imitate Miss Sloper to throw us off the scent. And doing a creditable job of it, I might add."

"I can scarce believe it!" I said.

"Ah, my dear fellow," Holmes said indulgingly, "as an occasional churchgoer you may well be familiar with hearing the sound of male altos singing service music within a choir — your Walmisley, your Wesleys father and son, your Stainer or Stanford. All well and good. But I daresay you have not had the pleasure, as I have done, of hearing a countertenor in full soloist mode singing a fully embellished Handel aria.

"For that is what we heard. You will recall that those final versions of "refiner's fire" were quite extravagant in their performance. I suppose Mr. Lambe, his emotions already heightened, finally felt a certain freedom to fully express himself musically."

"Astounding!" I said. "Hard to believe that a man would kill over mere musical differences."

"Artists do have their passions, Watson. And it is not always

—169—

ours, as non-artists, to understand them. We may yet see a day — I hope we do — when the countertenor voice fully regains the respect it once had among musicians as a soloist voice. But that day is not yet come.

"In the meantime, it's a great pity that the world has lost the voice of Miss Sloper. I'm not sure who will take her place for the *Messiah* performance to come in a few days, assuming it will go ahead. But I'm sure there are several capable contraltos, even without her reputation, who could step into the role. Alas, it is now even less likely to be a countertenor.

"But perhaps the greater pity is that Mr. Lambe will likely never get his own chance to sing before the public and display his vocal skill — which you will have to admit is considerable. Perhaps the prison will have a choir where he can stay in practice."

"I should hardly think so," I said. "Still, I'm baffled that all of this has led to the demise of such a talented singer."

"Never underestimate the power of jealousy and resentment, Watson," Holmes said. "Perhaps in end, the thought of a contralto usurping him was something that, as a countertenor, he could just not abide."

# Books by David W. Barber
## with illustrations by Dave Donald

*(available in print and as ebooks from Indent Publishing)*

*A Musician's Dictionary*
(1983)
(Revised and expanded in 2011 as
*Accidentals on Purpose: A Musician's Dictionary*)

*35th-Anniversary Edition*
*Bach, Beethoven and the Boys:*
*Music History as It Ought to Be Taught*
(1986, 2021)

*When the Fat Lady Sings:*
*Opera History as It Ought to Be Taught*
(1990)

*If It Ain't Baroque:*
*More Music History as It Ought to Be Taught*
(1992)

*Getting a Handel on Messiah*
(1995)

*Available as ebooks from Indent Publishing*

*Tutus, Tights and Tiptoes:*
*Ballet History as It Ought to Be Taught*
(2000)

# Other Books by David W. Barber

*The Last Laugh:*
*Essays and Oddities in the News*
(2000)

*Quotable Alice*
(2001)

*Quotable Sherlock*
(2001)

*Quotable Twain*
(2002)

*The Adventure of the Sunken Parsley:*
*and Other Stories of Sherlock Holmes*
(2011)

*Better Than it Sounds:*
*The Music Lover's Quotation Book*
(2013)

# About the Author

DAVID W. BARBER is a journalist and musician and the author of more than a dozen books of music (including *Accidentals on Purpose: A Musician's Dictionary*, *When the Fat Lady Sings* and *Getting a Handel on Messiah*) and literature (including *Quotable Sherlock* and *Quotable Twain*). Formerly entertainment editor of the Kingston *Whig-Standard* and editor of *Broadcast Week* magazine at the Toronto *Globe and Mail*, he's now the assistant editor of arts and life for Postmedia newspapers and a freelance writer, editor and composer. As a composer, his works include two symphonies, a jazz mass based on the music of Dave Brubeck, a *Requiem*, several short choral and chamber works and various vocal-jazz songs and arrangements. He sings with the Toronto Chamber Choir and a variety of other choirs on occasion. In a varied career, among his more interesting jobs have been short stints as a roadie for Pope John Paul II, a publicist for Prince Rainier of Monaco and a backup singer for Avril Lavigne.

Find him on the Web at BachBeethoven.com

or IndentPublishing.com

or follow him on Facebook (David W. Barber)

or Twitter (@bachbeethoven)

Manufactured by Amazon.ca
Bolton, ON

29315228R00101